BLACK TIDE

Also by Anthony M. Strong

The John Decker Thriller Series

What Vengeance Comes

Cold Sanctuary

Crimson Deep

Grendel's Labyrinth

Whitechapel Rising

Black Tide

Ghost Canyon

Cryptid Quest

John Decker Series Prequel

Soul Catcher

The Colum O'Shea Series

Deadly Truth - Coming Soon

The Remnants Series

The Remnants of Yesterday

Standalone Books

The Haunting of Willow House

Crow Song

BLACK TIDE

ANTHONY M. STRONG

WEST STREET
PUBLISHING

West Street Publishing

Cover art and interior design by Bad Dog Media, LLC.

ISBN: 978-1-942207-16-0

For Sonya, who finally read one without knowing the whole story first. Also for Izzie and Hayden, who would rather I was taking them for walks than writing.

BLACK TIDE

Prologue

February 1943

THE AVRO LANCASTER bomber sliced through the frigid deep winter night on the way to Frankfurt, flying near its altitude ceiling of a little over 24,000 feet to avoid anti-aircraft fire. To the left and right, more bombers flew in tight formation, while below, the Belgian countryside slipped by unseen thanks to a thick layer of cloud cover. In the pilot's seat, Flt. Lt. Ernest Latimer stared out uneasily into the pitch-black sky. They had left the relative safety of the English Channel far behind and would now be vulnerable to attack by Luftwaffe interceptors. But only if the Germans detected them, which Ernest hoped would not happen, at least until they dropped their payload. At that point, the element of surprise would be lost, and all bets were off. But for now, everything was quiet.

"I saw Betty last night," said the flight engineer, Sgt. Frank Ward, from the second dickie seat to Ernest's right. "She was in a mood, I'll tell you. She could barely keep her hands off me when I walked her home. Let me kiss her and everything. She always gets like that before a sortie. Keen as mustard. I swear, it's like she doesn't think she'll ever see me again."

"What have I told you about talking like that." Ernest glared at the flight engineer. "It's bad luck."

"I was just stating a fact. It's true. She gets all worried every time there's a mission. Besides, nothing's going to happen. We'll come home safe and sound just like always. Best bomber crew in the squadron, we are."

"Luck. That's all it is. We've shared the skies with plenty of crews that didn't make it home."

"Long may that luck hold." Frank sniffed and wiped his nose with the back of his hand. "To tell the truth, I thought it would all be over by now. Who knew the Krauts would be this persistent. I figured a few months of fighting, a year tops, and they'd throw their hands up. It's a shame they didn't learn their lesson after the last time we gave 'em a good hiding. It'll be four years this September. It's getting tiresome, I'll tell you."

"What else have you got to do?" asked Ernest.

"I suppose." Frank chuckled. "The RAF would be a pretty good flying club if it wasn't for those pesky Messerschmitts." He lapsed into silence and studied his own reflection in the cockpit window. At last, he spoke again. "I think I might ask Betty to marry me."

"Now why would you want to go and do a harebrained thing like that?" Now it was Ernest's turn to chuckle. "The skirts love a man in uniform."

"Especially if that uniform's American," Frank retorted.

"You're not wrong there, lad." A new voice drifted from beyond the curtain blocking off the navigator's station. The fabric swished back to reveal Tommy Corker, otherwise known as Fish, not because he liked to swim, but because of his ability to sink pints at the Kings Arms, which was legendary. He sat perched at the chart table, crammed between the cockpit and the wireless operator's station. Above him the astrodome, used for celestial navigation, was nothing but a dark hole in the plane's fuselage. "It's bloody impossible to pull when the Yanks are in the pub, and since they only fly daytime raids, they're always in the pub."

"Which is why I'm sticking with Betty," Frank said. "It's just easier."

"And because you love her too, right?" Tommy shook his head, bewildered.

"Well, yes, there is that."

"Spoken like a true romantic." Ernest glanced back at the navigator. "Are we close?"

"We're over the German border and in the rats' nest." The joviality had fallen from Tommy's face. He now looked scared. "Almost on top of it."

The seven-man crew fell silent, their concentration now focused on the job at hand. To complete the bombing run, they would have to break cloud cover. Ernest closed the throttles and allowed the plane to start its descent in anticipation of the Master Bomber's orders. Below them would be small villages and towns, while up ahead sat Frankfurt. Their target. He could see the other bombers following suit and dropping lower as they prepared to release their payloads of 500lb bombs. One plane flew too close, threatening to drop right on top of them, and Ernest jabbed his left rudder with a curse. The Lancaster reacted, pulling away at the last minute and avoiding a midair collision.

"Phew. That was a close one," Ernest said, wiping a sheen of sweat from his forehead.

"I swear, they're giving the new pilots less and less training." Tommy looked up from the chart table. "I know we're short of men and all, but they should at least give them an eyesight test before putting them in the cockpit."

"I blame the Germans myself," Ernest replied. "If only they'd be good sports and stop shooting us down, we wouldn't need new pilots."

"Chaps, were not out of the woods yet." Frank was looking up through the cockpit canopy from his lower position in the collapsible seat next to the pilot. His eyes were wide with surprise. "There's something coming down toward us. I've never seen anything like it."

"Stone the crows." Ernest followed the flight engineer's gaze and for a moment he could not comprehend what he was looking at. Above them, dropping out of the moonless sky, was a spherical red orb. "What in blazes is that?"

"I wish I knew." Frank shifted in his seat, nervous, as the orb dropped closer.

"You think it's a new German weapon? Some kind of defense system?" Tommy was craning his neck to see. He stood and pushed his head into the astrodome to get a better view. As he did so, the glowing red orb drew level with their aircraft.

It stayed that way for a few seconds, matching their course and airspeed, and then without warning, shot off at ninety degrees, weaving in and out of the tightly packed planes at impossible speed.

Ernest held his breath, waiting for the sphere to impact one of the forward bombers and send it crashing to the ground in flames. But it didn't. Instead, the unusual object pulled ahead of the squadron, turned, and shot straight up into the firmament where it disappeared from view.

"It's gone." Tommy dropped back down into the cabin and took his seat again. "A pretty useless secret weapon, if you ask me."

"Maybe not. We have more company coming straight for us," Ernest said, watching the Lancaster ahead of them billow into a sudden ball of flames and spiral downward, leaving a bright orange streak as it headed into oblivion. "And this time there's no doubt who they are and what they want."

"Night fighters." Frank's voice was laced with fear. The dreaded Luftwaffe BF 109 Messerschmitt's were equipped with radar, allowing them to see the incoming bombers before they even knew there was a problem. That, coupled with their superior armaments, made them a formidable foe. "If we don't get out of the way, we won't stand a chance. The buggers will shoot us to pieces before we even get a look in."

"Already taking care of it." Ernest pulled back on the stick. The plane's nose lifted, taking them back up and out of the line of fire. His heart began to beat slower and for a few seconds he thought they had avoided trouble even as the bombers that remained at lower altitude were being swiftly picked off, their gunners unable to find the marauding defenders thanks to a combination of darkness and the longer range of the German guns.

But then Tommy was leaping up again and peering through the astrodome's spherical glass. "I don't want to worry you, fellows, but that red ball is back, and it's brought some friends along."

Ernest peered upward to see the glowing red orb dropping back toward them, surrounded by four more pulsating spheres. They raced downward toward the fray, zigzagging between the aircraft, and making sharp turns that would have ripped a regular plane apart. "That nails it. They must be some sort of weapon."

"I don't know," Frank said. "I've heard the American fly boys talking in the pub. They've seen them too. They call them foo fighters. They've shown up even when the Germans aren't around, and they certainly aren't ours."

"Whatever they are, they're getting in the way." Ernest pushed on the stick to avoid an orb that had dropped directly in their path. The plane's nose dipped, and the orb slid momentarily upward, out of view. Below them, more of the incandescent balls were streaking in and out of the bombers still at a lower altitude, hampering their efforts to fend off the attacking fighter planes.

"Look out." Frank's eyes flew wide with terror. He pointed thirty degrees down and to their left.

Ernest followed the engineer's gaze and saw, to his horror,

an ominous shape flitting through the darkness below them. The unmistakable outline of an ME-110. If it got under them, it would use its upward facing 20mm cannons to rip into the now defenseless Lancaster's belly.

He did the only thing he could. He pulled hard on the stick and pushed the plane back upward in a fast ascent, just as the Messerschmitt opened up. Bullets streaked through the sky. A curtain of death that advanced as the enemy aircraft drew near. But that was not the worst of it. The orb that Ernest had tried so hard to avoid was too close. Even with its greater maneuverability, it was caught off guard by the Lancaster's sudden course change, and the German bullets that slammed into it from below.

The orb's pulsating red light filled bomber's the cockpit.

Ernest let out a strangled cry.

He made a frantic attempt to turn the plane to the right and avoid a collision. But it was too little, too late. The bomber's wing tipped up as the plane banked. It smacked into the sphere, which was not as amorphous as it initially appeared. An engine flared up. Part of the wing tore away and dropped out of sight.

For a terrible moment, time ground to a halt.

Ernest glanced at his engineer, saw the terror on his face.

The rear gunner screamed as rounds from the Messerschmitt tore through their fuselage and peppered him.

Tommy cried out, a desperate prayer escaping his lips as the realization of their predicament dawned upon him.

Then the Lancaster's nose dropped one last time and the plane, unable to keep level flight with half a wing missing, twisted sideways and fell in a sickening, lurching spiral.

Ernest gripped the stick and fought to right the stricken bomber, but it was useless. While next to them like some aerobatic dance partner was the orb—red glow fading now to reveal a spherical metallic craft, the likes of which Ernest had never seen—accompanying them into oblivion.

Dawn. Smoke hung over the field, acrid and black. A deep trough cut through the landscape, starting near a copse of fir trees and ending at the shattered remains of an Allied bomber half-buried in the earth near a narrow winding stream.

Gunter Lang and his son, Elias, trudged across the muddy pasture, which was still wet from an earlier rainstorm. In his hand Gunter carried a pitchfork. He didn't think anyone would still be alive inside the burned and broken plane, but he wasn't taking any chances. As they drew close, he quickened his pace and took up a position ahead of his son, shielding him just in case. But there was no need. The bomber had all but disintegrated on impact. The tail section, including the shattered gunner's position, lay twenty feet from the main wreckage. A wing had clipped the ground and come free, tumbling end over end and landing in the stream, propellers bent back upon themselves. The cockpit was unrecognizable. Nothing but a mass of tangled metal. The fuselage was buckled, its back broken. A dead airman hung from the open side door as if his lifeless body had tried to escape its own horrific end.

Gunter relaxed a little. There was no danger here beyond the obvious hazards of torn metal and spilled fuel. Or so he thought until he saw the second object sitting upright in a shallow crater a little further away.

A chill wormed its way up Gunter's spine.

This was like nothing he had ever seen. It was a perfect sphere, with what looked like geometric patterns etched across its surface. It was large too. At least twenty feet tall.

He approached the strange orb and stopped short, peering up at it. Beside him, his son let out a gasp.

"What it is?"

"I don't know." Gunter rubbed his chin. "Never saw anything like it."

"We should go now." Elias took a step backwards.

"Not yet." Gunter inched forward. His foot slid at the edge of the crater. He steadied himself, then turned to his son. "Stay here."

"Papa, don't go down there." Elias looked scared. "Please?"

"There's nothing to worry about, I promise. I'll be back in a moment." Gunter steeled himself, then stepped into the crater, skittering down the slope amid a cascade of loose rocks and soil. Everywhere else, the ground was soaked. Here, it was dry, the rain vaporized by the intense heat when the object crashed to earth.

Gunter was at the sphere now. He reached out, touched a palm to it. Felt a throbbing pulse from within. Something was running deep inside the orb. He pulled his hand away, surprised. Then he heard a rumble of engines. Shouts. He turned, just in time to see his son at the edge of the crater, flanked by men in dark uniforms, twin lightning rod patches sewn to their sleeves.

The Waffen-SS. Heinrich Himmler's dreaded elite troopers.

They aimed their guns downward into the pit.

He swallowed hard and raised his arms, eyes flitting between the soldiers and his terrified son. If they were lucky, he and Elias would live to see another dawn.

Chapter 1

July 1944

Commander Hermann Richter stood on a gantry inside the cavernous Dora 1 submarine pen in Trondheim, Norway, and watched supplies being loaded into his boat sitting some fifteen feet below. To his right, First Watch Officer, Otto Sauer, looked less than pleased.

"A week?" Otto rubbed his hand over the three-day growth of stubble that lined his chin. "It's not enough time. The men have barely had any shore leave. They're exhausted."

"The men will be fine, I'm sure." Richter didn't need reminding how unusual it was to head back out after only seven days in port. U-975, moored in a bay next to his own vessel, had been docked for almost a month and might stay there for a month longer until her captain received new orders. "This is what they signed up for."

"They didn't sign up to spend so long at sea without even enough hours to see their loved ones between patrols. No other crew in the Kriegsmarine is expected to perform under such conditions."

"Which is why I handpicked every man on this boat. They are the best the navy has to offer. You should know, you helped select them."

"All I'm saying is that we could give it a little more time before sending our men back into battle. If only to aid morale."

"That is not my decision," Richter said. "The powers that be are eager to exploit our unique capabilities, and I understand their logic. The tide of war is changing. We're not in the Happy Times anymore, when we could attack a Liberty ship or a freighter and be away before they even knew we were there. The Allies have gotten too good at finding us. Sinking us. They have sonar. Depth charges. Long-range bombers. The wolf packs are too vulnerable. They're being decimated on a daily basis."

"You really think one submarine can make a difference to that?"

"This one can." Richter adjusted his cap and then folded his arms. "Strike hard and strike fast. There's no need for a wolf pack. It's like the old days, at least for us. In and out before the Allies can even react. How much tonnage have we sunk in the last three patrols?"

"More than any other U-boat, by far."

"Exactly. Thousands of tonnes. We sent two merchant vessels and a tanker to the bottom on our last patrol. I'd like to see another crew do that."

"I'm not disputing the effectiveness of our boat. If every sub in the fleet had this technology, the war would be over in months." Otto smiled at that thought. "Weeks, even."

"If only that were possible," Richter replied. "But we are, and will always be, a one off. Our contribution shall be immeasurable."

"I understand, of course." Otto's expression turned serious once more. "I just think we are pushing the men too hard."

"What you or I think doesn't matter. In an ideal world, I would love to give the men more leave. I would give them a month with their families if it were up to me. They have fought hard and they deserve it. But we have our orders." Richter glanced down towards the attaché case sitting at his feet. "A fast convoy has been brought to my attention. Four days out and heading for the English Coast. Liverpool, to be precise. They're protected by an escort group composed of destroyers and corvettes. They've already thwarted one attack and sent forty-three brave submariners to the bottom. I possess the current coordinates of this convoy and have extrapolated their position twenty-four hours from now based on their current speed of eleven knots. Under normal circumstances, we could never reach the convoy before it arrives in port. But this is not an ordinary submarine."

"On that, we agree." The smile was back on Otto's face.

"Rear Admiral Dönitz is most anxious that we reassert our dominance over the supply routes. We will start with this convoy, swat them like flies, and then go in search of other prey."

"Our orders come from on high, then."

"They do, indeed." Richter nodded. "But have no fear, old friend, it will be a short patrol. Only a few weeks. After that we shall return in triumph and I shall insist the men get a longer break."

"That's good to hear." Otto glanced toward his commander. "When do we depart?"

"An hour before dawn. We shall head away from the coast and chart a course southwest toward the Faroe Islands before we engage the device."

"I see," Otto said. "We have a few hours then. You should go see your wife. I will stay and supervise the loading of provisions."

Richter stared down at the U-boat. "You're a good man, Otto. The most capable first officer in the fleet by far."

If the compliment pleased Otto, he did not show it. "I'm merely doing my part."

"And I, mine. I admit it would be nice to see Liana once more before we leave, but I've already said my goodbyes. The men cannot go home, and so neither shall I."

"Then we shall stay, together. For the glory of the Reich."

Richter lifted a hand, his fingers finding their way to the Reichsadler sewn under his right lapel, the heraldic eagle with outstretched wings. He looked toward the U-boat and smiled. "For the glory of the Reich."

Chapter 2

It was almost midnight. They had been trailing the Allied convoy for nine hours, moving into position and waiting for the perfect moment to strike. In the control room, Commander Richter was nervous. Not because he thought they would fail—he knew they would not—but because only a fool would have no fear in a situation such as this. After all, the submarine fleet had the highest mortality rate in the entire navy. Even with the tactical advantage of the device installed in their engine room, Richter knew the risks. He stood in silence and repeatedly clenched his fists, a stress habit he'd picked up many years before and never shed. It was the only outward sign of his inner turmoil.

They were running at periscope depth and had gone undetected as they slipped through a gap in the convoy's protective escort and closed in on the defenseless merchant ships beyond. That would change the moment they made a move to engage. His attack plan was dangerous. For a lesser U-boat it would be suicide, especially since there was no wolf pack to offer backup. Richter and his men were on their own. Yet he trusted his instincts, and his ability to get them out of trouble. He also trusted the unique technology fitted to his sub. It would work just as it had on the three previous war patrols. Even as enemy destroyers and sub-hunter planes bore down upon them, Richter and his crew had slipped away unscathed. Like they were never there. Ghosts.

First Watch Officer, Otto Sauer, lowered the attack periscope and stepped away. "The freighter is dead ahead. She's still moving at ten knots and zigzagging with her lights dimmed, but we have a clear bow shot if we move fast. This is what we've been waiting for."

Richter remained silent for a moment, weighing the options. But his second in command was right. This was their opportunity. He tensed his fists again, then instructed the firing crew to prepare the torpedoes. That done, he turned to observe the helmsman, who was busy adjusting trim to compensate for the now flooding forward tubes.

This was the moment every commander in the submarine fleet lived for. The kill. He took a deep breath and closed his eyes. He visualized the freighter in his mind's eye, crossing their path with its captain standing proud on the bridge, blissfully unaware of the danger that lurked off his starboard side. He felt a flicker of empathy. They might be at war, but this was a fellow seaman. No sooner had the thought entered his head, than it was gone, replaced by a grim resolve to fulfill his mission. Richter opened his eyes and raised an arm, then dropped it in a downward chop as he barked the firing orders. "Torpedo one, off. Torpedo two, off."

The sub shuddered as twin shafts of death slipped from the tubes and streaked away through the water.

Richter moved to the attack periscope and raised it. Ahead of them he could see the freighter as a dim outline set against the night sky.

Next to him, Otto counted off the seconds as the torpedoes sped toward their mark. He reached the number eight before his voice was drowned out by an ear-splitting boom.

An orange fireball erupted from the freighter's midsection. Richter gripped the periscope and tensed, keeping his eyes pressed to the ocular box, even as the shock wave slammed into them. The sub rocked and lurched. A mini tsunami washed over the periscope, blocking Richter's view of the freighter. Then another wave, and one more after that. When the view cleared, the freighter was still there, but she was low in the water and listing heavily to one side with fires raging across her decks. A pall of thick smoke rose into the sky, blocking the crescent moon. Whatever she was carrying was volatile. Richter guessed it was munitions on their way to England to aid the war effort. Instead, they had ripped through the ship and broken its beam. There would be men struggling to stay afloat in the oily water. Those the initial blast hadn't killed, that was. If they were lucky, one of the other ships in the convoy would swing around and pick them up. If they were not, they would freeze to death in the frigid Atlantic. Either way, Richter had done his job. There were other targets in the convoy, and he still had twelve torpedoes between the forward and aft tubes, but for now Richter was satisfied to slip away into the night.

Except it wouldn't be that easy.

From somewhere off their port side came a second explosion, this one nowhere near the freighter.

Depth charge.

He grunted and swung the periscope around, horrified to see a United States Navy destroyer flanking them. Further away, but approaching fast, he saw two more escort vessels.

Even though he was sure they would escape, he felt an involuntary shudder of fear. He retracted the periscope and shouted toward the chief engineer. "Flood the tanks."

A second boom jolted the sub. The destroyer's aim was wide, but it was getting closer with each charge it lobbed from the K-guns mounted on its deck.

The sub tilted and dropped downward into the blackness

as the ballast tanks filled with seawater. Crew members scurried toward the forward torpedo room to weight the front of the boat. The diesel engines cut out, filling the sub with an eerie silence. They were now on battery power.

"We should engage the device." Otto braced himself, legs apart, near the pressure bulkhead hatch.

"Where the hell did that destroyer come from?" Richter glared accusingly at his first officer. "I thought we slipped through undetected."

"This isn't the time," Otto growled. He spun toward the navigator, who hunched over a control panel with two rows of dials. "Can we activate the transit device yet? Are the coordinates set?"

"Working on it." He turned dials and consulted a notebook filled with calculations. "Almost there."

"Make it quick, lad." Richter felt the boat's stern drop as the sub leveled off. They were deep now, almost at crush depth. Close to seven hundred feet. Tortured groans reverberated through the confined space as the hull pushed back against the ocean's immense weight. Water seeped in, dripping onto the gantry through every seam and bulkhead.

We're nothing more than a submerged pepper pot, thought Richter, *and if we go any lower, we'll be a flat one at that.*

He knew this was not accurate though. If they went below their crush depth, they would implode. The hull would rip itself open like an overripe peach hitting a wall. Not that any of them would be around to notice. They would be killed instantly. But this wasn't the real danger. The destroyers above were blanketing the ocean with depth charges. They could hear the booms as the pressure-sensitive bombs detonated. None had dropped low enough to find them yet, but it was only a matter of time.

Which was why they couldn't stay where they were.

They also couldn't risk starting up their electric motors and moving. This would give their position away.

The transit device was their only hope of a silent escape.

Which was why Richter kept on clenching his fists until the navigator glanced up at him and nodded. Richter nodded back, a silent command to engage the device and get them the hell out of there.

The navigator checked his dials one more time, consulted his notebook, then depressed a red button on the console.

A hum reverberated throughout the boat. It started in the engine room and spread forward, filling the air with a strange and tingling warmth as it did so.

Richter finally let his hands relax.

In another moment, the hum would reach a crescendo, and then they would flee to safety, leaving the destroyers above to hunt in vain. It had worked three times already, and he now knew that it would work again. His chest swelled with pride. They had snuck inside the cordon of escort vessels and notched up another kill. A lone wolf in the henhouse. He imagined the accolades that would await them when they returned to base. Four war patrols, each one sending more tonnage to the bottom than any other sub in the fleet. He would be a hero. He smiled at that.

The smile didn't last long.

Another thunderous boom, this one close enough to shake the sub.

The hum reached its peak. Higher pitched and somehow more urgent than it had been before. He felt the decks rattling, the hull groaning, as the device kicked in. And he felt something else. The rumble of another explosion. This one much too close. It sent the boat lurching sideways through the water.

Something fell in the galley, clattering to the deck.

The lights flickered and went out, then came back on, even as the hum dipped and faltered.

Richter looked toward his first officer, saw the fear on his face.

A sailor screamed.

Richter clenched his fists one more time. A memory of Liana, and the kiss they shared on their last afternoon together, brought a tear to his eye. Then the world around him fractured in a flash of searing white light.

Chapter 3

Present Day

THE U-BOAT SAT on the ocean floor at the edge of the continental shelf, a relic from a bygone age that had waited in the darkness for over three quarters of a century, until a trawler snagged its nets in her conning tower.

Mackenzie Peters, informally known as Mac to pretty much everyone who knew her, was in the control room photographing every inch of the equipment in close up. She had spent the previous day spatially mapping the interior with a tripod mounted 3-D camera to create an interactive computer-generated model. It was mind-numbing work, carefully placing the camera, and then exiting the space so she wouldn't be in the frame as the photographic head rotated three-hundred-and-sixty degrees to record the environment in stunning high definition. Once the rotation was complete and the data captured, she would venture back and repeat the process, moving the camera only a few feet. She did this repeatedly, along the entire length of the boat. Once finished, they would stitch the images together to create a virtual recreation of the entire submarine from stem to stern. This would allow the researchers to explore the sub whenever they wanted, even long after they had left the actual vessel behind and returned to the surface. It was an invaluable tool.

Mackenzie stooped and photographed a set of dials that might once have shown the pressure in the submarine's ballast tanks. Not that she was an expert on such things. She was merely a research assistant. A willing body to do the grunt work the actual scientists did not wish to bother with. Which was how she'd ended up alone with her camera snapping pictures of control panels, dials, and valves. But that was fine. She was only twenty-three years old and had many years to advance her career and become the person leading the expedition instead of the one doing all the dirty work.

She straightened up and stretched. Hours in the cramped space had left her back aching. A couple more hours and she could knock off and escape the claustrophobic confines of this ancient relic sitting on the seabed.

She checked the latest batch of photos, flipping through them on the camera's view screen to make sure they were in focus and she had missed nothing, before moving on to the next instrument panel. She pressed an eye to the viewfinder and was about to snap a picture of yet another old-fashioned looking dial, when she heard a noise to her rear.

It wasn't much, just a light shuffling sound, as if someone were walking up behind her. She lowered the camera and turned around, expecting to see one of the other researchers, but there was no one there.

"Hello?" Her voice echoed through the sleek metal tube that formed the submarine's hull, but she received no reply.

"Is there someone in here with me?" She listened a moment, peering past the squat, cylindrical periscope apparatus, toward the back of the sub. The pressure bulkhead hatch leading to the aft battery room was open, providing a clear line of sight all the way back to the galley. They had strung work lights throughout the vessel. Bare bulbs hanging in yellow cages from the ceiling of each compartment. These lit the interior in a bright white glow that revealed the sub's cramped spaces and apparatus in sharp relief. She appeared to be alone.

Shrugging, Mackenzie turned her attention back to the console. She raised the camera again.

The shuffling repeated, louder this time.

There was someone here, after all.

Mackenzie lowered the camera again and whirled around, just in time to see a shadow leap up the galley wall. She drew in a sharp breath.

"If there's someone in here, you need to show yourself," Mackenzie said, wondering if Pavel, one of the research team's two marine archaeologists and a known prankster, was messing with her. "Stop playing around. You're not going to scare me."

As before, there was no response.

"Come on guys, this isn't funny." She was the youngest member of the team. That meant she was fair game for hazing.

From somewhere deep within the sub there was a clang of metal upon metal, as if someone had dropped a wrench or a hammer.

"Enough is enough. Cut it out," Mackenzie shouted. The words echoed back to her. She placed the camera down and made her way toward the pressure hatch. She could feel her heart beating fast against her rib cage.

She stepped through into the battery room then proceeded to the galley, a space so small she found it hard to believe it was used to prepare meals for forty-five crew members.

She came to a halt and studied her surroundings but saw nothing. The sub was quiet and still. Maybe it was just her imagination playing tricks. After spending days cooped up in here, no wonder she was jumpy. Who wouldn't be? The submarine was creepy, especially when she was the only one working in it. And this wasn't the first time she had felt like someone was watching her.

"Get a hold of yourself, Mac," she muttered into the emptiness. The self-admonishment did little to ease her concern. Not that it mattered, she would have to suck it up and keep going. She still had three more instrument panels in the control room to photograph before knocking off. She tried to push the unsettled feeling away. There was no point in creeping herself out. She turned back toward the battery room.

It was at that moment the work lights flickered and went out.

Mackenzie resisted the urge to scream. The sudden darkness was absolute. It was so thick she couldn't even see her own hands as she groped ahead for any surface to latch onto. Finally, she felt cold, smooth metal under her fingertips. The bulkhead separating the galley from the battery room. She inched her fingers along until she found the opening. She stifled a sob, tried not to give in to the panic that rose within her, ignored the overwhelming urge to flee headlong. The sub was a death trap without the lights on. There were too many places she could run into an overhead pipe, a piece of equipment, or fall and crack her head. The last thing she wanted was a concussion, or worse, a fractured skull.

She eased her way past the bulkhead and into the battery room. She had no idea why the lights had gone off, but she knew one thing. She had to get back to the control room, above which sat the conning tower. Once there, she could climb the metal ladder through the sub's conning tower to the access hatch. The only way out.

She felt her way along, hand over hand, moving slowly lest she trip and fall. Then, before she'd reached the bulkhead hatch leading to the control room, the shuffling noise came again. Robbed of her eyesight, it sounded much worse.

Mackenzie froze.

Her breath came in short, ragged gasps, way too loud.

She shivered. It felt cold. Freezing, in fact. It was always chilly in the sub, but this was noticeable, like the temperature had plummeted in a matter of seconds.

She forced herself to move again, took a step forward. Then she felt a light touch brush her shoulder.

This time she screamed.

Fingers closed around her arm and yanked her backwards, away from the control room and any chance of escape.

She flailed, twisting in the viselike grip. She pummeled the air with her free hand clenched into a fist, desperate to break free, but her frantic blows found only empty air. Then, suddenly, the hand released its grip.

Mackenzie stumbled backwards, carried by her own momentum. Her foot snagged something in the darkness, and she tumbled, her rump smacking hard on the deck.

She cried out as a jolt of pain shot up her spine.

Just as the lights came back on.

Mackenzie squeezed her eyes shut against the sudden brilliance, then opened them again slowly. She was in the battery room near the galley bulkhead. Just as before, she was alone.

She sat there for a moment, dazed, her ass smarting where it had contacted the deck. Then she noticed that her arm ached too. She pushed her sleeve up to reveal an angry red weal. A weal in the shape of crushing fingers.

Chapter 4

JOHN DECKER PACED BACK and forth on the dock in the coastal district of Kourou in French Guiana and glanced at his watch. It was a quarter past eleven in the morning, and the person he was here to meet was late. On the outskirts of town stood the Guiana Space Centre, the European Space Agency's primary facility, where towering Ariane and Soyuz rockets blasted off to slip the bonds of Earth's atmosphere. But here, at the water's edge, the vehicles were much less high tech. Mostly fishing boats that lined the landing piers near the fish market, their brightly colored hulls a stark contrast to the muddy brown waters laced with Amazonian silt spewed from the mighty river's mouth hundreds of miles to the south.

He had flown overnight and arrived earlier that morning, landing in Cayenne, capital of the French overseas region wedged between Suriname and Brazil, and met a car prearranged by Adam Hunt for the hour-long journey north up the coast.

Now he contemplated calling his superior to inquire regarding why his next ride, to the marine research outpost, was fifteen minutes late. But then, as he was reaching for his phone, he saw a figure striding along the pier toward him.

Dressed in khaki pants and a short-sleeved white shirt, the man who now approached was clearly no fisherman.

"You must be John Decker." the man said as he drew near.

Decker nodded and slipped the phone back into his pocket.

"Pavel Kovalenko." The man said in an American accent. He held out a hand in greeting. "I guess I'm your sea taxi."

Decker gripped the hand and shook it. "Russian descent?"

"Ukrainian. My parents came to the USA when I was eight years old." Pavel motioned toward a large vessel tied up at the end of the pier that Decker had assumed was a commercial fishing trawler. "Are you ready to go?"

"Lead the way." Decker bent and picked up a travel bag that sat at his feet and followed Pavel to the ship. Now that he was closer, Decker realized it was anything but a commercial fisher. The hull was too clean and well-kept, the paint bright and new. A wide red stripe ran along the side of the boat, ten feet above the waterline. Painted in tall black lettering near the prow was the vessel's name. Sheena.

As they walked up the gangway, Pavel spoke over his shoulder. "Welcome aboard the pride and joy of the Maritime Exploration and Recovery Organization, and the workhorse that makes our research possible. She's named after the director's first pet. A sheepdog he owned when he was a young boy."

"You must be well-funded," Decker commented, as they stepped through a hatch and into the ship.

"The perks of being a nonprofit. We have grants from NOAA, The Smithsonian, and a dozen universities including Oxford and MIT." Pavel ushered Decker along a narrow corridor to a stateroom at the back of the ship that contained a narrow bunk, chair, a locker, and a twenty-inch TV mounted on the wall. "Not to mention CUSP, who are footing the bill for this particular expedition, as I'm sure you already know."

Decker nodded. "Speaking of which, where exactly are we going?"

"Seventy-five miles due east off the coast. Out near the continental shelf. It will take us just under four hours to reach the research station once we get underway. We'll be casting off soon. I have some work to attend to, but you're welcome to relax here during the journey. I'm sure you're tired after your journey."

"A little." Decker was still holding his bag. He placed it on the floor.

"Excellent. I'll return when we get close to our destination. In the meantime, make yourself at home. The accommodations aren't exactly luxurious, but they are comfortable enough. We have a surprisingly good Wi-Fi signal throughout the ship, and the TV has both Hulu and Netflix, if you're looking for a way to pass the time. None of the premium movie channels though, I'm afraid." He grinned. "We're not *that* well-funded."

"Don't worry about me, I'm sure I'll be fine," Decker said.

Pavel nodded. "One last thing. If you need to make any phone calls, better make them now. Once we get out to sea, there won't be any signal, and after we reach our destination communications will be severely limited. No phone, no internet. Nothing. There's a low frequency radio, but it's a real power hog, so we use it sparingly."

"Thanks for the heads up, but I made my calls on the drive up here from Cayenne."

"Good to hear," Pavel said. "I'll leave you in peace then."

"Sure." Decker watched him depart before crossing to the bunk. He sat on the edge. The mattress was thin, but comfortable enough. He fluffed the pillow and lay back, then closed his eyes. From somewhere deep in the ship came the rumble of engines. He felt a subtle sway. They were underway. He wondered what awaited him at the other end of their journey. Adam Hunt, as always, had provided the bare minimum of details. What he had told Decker sounded far-fetched. The research facility was being plagued by what Hunt described as spectral apparitions. In other words, ghosts. Decker wasn't sure he believed in such things, but he was curious, nonetheless. Especially given the focus of the expedition's attention. A sunken World War II Type VII U-boat in almost pristine condition. He couldn't help being intrigued. Even so... Ghosts haunting a newly constructed research facility? He knew better than to dismiss such things, however. After all, he'd only recently returned from London, and a brush with the real Jack the Ripper. Before that, it was Grendel. A haunting seemed infinitely more plausible than a vampiric Victorian serial killer surviving through the ages, or a mythological creature that tortured the Danes turning out to be real. If past were prologue, this assignment would prove no less interesting.

He closed his eyes and drifted off to the gentle to-and-fro of the ocean. The next thing he knew, there was a light knock at the stateroom's door. He sat up, then swung his legs off the bed, surprised to see that almost four hours had passed while he slept.

"Hey." Pavel stood on the other side of the door. "I left you as long as I could. We're coming up on the facility coordinates now. You ready to roll?"

"Ready and willing." Decker grabbed his bag and followed Pavel through the corridor and up two flights of metal stairs to the ship's wide foredeck. They were far out into the ocean, with no land visible. Choppy waves smacked against the side of the hull, sending salty spray over the railings.

"Sorry it's a bit rough. There's some weather coming in," Pavel said, gripping a rail to steady himself. "If you'd gotten here a day from now, we wouldn't be able to get you down there."

"Down there?" Decker realized for the first time that he could see no other ships or structures. He wasn't sure what he had been expecting, but the lack of a visible research facility surprised him.

"Down there indeed. Straight down." Pavel nodded toward a bulbous and squat submersible tethered to the deck with thick cables. A gantry loomed overhead; the arm lashed immobile. "A hundred and seventy-five meters down, to be precise. That's almost six hundred feet."

"We're going underwater?" Decker observed the mini-sub. He felt his gut tighten. "In that?"

"Damn right we are." Pavel chuckled. "That's where the U-boat is. And our research station. It's tethered to the ocean floor."

"You're kidding me."

"I most certainly am not. Habitat One is a completely self-contained sub-aquatic outpost that can support a research team for up to six months at a time. So long as we get regular supplies, that is. Usually every two weeks. That's where the submersible comes in."

"You're being serious. We're really going down to the ocean floor in that bean can?"

"Absolutely, we are," Pavel replied. "Don't worry, I'm a pretty good pilot. I haven't lost a submersible yet." He slapped Decker on the back and shouted over the wind. "Had a close call once, but that's a story for another day. I'll get us down there in one piece, have no fear."

Chapter 5

HALF AN HOUR LATER, Decker sat strapped into the pint-sized submersible with Pavel Kovalenko beside him in the pilot's seat. They were high off the ship's deck, hanging from a boom arm that was slowly swinging out and away from the vessel's side, ready to deposit them in the water.

"You know what you're doing, right?" Decker asked. He wasn't exactly nervous but possessed a healthy measure of apprehension. The last time he'd been underwater, albeit in a diving suit instead of a submersible, a genetically engineered prehistoric alligator had been eyeing him up as a quick snack.

"It's all good." Pavel glanced sideways toward him. "I've done this a thousand times."

"Sounds like I'm in expert hands then," Decker replied. He craned his neck to look down at the ocean's surface, and the swells that raced and crashed across it. "Looks pretty choppy down there."

"Only on the top." Pavel was flipping switches. "Once we get twenty feet down, it will be like a milk pond. By fifty feet you'll forget the surface was even there."

"I doubt that." The sub lurched to the right, caught in a

gust of wind. Decker tensed and gripped his armrests, but Pavel appeared unfazed.

"The descent will be smooth, I promise, albeit dull. Once we get below around three hundred feet, it will start getting pretty dark. By the time we reach the research station there will be barely any perceivable light filtration at all, so not much to see outside. At least without the spotlights."

"That sounds terrifying," Decker joked, although a small part of him meant it.

"Not at all," Pavel replied as the sub started its descent toward the ocean. "It's actually quite a calming experience. Serene even."

"I'll take your word for that." Through the submersible's semi-spherical acrylic-glass front viewing window Decker watched a bright orange rigid–hulled inflatable in the water below them, and a pair of scuba divers waiting to free their craft from its cables.

"Ready or not, here we go." Pavel was tapping commands into a touch screen mounted on the sub's dash, at the same time as they broke the water's surface and sat bobbing up and down while the divers fussed around them.

Moments later, their tethers released, Pavel gave a quick thumbs up to the nearest diver, then waited as they retreated. Once they were safely back on the ship's boat, he filled the ballast tanks beyond neutral buoyancy and guided them beneath the waves. They dropped through the water. Without a visible point of reference, Decker could not tell how fast they were descending.

At one point, less than a minute after they had entered the water, Pavel let out an exclamation and pointed. "Look, over there, off to our left."

Decker followed the pilot's gaze and saw a chilling shape gliding toward them. "Is that what I think it is?"

"Great white shark. He's curious about us."

"Let's hope he's not too curious."

"It's all good. He'll probably hang out a while and then decide we're not worth bothering with. Even if he thinks we look like a tasty meal, he won't have much luck. Bela's pretty tough."

"Bela. Let me guess, your director's mother?"

"Good guess, but only half-right. Actually, he named the submersible after both his parents. Belinda and Lawrence."

"The first two letters of each name. Clever." Despite Pavel's assurances, Decker kept one eye on the shark as it made a close pass in front of them. "How long will it take us to reach Habitat One?"

"About ten more minutes, give or take."

"That quick?" The shark was losing interest now. Having circled several times as they dropped, it gave a flip of its powerful tail fin, and was soon lost to the deep blue ocean twilight.

"I could bring us down quicker if I needed to, but I like to take my time and make sure that Bela is running at optimal performance levels."

"I'm pleased to hear that." Decker peered around, watching the occasional silvery fish dart in front of them. "You were right, by the way. It is serene down here."

"What did I tell you." Pavel was concentrating on the touchscreen, tweaking their descent where necessary. Slightly behind them and mounted on both sides of the submersible, directional propellers adjusted to keep them on the correct heading.

Decker fell silent and let him work. Outside their protective bubble, the water grew steadily dimmer, turning from a light blue with shafts of sunlight slanting downward, to teal, and then a deeper navy blue. Eventually they reached a depth where the sunlight petered out almost entirely and gave way to gloomy darkness.

"It looks pretty bleak outside, but this is nothing compared to the deep ocean," Pavel said after another minute had passed. "Beyond the continental shelf, on the abyssal plain, the darkness is so absolute that you'd think all of creation had winked out and left you in a void of swirling nothingness. Down there, it's easy to imagine you're the last person left on Earth."

"Sounds charming." Decker realized he'd been gripping the armrests the entire time they'd been dropping into the abyss and finally let his hands relax. "I assume you've been there, by the way you talk."

"A couple of times. I once dived a wreck dating back to the first world war. A cruiser sitting at a little over seven thousand feet. It was magnificent and frightening all at the same time." Pavel's fingers danced across the touchscreen, and spotlights mounted to the submersible's roof and belly winked on, illuminating the surrounding space.

It surprised Decker to see they were approaching the ocean floor already. The submersible dropped the last twenty feet as its propellers swiveled horizontally to stop their downward movement. Ahead of them, lit by the mini-sub's powerful halogen lamps, was a sandy expanse interspersed with rocks. And sitting upright, as if some celestial hand had gently placed it there, was the hulking, ominous outline of a German U-boat.

Chapter 6

THE SUBMARINE LOOMED large in the smaller submersible's viewing window. As they grew close, it filled their acrylic-glass bubble, forcing Decker to lean forward to look up at the hulking wreck.

Pavel turned their submersible and guided it along the line of the bigger vessel's pressure hull, providing Decker with his best glimpse yet of the World War II submarine.

"What do you think of her?" Pavel asked, a slight smile on his face. "Quite a sight, yes?"

"In a chilling sort of way." Decker nodded in agreement. The sub's preservation amazed him. The hull was dark and smooth with nary a sign of deterioration or rust. Even the wire antenna running from the bow to the conning tower was still intact. "It looks so new, like it could start its engines and make an escape."

"Isn't it incredible?" Pavel's face was bright with wonder. "I've dived on two other U-boats and they didn't come close to this one by far. That's just one of the mysteries we're here to solve."

"Have you found an answer yet?" Decker asked.

"Not even close. This submarine should be falling apart by

now, corroding away. Yet here she is, as if she slipped from the Nazi submarine pens only yesterday. Her hull hasn't even been breached."

"You mean she can still hold pressure?"

"She does. The U-boat is completely dry inside."

"Now that, I find unbelievable." Decker shook his head and watched as Pavel let the submersible drift higher until they were moving up alongside the conning tower, their lamps playing across the U-boat's pristine skin.

"I did too, until I saw it with my own eyes," Pavel replied.

They were at the top of the conning tower now, except Decker couldn't see it. There was a structure built around it. An enclosed cylinder that capped the tower and hid the hatch leading inside the boat. "Is that an airlock?"

"Not quite. Like I said, the boat isn't flooded. It never was. When we first arrived on site, we noticed the hatch was still sealed."

"That's not unusual though, is it?"

"No. A lot of U-boats are found with their hatches closed. But there is always hull damage, sometimes quite extensive. Not this one. We ran tests and determined there was still air inside, crazy as that was. That's when we built the umbilical."

"The umbilical?" Decker asked. "What's that?"

"I'll show you." Pavel steered the submersible away from the conning tower and around to the other side of the sub.

Now Decker saw what the pilot was talking about. Attached to what he had assumed was an airlock, was a tube that ran at least a hundred feet over the seabed, supported by stilts. Beyond this was the research station.

Habitat One.

It sat on the ocean floor. A central core surrounded by four large windowless cylinders, each one at least fifty feet long and twenty-five feet tall, that radiated out like the spokes of a wheel. The whole thing stood on a network of girders that kept the facility level on the bottom. Within these, and underneath the primary structure, he could see tanks that surely contained oxygen and fresh water for those living on the research station. "This is amazing. I don't know what I was expecting, but you've exceeded it."

Pavel grinned. "That tube running from the U-boat to the habitat is the umbilical. It's fully pressurized, as is the U-boat."

"Does that mean you can go from the research facility directly into the U-boat?" Decker asked.

"Absolutely." From the tone of Pavel's voice, he was having fun showing Decker this engineering marvel. "Naturally, we have emergency hatches that can be closed to protect the habitat from a flooding event or hull breach."

"I'm pleased to hear that," Decker commented. He turned his head to examine the submarine once more. "I hope you'll give me a tour of the U-boat. I have to admit, I'm fascinated."

"Naturally." Pavel pushed on the joystick and steered the submersible toward the research station. "But first things first, I need to get you aboard the habitat. My little sightseeing trip around the U-boat has made us late. Claudia will be wondering where we are."

"Claudia?"

"Our team leader. A word of advice. When we get aboard, there will be a folder in your bunk room listing what you can and cannot do while you are on Habitat One. Most of it is common sense when you're in a pressurized environment this far underwater, but even so I suggest you look through it and make sure you follow the rules. Claudia runs a tight ship and won't hesitate to chew you out if you don't."

"I'll remember that," Decker said.

They were approaching the habitat now. Decker saw a docking port on the underbelly of one of the four cylinders. Pavel eased back on the joystick and brought the main, then maneuvered the submersible until the port lined up with their own hatch. There was a shudder and a clunk as they docked. Once they'd stopped moving, he released his grip on the joystick and flipped several switches, deactivating most of the sub's systems and powering down the thrusters. Then he turned to Decker. "We'll need to give it a few minutes for the pressure in the sub to equalize with the facility, and then they'll open the hatch and let us out." He glanced up through the submersible's bubble, a smile on his face. "Welcome to Habitat One, Mr. Decker. Your new home away from home."

Chapter 7

CLAUDIA LANDRY STOOD on the lower level of Annex C, one of the four cylindrical modules that made up the crew compartments of Habitat One and listened as the mini-submersible, Bela, docked with the facility underneath them. Next to her, standing with his arms folded, was Thomas Barringer, who had joined the team as a weapons expert and also provided muscle for most of the heavy lifting needed around the facility.

"Are you sure we need an investigator poking around down here?" Thomas asked as they waited.

"I haven't decided yet," Claudia admitted. She watched a pressure readout adjust itself on a wall-mounted touchscreen monitor. Twin red bars that showed the atmosphere within the sub and also the facility. When they turned green, it would be safe to release Pavel and his passenger from the submersible. "I'm not disputing that some weird stuff has happened, but I'm surprised my reports were taken seriously enough to warrant this reaction."

"That depends who you're submitting the report to." Thomas eyed the access hatch set into the floor. "I know I'm not officially here in a security capacity, but I had a colleague topside do some digging on John Decker. I spoke to him a few minutes ago on the VLF radio. It made for a fascinating conversation."

"We have a few minutes to whittle away. Would you care to elaborate?"

"Mr. Decker has quite the colorful background. An ex-NYPD homicide cop who quit the force after a baffling incident involving an Egyptian cult that led to the indictment of his partner on attempted murder charges. After that he returned to his hometown and took a sheriff's job. That ended after he shot and killed an old woman that he claimed was some sort of werewolf."

"That's enough. You're pulling my leg."

"Hand on Bible, I'm not. Turns out the old woman somehow tore the town's mayor apart and chewed on him. DNA evidence proved it. That was the only reason he didn't end up making license plates. But it gets even weirder."

"It will need to be pretty weird to top what you've already told me."

"It is. According to the dark web, John Decker was then recruited by a shadowy black-ops organization, presumably CUSP given his current employment status, as some sort of monster hunter. It's all very conspiratorial. Nothing official. Mainly posts on right wing websites and message boards where geeks like to hang out. Outlandish crap mostly."

"In other words, the rumor mill."

"Even rumors often have a basis in fact."

"Then if I'm hearing you right, what you're trying to tell me is that the organization footing the bill for this expedition has sent a monster hunter down here to look for ghosts on our U-boat."

"I'm saying no such thing. I'm merely reporting the chatter my colleague uncovered on the web. Personally, I think that John Decker was just doing his job and got shafted for it. The NYPD didn't drum him out. He quit after becoming disillusioned. As for the incident in his hometown of Wolf Haven, he took down a vicious murderer, regardless of her age. The fact they made him a scapegoat is more a stain on his superiors than on him. As for his role with CUSP, I have no idea, but I find it hard to believe they employed him as a monster hunter."

"Either way, we're about to find out," Claudia said, noting that the pressure between the submersible and the facility was now equal. "I must admit that I'm a mite curious."

"You and me both." Thomas kneeled next to the docking hatch and rotated the release handle, grunting with the exertion. As soon as the locking pins released, he heaved the heavy circular metal door up and out of the way. Beneath, a short tube with rungs affixed to the side led to a second hatch, this one atop the sub.

For a moment nothing happened, then they heard the clunk of bolts snapping back and the lower hatch swung away with a whoosh as the airtight seals disengaged.

Claudia walked to the edge and looked down into the sub, and the two faces peering back up at them. Pavel Kovalenko, marine archaeologist and sub pilot, and John Decker, their newly arrived ghost hunter.

Chapter 8

CLAUDIA LANDRY, leader of the team investigating the sunken German U-boat, and the woman in charge of the facility he was now entering, waited for Decker to climb out of the sub and then met him with an extended arm. "Welcome to Habitat One, Mr. Decker. I hope your journey to get here was a pleasant one."

"I've had worse," Decker replied. He took the proffered hand and shook it, surprised at the strength of Landry's grip. Next to her stood a burly man who merely nodded a greeting. "That U-boat you have out there is quite a sight."

"Isn't she, though," Claudia replied before turning her attention to Pavel, who was heaving himself through the hatch and into the facility. "I assume that's why you're tardy."

"I gave our visitor a quick once around the sub." Pavel closed the hatch and spun the top handle to engage the locking mechanism once more. "I hope you don't mind."

"Not at all," Claudia replied, although Decker sensed a hint of annoyance in her voice. "It will make it that much easier to bring Mr. Decker up to speed."

"Please, call me John."

"Very well."

"I'm surprised we had to wait for the pressure in the sub to acclimatize to your facility," Decker said.

"It's not really necessary," Claudia replied. "It's more of a precaution, really. We keep the habitat at one atmosphere, just like the submersible. There may be a slight pressure differential between the two, but nothing like the multiple atmospheres you would experience on the bottom as a diver."

"I see." Decker nodded. "That's why you have the umbilical going out to the U-boat."

"Precisely," Claudia said. "As I'm sure Pavel already told you, the U-boat is in pristine condition and can still hold pressure. We can walk right on over there and straight into the U-boat whenever we want. It makes things much easier."

"Which is why Habitat One was deployed to this location." The burly man spoke for the first time. "Given the unique condition of the wreck and the complexities of diving to such a depth, it made sense." Now he finally held out a hand for Decker to shake. "I'm Thomas Barringer."

"Ah, yes." Decker remembered the name from the briefing file he'd read on the flight down to French Guiana. "You're the Munitions Systems Specialist."

"I am, indeed. Weapons expert, military advisor, and hired muscle." He grinned. "I'm also the guy that opens pickle jars when no one else can."

"And a fine job you do, too." Claudia laughed. "If it wasn't for you, our sandwiches would be twenty percent less appealing."

"I aim to please." Barringer glanced toward a watertight door that led out of the docking room. "Now that we're all aboard and safe, if you'll excuse me, I have other duties to attend too."

"Of course," Claudia said. "I won't keep you any longer."

"Thank you." Barringer turned to leave.

Claudia reached out, touched his shoulder. "You'll keep me appraised of the progress with the torpedo?"

"Naturally." Barringer nodded. "I'll let you know if I come across anything interesting."

"Torpedo?" Decker watched Barringer leave and then turned his attention back to Claudia. "Are you having an issue?"

"Nothing of the sort. When we first boarded the submarine, it still had twelve intact torpedoes on board. That means there were twelve potentially lethal and aging warheads that might go off at any time. The torpedoes weren't armed, of course, but even so they needed to deal with them before we could safely work inside the sub. To that end, we removed the explosive charge, and also the contact and magnetic detonators."

"Makes sense," Decker said.

Pavel jumped in. "Since barely any of these torpedoes have survived intact, we're now stripping one down into its component parts to see exactly what made it tick. Pretty exciting stuff."

"Sounds fascinating."

"You don't have to humor him, John," Claudia said. "I'm sure that you will find most of the work we do here to be rather dull. I'm also sure that you are eager to get started on your own work."

"I am," Decker replied. "I'd like to begin by having a chat with each of the team members."

"Very good." Claudia motioned toward the door. "I'll take you to your quarters and give you time to settle in, and then you can begin."

"Lead the way." Decker picked up his bag.

"Follow me then," Claudia said, turning toward the door and stepping through. "The crew accommodations are on the other side of the main hub. In Annex B on the upper level.

We have space for ten crew members, but there are only seven on board right now. The bunk rooms are spartan but comfortable enough."

"Thank you." Decker followed Claudia along the corridor with what looked like storerooms on both sides. Soon they reached the central hub, a circular space with hatchways that led off in all four directions, and a second level accessed by a curving staircase that hugged the wall. There were four more hatches on the second level. Claudia led them around the second-floor gantry to a hatchway with the words Annex B level 2 stenciled above it. A sign affixed to the wall next to the hatch read, crew quarters.

"There's a binder in your bunk room that contains the rules and procedures for the facility. Please look through it and familiarize yourself with them. For example, there's no smoking anywhere on the habitat, for obvious reasons."

"No worries there," Decker replied as they navigated a narrow corridor with four hatchways on each side. "I don't smoke."

"Pleased to hear it." Claudia led him to the furthest door on the left. "That's good to know. There are plenty of other rules that every member of the crew must adhere to, many of them not so obvious, but all designed to keep everyone safe."

"I told you she was a stickler for rules," Pavel chipped in from behind Decker.

"Pavel, don't you have somewhere to be?" Claudia glared at him. "I'm sure you have plenty to keep you busy."

"Fine, I'm going." Pavel grinned and slapped Decker on the back. "I'll be back later, my man. I have a bottle of whiskey hidden in my bunk room. I'll bring it around and we'll have a drink together after my shift is over."

"It's a date," Decker said. "Looking forward to it."

"You know you're not supposed to have alcohol down here," Claudia said.

"Lighten up, will you," Pavel retorted. "The crew needs to relax after hours. Besides, I know for a fact you have a couple of bottles of gin stashed under the bunk in your room. I was the one that smuggled them down here in the submersible." With that, Pavel turned and hurried off, leaving Decker alone with Claudia.

Chapter 9

DECKER WATCHED Claudia depart and pulled the pocket door separating his new quarters from the corridor beyond closed. He looked around the cramped room. In a facility such as this, every square inch counted, which meant the crew quarters were small and utilitarian. There was a built-in bunk against one wall. At its foot was a floor to ceiling metal locker. There was a narrow shelf on the wall above the bunk, upon which was a digital clock. Running along the other wall was a ledge that served as a compact work desk with a TV mounted above. The only piece of free-standing furniture was an office chair with a mesh back support and adjustable armrests. As Claudia had promised, a binder sat on the desk. After depositing his travel bag in the locker, he sat down and flipped through it.

The first section outlined the rules and regulations. No smoking. No drugs except prescription medication. No alcohol. There was also a code of conduct, which included a moratorium on romantic liaisons with other crew members. Most of the rules, such as the ban on smoking in an oxygen-rich environment, made sense. The prohibition on alcohol appeared to be less stringently enforced, especially given that

Claudia Landry, the woman in charge of the research project, possessed her own illicit stash of gin. He suspected she turned a blind eye to the alcohol on board in order to allow the rest of the team, faced with the prospect of many weeks enclosed in the habitat's claustrophobic and remote environment, a way to blow off steam.

The second section contained a plan of the entire facility, showing its modular design and the various sections. All four cylindrical sections contained two levels, accessed from the central hub. The lower level of Annex A held the moon pool, which allowed access to the ocean. There was also a hyperbaric chamber and storage for diving gear. The second level contained a pair of labs for preserving artifacts and a room labeled *Trunk Access Chamber*.

Annex B contained the living quarters. The bunk rooms occupied the second level, along with two bathrooms and a separate washroom with a shower. To conserve water, showers were restricted to twice a week. The lower level contained a mess hall, which also doubled as the crew lounge, and a galley. The other two sections of the facility, annexes C and D, contained the docking area where he had boarded, storerooms, workshops, offices, a large dry pantry, and other miscellaneous spaces including an exercise room. There was also a server room which contained the computers that controlled the environment and performed the thousands of unseen tasks that kept everything running. Nearby, the mechanical room housed a generator that provided power to the habitat. It also ran the air pumps and oxygen generators that kept the habitat pressurized and livable.

The last page of the binder contained information regarding the differentiation between day and night. Since the facility had no access to sunlight, and therefore no way to regulate sleep, the facility maintained an artificial schedule. The habitat's twelve-hour daytime shift, during which the researchers rose, had breakfast, and worked, ran from 7 AM to 7 PM base time. After that there was time to eat an evening meal and engage in social activities. The lights dimmed at midnight throughout the facility to create the illusion of night. It was something Decker hadn't thought about before, but it made sense. When their circadian rhythm was interrupted, people did not perform at their best.

He put the folder down and removed the laptop from his travel bag. He opened the report Adam Hunt had provided and studied the crew manifest. Of the seven personnel living on Habitat One, Mackenzie Peters, a research assistant, and the youngest member of the team, had endured the most disturbing incident so far. Over the next twenty-four hours he planned to interview the entire crew one by one in order to understand the true scope of what they were experiencing, but he would start with Mackenzie. Hopefully this evening, but if not, first thing in the morning.

He glanced at his watch. It was almost seven and the habitat's workday would finish soon. Evening meal would be served shortly. At that thought, his stomach growled. Decker hadn't eaten since landing in French Guiana twelve hours earlier. He was starving.

Decker closed the laptop, went back to the locker, and found a fresh shirt in his travel bag. Then he picked up his cell phone, which had no signal but would allow him to record his thoughts and impressions. He could also record any pertinent conversations with the crew. He slipped the phone into his pocket, smoothed a crease from his newly donned shirt, and left the bunk room, sliding the door closed behind him.

Chapter 10

DECKER DESCENDED from his second-floor bunk room to the level below. The mess hall was one large room with a long table and chairs occupying one half, and a recreation lounge in the other. There was a bookcase filled with books, a 60-inch TV mounted to the wall, and a foosball table. A sofa and several chairs also occupied the space, providing comfortable seating. A set of double doors on the far wall led to what Decker assumed was the galley.

When he entered, most of the crew were already there, gathered around the table, including Pavel, who looked up with a grin. "Come on in, Mr. Decker. Join us.

"Thanks." Decker took a seat and looked around the group. There were only five people at the table. Two were missing, including the team leader, Claudia.

"Let me introduce you to the gang," Pavel said. He introduced each team member one by one, starting with a young woman with short cropped brunette hair who Decker guessed was in her mid-twenties. "This here is Mackenzie Peters. Mac to those who know her. She's the baby of the team. Like our bratty little sister."

"Thank you for that charmingly inappropriate introduction," Mackenzie said, lightheartedly. She looked at Decker. "Aside from being a surrogate baby sister to the rest of the crew, I'm a research assistant. If there's boring work and no one else wants to do it, I'm your gal."

"Please to meet you, Mackenzie," Decker said.

"Right back at you," Mackenzie replied.

"Moving on," Pavel said. "Next up is Patrick Marchant. He's our translator and historian. Everything on the sub is in German. He tells us what it all means. When it comes to the history of U-boats, if he doesn't know it, no one does."

"I'm also translating several interesting documents found on the submarine, including the commander's logbook," Patrick said in a thick French accent.

"Ah yes, the historian," Decker said. "Until I read your bio in my briefing file I assumed you would be German, given your area of expertise."

"Just because the boat is German doesn't mean I need to be." There was a fleck of annoyance in Patrick's voice. "Actually, my grandparents were members of the French Resistance back in the war. That's what sparked my interest in military history. I'm fluent in three languages. German, French, and English. I can also get by in Czech."

"I apologize, I didn't mean to offend."

"No offense taken," Patrick said, but Decker sensed he might have made an enemy.

"All right, then." Pavel jumped in, eager to move the introductions along. He turned his gaze toward another young woman wearing blue overalls. "This here is Lauren Borne. She's our ETO."

"And that is?" Decker asked. He had briefly skimmed her profile in the file Adam Hunt provided, but still didn't know what an ETO was.

"Electro Technical Officer," Lauren said. "I keep Habitat One up and running. I make sure the air filtration is working, that we have plenty of fresh water in the tanks, and that the generator doesn't quit on us."

"Sounds like an important job," Decker replied.

"I'm a glorified engineer. If it goes wrong, I fix it, from a pressure hull repair to a blocked toilet."

"Good to know," Decker said.

Pavel motioned to the last member of the team sitting at the table. "And of course, you've already met Thomas Barringer."

"I have, indeed." Decker nodded a perfunctory greeting toward the stocky Munitions Specialist. "I'm surprised Claudia Landry isn't here yet."

"She might join us, she might not," Mackenzie said. "She often eats alone in her office over in C. I think she prefers the company of a computer screen to that of her colleagues."

"It's nothing of the sort," Pavel said. "She gets immersed in her work, that's all."

"She should be here with the team. She's always talking about harmony, and everyone getting along together. Maybe she should set an example."

"So, she's not good in social situations. Who cares?"

"Why are you defending her?" Mackenzie looked at Pavel and narrowed her eyes.

"I'm not," Pavel retorted. "I just think you're making a mountain out of a molehill."

"Which is exactly what she said I was doing when the lights went out on the sub." Mackenzie leaned back and folded her arms across her chest. "But I wasn't, and I have the bruise to prove it."

"Look, I don't know what happened over on the sub, but —" Pavel began, but at that moment the galley door opened, and a stocky gentleman emerged carrying a tray loaded with steaming dishes and a stack of plates. He wore a white apron. His head was bald and smooth, the stark overhead lights glinting off it.

"Hallelujah. Just in the nick of time," Lauren murmured. "Now maybe we can eat instead of squabbling."

"Food's up, amigos," the bald man said as he deposited the dishes and plates in the center of the table. "I made my special three cheese macaroni in honor of our visitor. There's also barbecued ribs, garlic bread, and arugula salad."

"Yum. Sounds delicious," Lauren said with a grin on her face.

"Everything I make is delicious." The bald gentleman reached into his apron pocket and pulled out a fistful of silverware. He placed the knives and forks on the table.

Pavel turned to Decker. "John, say hello to the last member of our happy family. Bertram Carson. He's our steward. Without him we would starve to death and there would be no toilet paper or clean sheets."

"You might say he's the most important member of the team," Thomas said with a smile.

Bertram ignored the flattery and focused on Decker. "Pleased to make your acquaintance."

"Right back at you."

Bertram nodded toward the gathered group. "If the rabble here get too excitable, just tell them to can it. They haven't had anyone new to talk to in weeks."

"I'll keep that in mind," Decker replied.

"Now if you'll excuse me, I have to make a quick trip over to Annex C with the boss's meal."

"What did I tell you," Mackenzie said.

Bertram ignored the comment. "Dig in, guys. I'll join you as soon as I get back." With that, he turned and retreated into the galley. A moment later he reappeared, heading in the other direction with another tray.

"Okay, then. Why don't I do the honors," Pavel said. He pulled a serving spoon out of the macaroni. "Who wants the first helping?"

Chapter 11

THEY ATE MOSTLY IN SILENCE. After they finished the meal, Bertram jumped up and cleared the table.

"Would you like some help with that?" Decker asked.

"Not at all. Stay there and let your food go down," Bertram replied as he piled the dirty plates one on top of the other. As he headed toward the galley, he shouted over his shoulder. "The rest of you guys could learn a thing or two from the newcomer. Not a one of you has ever volunteered to help me clear up."

"And with good reason," Thomas called jokingly after him. "You don't buy a dog then bark yourself."

"Yeah, yeah." Bertram kicked the galley door open with his foot. "You better watch out, or tomorrow's breakfast will be a big bowl of nothing with a side order of make it yourselves."

Thomas watched the jovial steward depart and then clapped his hands together. "Okay then, who's up for a beating at foosball. I shall crush all takers."

"Not likely. I've beaten you six out of the last seven games," Lauren replied.

"Why not," Patrick said. "I'll take you on."

"Count me out." Pavel grimaced. "I can't stand foosball."

"Then we need one more to make up the teams. Mac, you up?"

"I don't think so, not tonight." Mackenzie pushed her chair aside and stood up. "If it's all the same with you all, I think I'm just going to head back to my bunk room."

"Are you feeling okay?" Thomas asked, a look of concern on his face.

"I'm fine. It's nothing. Just not in the mood to play games, that's all," Mackenzie replied before turning and heading for the hatchway.

"All right then." Thomas motioned toward Decker. "You're our fourth man. You can play on my team."

"In a few minutes, maybe," Decker said, watching Mackenzie step into the hub and disappear toward the stairs leading to the second level. He pushed his own chair aside and stood up. "If you'll excuse me, I'll be back in a little while."

Decker dropped his napkin on the table and hurried after Mackenzie. He caught up as she was entering the crew quarters.

"Hey."

She stopped and looked around, surprised. "Aren't you supposed to be helping Thomas kick everyone's ass at foosball?"

"That can wait." Decker stopped and caught his breath. "If you don't mind, I'd like to have a quick chat with you first."

"Oh." Mackenzie looked taken aback. "Have I done something wrong?"

"Why would you say that?" Decker asked.

"Because you showed up here after I filed that report about the incident on the sub. I figured they sent you to make sure we keep quiet."

"That incident is part of the reason I'm here," Decker

admitted. "But it's not the only reason. There have been other incidents as well."

"Like people getting spooked or thinking they're being watched? Claiming the sub is haunted? That's nothing like what happened to me. Someone physically attacked me."

"Which is why I want to talk to you first," Decker replied in the most soothing voice he could muster. "I'm not here to tell you it didn't happen or to do damage control. I'm here to understand what's going on."

"All right then," Mackenzie nodded toward one of the bunk rooms. "Can we do in my quarters? It will be more comfortable than standing in the corridor."

"Sure." Decker followed her inside and slid the door closed, then took his phone out. "Do you mind if I record our conversation?"

"Knock yourself out." Mackenzie hopped up onto her bunk and sat cross-legged with her back against the wall. She nodded toward the office chair tucked under the desk. "Take a seat."

"Thank you." Decker pulled the chair out and sat down. He placed the phone on the edge of the bed, in between them. "Why don't you tell me what happened."

"If you've read the report, you already know. I was in the sub, the lights went out, and then someone grabbed me."

"Claudia seems to think that you might have just gotten spooked and tripped in the dark."

"Claudia doesn't want to admit what we all know, even though she's had experiences herself."

"And what is that?"

"That there's something not right about that sub. There's something on it. I don't know if you'd call it a ghost, but it's there. I've felt it here as well, on the habitat. Some of the others have too."

"And how are they taking it?" Decker leaned forward. He'd read the report regarding what had happened to

Mackenzie on the sub, and didn't think she was making it up, but he also knew that things weren't always as they seemed.

"They don't like to talk about it. They're professionals. Stuff like ghosts and ghouls, things that go bump in the night, don't fit into the scientific view of the world that most of us down here adhere to. Deep down though, most of them believe. Claudia can't accept the possibility that the sub is haunted, and Patrick does his best to flat-out deny it, although I know he's scared. But I know what happened to me, Mr. Decker. I didn't get spooked and run into a pipe and crack my head. I didn't panic because the lights went out. There was someone there with me, and I can prove it."

"How can you do that?" Decker asked.

"I'll show you." Mackenzie unbuttoned the sleeve of her shirt and pulled it up to the shoulder. She held her arm out for Decker to see. "I didn't get this by tripping and falling on my ass. It's been several days and the bruises are still there, although not as bad now."

Decker leaned closer and studied the angry purple blotches on Mackenzie's arm. There were four distinct marks where fingers might have squeezed down. And on the other side of her arm, another bruise in just the right place for a thumb.

"Mind if I photograph this?" Decker asked.

"Be my guest," Mackenzie replied.

Decker picked up his phone and took a few quick shots, then placed it back on the bed in between them. "All done."

"Now do you believe me?" Mackenzie asked, rolling her sleeve back down.

"I never said I didn't believe you." Decker met the younger woman's gaze. "And I promise, I'm going to do the best I can to find out what's going on around here."

"That's good to hear," Mackenzie said. She yawned. "If it's all the same with you, Mr. Decker, I'd really like to get some sleep now. Claudia's been running me ragged. Maybe we can finish this interview tomorrow?"

"Tomorrow it is," Decker nodded. "And please, call me John, okay?"

Mackenzie nodded.

"Good." He scooped up his phone and stood up. He stepped out in the corridor, closing the door behind him. He was about to retreat to his own bunk room when Pavel appeared in the hatchway at the end of the corridor.

"There you are. You never came back to join the game. They're playing a man short down there."

"I'm sure they'll live," Decker replied. "I've been awake for almost twenty-four hours. My bunk sounds pretty appealing right now."

"In that case, I think it's time for a quick nightcap." Pavel ducked into his own bunk room and returned a few moments later with a bottle of bourbon and two glasses. When he saw the look on Decker's face, he held a hand up. "I know, I know. You're tired. One drink and I'll leave you alone. Besides, a shot or two of this stuff, and you'll sleep like a log."

Chapter 12

THE SIREN JOLTED Decker from his sleep. At first, he wasn't sure what the jarring sound was, but then he snapped awake and sat up as realization dawned. An emergency alarm was going off. A warbling klaxon that rose in pitch, then dropped again.

As he swung his legs off the bed, he glanced at the clock. 3:20 AM. It was still the middle of the night. His gut tensed. Whatever was happening could not be good. They were hundreds of feet beneath the Atlantic, sitting on the ocean bed. Had there been a hull breach? Was the facility filling with water even as he sat there contemplating the sudden intrusion into his slumber?

Decker looked down at the floor, afraid he would find sea water inching under the bunk room door, but everything was dry. He breathed a sigh of relief. Then he remembered they were on the second level. For all he knew, the galley and mess hall below them were already flooding. He didn't know what the evacuation procedures were and couldn't remember if there was even a section covering such things in the folder he'd browsed earlier. As far as Decker knew, there was only one way off the facility. The submersible that had brought him down here in the first place, and it only had two seats. Not that it mattered. If the accommodation annex was flooding, the docking bay would also have flooded, cutting the submersible off.

He jumped out of bed and threw his clothes on, then pulled the bunk room door open and stepped out into the corridor. He wasn't the first one there. Pavel was in his own doorway, looking confused. Mackenzie had exited her bunk room at the same time as Decker, and now stood bleary-eyed, wearing a pair of pastel blue flannel pajamas.

The rest of the crew were arriving now, some fully dressed, others still wearing their night attire. Everyone looked confused.

"Why is there an alarm sounding?" Bertram said as he stepped into the corridor.

"Beats me," Pavel responded. "I wish someone would turn the damned thing off, though. It's giving me a headache."

"It's the umbilical hatch alarm," Lauren said. "When the facility is in night mode, it goes off if there's a break in the door seal. It's a safety precaution to make sure we're alerted if the umbilical breaches and the hatch fails."

"Are you saying the umbilical has flooded?" Mackenzie asked, her eyes wide.

"Not necessarily. It could mean hatch integrity has failed, but it would also sound if someone opened the hatch without deactivating the alarm first."

Claudia pushed to the center of the group. "No one opened the hatch. There are eight of us here. We're all accounted for."

"Then let's get down there and see what we are dealing with," Thomas said.

"I second that," Claudia replied. She moved off toward the central hub.

"Exactly where does the umbilical connect to the habitat?" Decker glanced toward Pavel.

"Annex D, lower level." Pavel ducked into his bunk room and reappeared with a sweater, then hurried to catch up with the group. "I hate how cold it always is at night," he explained. "We lower communal area temperatures several degrees while we sleep to conserve power."

Claudia had reached the hub's second-level gantry. She paused and peered over the railing. "No sign of water on the lower deck. If the umbilical has flooded, then the hatches are holding, at least so far." She hurried around the gantry and onto the steps leading to the lower level.

Decker could sense the tension in the air. This was a serious situation. "Do you think it really has flooded?"

"I guess anything is possible," Pavel replied as they started down. "If so we're in a pickle. And not just because we won't be able to get to the U-boat anymore."

"How so?"

"Remember that foul weather I mentioned earlier?"

"Yes."

"The support ship won't be able to leave port for at least a couple of days. Even if we evacuate the facility, there won't be anyone topside to meet us."

Decker was about to ask exactly how they could easily evacuate when the alarm abruptly turned off.

The sudden silence was disconcerting.

Claudia came to a stop halfway down the steps with the rest of the group behind her. She peered over the railing again to make sure it was still safe to continue.

"Ah. So much better," said Patrick, the French historian, speaking up for the first time since the alarm had woken them. "I can finally think again without that incessant wailing."

"Why did it shut off again like that?" Mackenzie asked, nervous. "Is that what it's supposed to do?"

"Only if the situation resolves itself and the door seals are intact, or it's deactivated from the server room," Lauren replied. "If the hatch has failed, the alarm shouldn't just turn itself back off."

"Well, that's some good news, at least," Pavel said as they started moving again and reached the bottom of the steps and hurried toward Annex D. "Whatever happened isn't cataclysmic."

A narrow corridor ran the length of the module, with workshops on both sides. In front of them was a watertight bulkhead with a hatch set into it. The door stood open, and Decker could see a small room with a second hatch beyond. He guessed the room acted as a failsafe. If the outer hatch failed, the inner hatch would prevent the entire facility flooding. He wondered why they didn't keep it that way all the time. He soon got his answer.

"Why is the inner hatch open?" Thomas asked.

"It shouldn't be," Claudia replied. She turned to Decker. "Protocol requires that we keep the hatches closed, even if a researcher is over on the U-boat. It's a safety precaution."

"It was closed earlier, I swear," Thomas said. "I checked the entire facility, just like I always do, before going to bed."

"You're sure about that?"

Thomas nodded. "One hundred percent. It's part of my job and I take it seriously."

"Then how did it get open?" Claudia stepped past the inner hatch and into the chamber beyond. She peered through a small porthole set into the outer hatch. "The umbilical hasn't flooded. It looks fine."

"Just to be safe, I'll go up to the server room and check the air pressure before we open the hatch again," Lauren said.

"Good idea." Claudia turned away from the hatch and faced the group. "I have no explanation for what just happened here."

"I think I do." Thomas was looking down at the floor.

"Someone was over on that sub tonight, and they must've stepped in something."

Decker looked down and followed the Munitions Specialist's gaze. There, on the floor near the outer hatch, was a faint but clearly discernible oily boot print.

Chapter 13

MACKENZIE RETURNED to her bunk room and closed the door, then engaged the privacy lock. It was an insignificant gesture. The lock was flimsy. It was there to stop people barging in while she was undressing or sleeping, more than to provide any significant security. It would not hold up to a serious attempt to enter. It gave her some peace of mind, though.

The facility's walls were thin. She could hear the others returning to their own quarters, lingering in the corridor and talking in hushed whispers, but before long silence once again descended upon the crew annex.

She was shaken. More nervous than she cared to admit. The incident in the submarine several days earlier had left her nerves frayed, and now this. It appeared, for all the world, as if someone had opened the umbilical's main hatch and come aboard Habitat One. But that was impossible. Everyone on the facility had been present when the alarm went off. No one was missing. Even the newcomer, John Decker, had been in his bunk room. Except she could not think of another explanation for what had happened, especially given the discovery of a boot print.

A tickle of fear wormed its way up her spine.

Something was not right. The hand that grabbed her in the darkness on the submarine had not been a figment of her imagination. Was the owner of that hand the same person who came aboard the habitat tonight? If so, where had they gone after the alarm stopped sounding? More important, how had they gotten down here in the first place? There was only one way on and off the facility. The submersible. Unless you counted the moon pool, a barrel shaped opening in the floor of Annex A which provided direct dive access to the ocean. She wondered if someone could have entered there. But that made no sense either. They kept the facility at the same atmospheric pressure as the ocean's surface, but Habitat One sat on the seabed at a depth of over sixteen times that pressure. Anyone swimming down from above would suffer incapacitating decompression sickness within minutes of coming aboard. Unless they used the hyperbaric chamber, that was. But it would be next to impossible to escape detection for the hours of decompression such a dive would require. Not to mention the enormous complexity of descending that deep. It was no small feat and would be extremely dangerous for all but the most experienced technical divers. Even the specialist dive team who had spent a week aboard the habitat examining the exterior of the U-boat inch by inch had used atmospheric hard suits that limited their exposure to the incredible water pressure outside the habitat. The more she thought about it, the more she realized there was no way an intruder could have gained access without them knowing.

That only left one conclusion.

No matter how ludicrous it sounded, the U-boat, and by extension Habitat One, really were haunted. Mackenzie shuddered involuntarily at that thought. A flesh and blood intruder coming and going at will was a frightening enough proposition. This was somehow worse.

She glanced at the clock near her bunk. It was almost five in the morning, and now that her adrenaline had returned to normal levels, she could feel tiredness descending upon her once more. Worse, there were only a few hours left before the day shift began, and it was unlikely Claudia would make any concessions for the disturbance that had roused them from slumber. She went to the door and tugged to double check it was locked, then returned to her bunk and slipped under the covers.

She reached to turn the lights off but hesitated. Darkness was not her friend. Not tonight. Instead, she dimmed the lights to half brightness and lay there looking up at the ceiling, wondering if she would be able to fall back to sleep. As it turned out, the answer was no.

Chapter 14

BREAKFAST WAS ALREADY BEING SERVED when Decker arrived in the mess hall a little after eight the next morning. The entire crew was already there, including Claudia, who sat at the head of the table and watched him enter.

"Good morning, John," she said, motioning to a chair next to Mackenzie. "Join us, please. We're about to eat."

"Sounds good, I'm starving." Decker sat down.

"I trust you slept well enough after last night's excitement?" Claudia asked.

"Actually, I found it hard to fall back to sleep." Despite his tiredness, Decker had laid awake for over an hour after the early morning disturbance. "The alarm going off unsettled me."

"You aren't the only one," Mackenzie chipped in. "I couldn't sleep for the rest of the night. All I could think of was that footprint outside the umbilical hatch."

"Now that I think about it, there's a reasonable explanation for that. It was probably left by one of us." Thomas sat back in his chair and put his hands behind his head. "There's oil and gunk all over that damned U-boat. You'd think it would all be dried up long before now given how many years the thing has been sitting on the ocean floor, but it's not. Someone probably stepped in some before coming back across the umbilical."

"I suppose." Mackenzie didn't look convinced.

The galley door opened, and Bertram ambled through with platters of bacon, eggs, and hash browns, all sitting on a serving cart. He deposited them on the table with an apologetic look. "There's no toast, I'm afraid. I thought I'd taken a loaf of bread out of the freezer yesterday evening before I turned in for the night, but it wasn't there when I came down this morning. I must have forgotten."

"Not a problem," Thomas said with a grin. "As long as we have bacon, that is." Without waiting for an invite, he picked up his fork and speared several rashers.

"You can joke," Bertram replied. "But it's my job to make sure everyone is well fed. An army marches on its stomach, as they say. Or in this case, a research crew. I'll make sure it doesn't happen again."

"I'm sure you will." Claudia watched the rest of her team help themselves to food before she served herself.

"I'll be back with coffee." Bertram turned on his heel and disappeared back into the galley. A few moments later he returned with a carafe and a jug of cream, then took a seat opposite Decker and dug into the food.

"Now that we're all here, has anyone given any thought to what might have happened last night?" Thomas asked between mouthfuls. He glanced toward Lauren. "Is it possible the alarm malfunctioned?"

"Not likely." Lauren shook her head. "I'll run a full diagnostic after breakfast, but I can't imagine there's a fault."

"Is there a way to tell if someone actually opened the outer hatch?" Decker asked. "Are there surveillance cameras on the habitat?"

"Nothing of the sort." Claudia shook her head. "We have no need for them."

"The computer should have logged the incident," Lauren said. "But that will just tell us the how long the alarm was going off and confirm the hatch seals disengaged. It won't tell us if the hatch was actually opened."

"It must have been." Pavel glanced around the group. "The umbilical didn't flood, so the hatch seals didn't fail. Since none of us turned the alarm off, it would only stop if someone closed the hatch door."

"Unless there was a malfunction," Lauren said. "But like I said, it's highly unlikely and we can rule it out pretty quickly once I get to the server room."

"There was no malfunction. The inner hatch door was still open when we got there. Both hatches should have been closed, and Thomas said he checked them before bed."

"I absolutely did," Thomas said. "They couldn't have gotten open again on their own. Somebody must have opened those hatches, presumably to access the U-boat."

"Which we know is impossible because no one was missing when the outer hatch alarm sounded." Claudia finished her food and pushed the plate away.

"It's just another weird incident to throw on the pile," Lauren said. "Maybe we should just blame it on the resident ghost."

"There's no such thing as ghosts," Patrick retorted. "All this talk about strange occurrences and people seeing things, it's all hogwash."

"Really?" Mackenzie's face flushed red. "I suppose you think what happened to me over on the U-boat is hogwash too?"

"I think an impressionable girl barely out of her teens got scared when the power went out, and then she fell on her ass trying to run away."

"I wasn't running away. Someone grabbed me. How many more times?"

"Fine. Let's assume someone turned the lights off and

then attacked you. Who would that be? You were the only one on the U-boat." Patrick leaned back in his chair, a smug look on his face.

"Why don't you believe me?" Mackenzie glared at the Frenchman.

"Because your story doesn't make sense. You start wailing about being assaulted, and the next thing we know there's some government goon coming down here to investigate us." Patrick glanced toward Decker. "No offense."

"Kinda hard not to take offense at being called a government goon," Decker replied. "And FYI, I don't work for the government. I work for CUSP, the organization funding this little jaunt."

"And who do CUSP report to? I bet it's the Pentagon."

"Why would it matter who we report to, unless you have something to hide?"

"Bah, Americans. You're all the same." Patrick grabbed the carafe and poured himself a coffee, then stared down into it sullenly.

"That's quite enough, people." Claudia slammed a hand on the table. "Bickering among ourselves won't get us any answers."

"You're right, sorry," Mackenzie said.

Claudia turned to Lauren. "I want that diagnostic ASAP. Let's confirm if the alarm was a malfunction or not."

Lauren nodded. "I'll do it as soon as I leave here."

"Good." Claudia glanced around the table. "Does anyone else have anything to say on the subject?"

No one spoke.

"Excellent. In that case I don't want to hear any more talk about ghosts or things that go bump in the night. We will get to the bottom of whatever has been happening around here, with John Decker's help. That is the reason he is here. Nothing more. No one is under investigation."

"That's true," Decker said. He caught Mackenzie's eye.

She looked as small and scared as she had the previous evening when he spoke to her. "Whatever is going on, I'll figure it out and put a stop to it."

"Good to hear," Claudia said. She looked at Decker. "Now that we're done with breakfast, I'm sure you would find a tour of the U-boat most interesting."

Chapter 15

FOR THE SECOND time that day Decker stood at the hatch door leading to the umbilical, and beyond that, the U-boat.

Claudia gripped the door's release wheel and turned it counterclockwise to disengage the latches. That done, she swung the door open to reveal a long cylindrical tube with a walkway down the center. At the other end, sixty feet away, was another hatch identical to the one they had just opened.

"No alarm this time," Decker said.

"If the umbilical suffered a catastrophic event, the alarm would still sound if sea water breached the hatch seals," Claudia replied. "But opening the door during normal operating hours will not activate it. Physically opening the hatch will only activate the alarm when the habitat is in night mode. That's also true of the hatch leading to the submersible, and the hatch set into the watertight bulkhead at the moon pool."

"I see."

"It provides an extra level of security at night and ensures that all exterior hatch doors are closed and sealed before we go to bed."

"Makes sense." Decker watched Claudia step into the umbilical, then followed her.

Once they were both inside, she turned back to the hatch and pulled it closed, re-engaging the latches. "One of the most important rules is that you never leave an exterior hatch open under any circumstances."

"I'll remember that," Decker said.

"Make sure that you do." Claudia started along the umbilical walkway toward the U-boat.

Decker followed behind. It surprised him to feel the metal walkway under his feet shifting. He was about to ask if this was normal when Claudia spoke, anticipating his question.

"We built the umbilical to be flexible. It moves with the underwater currents."

"Like the way skyscrapers sometimes sway in high winds."

"Exactly. I'm not an engineer so I can't give you a technical answer, but apparently it's a safety feature."

"I should feel reassured, but I don't." The slight movement was making Decker feel uncomfortable.

"It takes some getting used to, I'll admit." Claudia chuckled. "We're walking across a narrow tube with nothing but a few inches of steel between us and six hundred feet of cold dark water."

"You're not making it any better," Decker replied.

"Sorry."

They had reached the far hatch door now. Claudia repeated the same process as the other door and swung it open to allow them entry to what Decker now saw was a small room completely encasing the top of the submarine's conning tower and bridge, including a 37mm Flak gun mounted on a platform behind the tower, its barrels still pointing skyward to defend from sub-hunting aircraft that would never come. He stepped inside and waited for Claudia to seal the hatch.

That done, she turned to him. "We built this special dry room around the tower and then pumped the seawater out. It's completely sealed against the ship's hull."

"This is incredible." Decker reached out a hand and

touched the smooth, cold skin of the U-boat. He pressed his palm against the metal, wondering what the submarine had done, and all it had seen, in its previous life as a hunter killer for the Kriegsmarine.

"Takes your breath away, doesn't it?" Claudia watched Decker with a bemused smile on her face. "Especially when you think of the evil men that created this machine."

"I wonder how many people died at her hands."

"A lot, I'll wager." Claudia walked to a set of metal steps that ascended the side of the conning tower and allowed access to the sub's own hatch. "Ready to see the inside?"

"Lead the way." Decker followed her to the steps. "I'm more than a little curious."

The U-boat's interior was cramped and claustrophobic. It made the small spaces on Habitat One look enormous. They entered through the conning tower and descended a ladder into the control room.

Claudia pointed to the work lights strung throughout the vessel. "Obviously, the U-boat's batteries are long since dead, so we ran an electrical line from the habitat."

"Makes sense." Decker glanced around. The tiny space was brimming with valves, pressure dials, and pipes. Too many to count. A pair of metal steering wheels sat in front of narrow chairs bolted to the deck. A small table on the opposite side of the compartment held several curling nautical maps. The dizzying array of controls baffled Decker. The only device he recognized was the periscope, but only because he'd seen similar contraptions in old war movies.

"To the front of the ship are the officer's and CO's cabins, and the forward torpedo room." Claudia motioned for Decker to follow her toward the front of the vessel. "There wasn't much space in the submarines, so most of the crew did not have their own quarters and shared what they called warm bunks. Since there were not enough beds for everyone, another crewmember would occupy the bunk as soon as the previous one vacated it. They slept fully dressed, had no way to clean themselves or shave, and didn't even have a change of clothes."

"Sounds utterly miserable," Decker said as they stepped past the officer's cabins. He noted that even these had no privacy, with only a thin curtain to separate the cabins from the rest of the sub.

"It was. The men were at sea for weeks with no access to even basic hygiene." Claudia led Decker away from the cabins and into a larger space that contained long metal cylinders with fins attached. Torpedoes. "Crew accommodation was on the other side of the control room in the sub's aft section, but once the U-boat had fired enough torpedoes, normally toward the end of a war patrol, they could unfold auxiliary bunks attached to the walls of this room to gain extra space for the men to sleep."

"Where was Mackenzie attacked?" Decker asked.

"Follow me, I'll show you." Claudia led Decker back in the other direction.

They stepped through a pressure bulkhead hatch, passed through the control room once more, and through another hatch into a space lined with bunk beds. Beyond this was the galley. The smallest room Decker had seen on the sub so far.

Claudia stopped and turned to Decker. "This is where she was when the lights went out."

"It would be pitch black in here without those overhead lights. She wouldn't have been able to see her own hands, let alone an attacker," Decker observed. "A terrifying prospect."

"I don't doubt she was scared," Claudia said. "I don't know what happened, but I'm sure none of my team attacked her."

"She never said they did."

"There's no one else who could have. We're alone out here hundreds of feet down on the ocean bottom." Claudia folded her arms. "I trust my team, John. Not to mention that they were all accounted for. Mackenzie was the only person on the U-boat."

"Speaking of people being on the U-boat," Decker said. "The report provided to me by CUSP stated that you never found a trace of the crew on this boat when you entered. Is it true that there were no bodies found on the sub?"

"That is correct." Claudia nodded. "We found personal effects. Letters, photographs of loved ones back home, comic strips and books. We even found a couple of harmonicas. But as for the crew themselves, nothing."

"Do you have an explanation for that?"

"The most logical explanation is that they abandoned ship. Maybe they got into a skirmish with an Allied destroyer, or a sub-hunting plane spotted them and started dropping depth charges. If they couldn't escape because of damage to the U-boat, they may very well have bailed. Perhaps an Allied vessel took them aboard and they became prisoners of war."

"Is that likely?"

Claudia shrugged. "The lifeboat canisters near the prow of the ship are still intact, so they didn't escape in those."

"That doesn't explain how this boat came to be on the sea bottom in such pristine condition," Decker said.

"I agree, it's perplexing." Claudia glanced around. "U-boat crews were under orders to scuttle their vessel rather than let it fall into Allied hands. They had explosive charges for that purpose. Another method was to flood the diving tanks and allow it to sink. There was a valve in the control room they could open to flood the vessel and help it go down quicker. Obviously, they didn't set charges or open that valve because we're standing here right now. My best guess is that the crew departed the sub, leaving one person to flood the tanks before escaping."

"And that person took the time to close and seal the main hatch?" Decker shook his head, bewildered. "That doesn't make a lick of sense. If they wanted to sink the U-boat, why not leave it open?"

"Your guess is as good as mine. It's the only explanation we've come up with for the lack of a crew aboard. Frankly, we expected to find a lot of bodies when we first entered. We originally assumed a mine or depth charge damaged their ballast tanks and prevented them from surfacing. In that scenario, the sub would sink to the bottom, and since we're still above its crush depth, the crew would have suffocated while trapped inside the hull with no means of escape. Other U-boats met that grisly fate."

"Not a pleasant way to go," Decker commented.

"Except that isn't what occurred here. All evidence points to the crew abandoning the submarine. I'm glad of it too." Claudia shivered visibly. "The thought of those men sitting in the dark on the ocean floor suffering a slow and agonizing death is dreadful, regardless of which side they were on." She fell silent for a moment, as if contemplating this. Then she touched Decker's arm. "Enough of this maudlin talk. I'll show you the engine room."

Chapter 16

LAUREN BORNE WAS in the Annex D mechanical sub-level, a tight chamber in the bowels of the habitat underneath the lower level, performing maintenance on one of the atmospheric circulation pumps that fed breathable air from the oxygen tanks back up into the facility. Access to the sublevel was through a trapdoor set into the floor of mechanical room D; a cubicle sized space next to the umbilical's inner bulkhead hatch. She was lost in her work, switching out a clogged air filter, which was why she didn't notice Decker's approach at first.

"Ahoy down there."

Lauren stopped what she was doing and glanced up.

"You're a hard woman to find," Decker said, peering down through the square opening in the mechanical room's floor.

"Not if you know what I do," Lauren replied. "I spend half my day crawling around under the floor with a wrench in my hand."

"I'll keep that in mind."

"Was there something I could help you with, Mr. Decker?"

"I keep asking folk to call me John."

"Very well, was there something I could help you with, John?"

"I hope so. If you have a few minutes. I've been talking to the team one by one, to get their take on what's going on around here and get a first-hand account of their experiences."

"How's that going?"

"I've spoken to Mackenzie and Claudia so far. You're my third port of call. Patrick is next in line."

"Good luck with that." Lauren let out a snorting laugh. "He's a cantankerous asshole at the best of times. Plus, he's choosing to ignore all the strange occurrences because they don't fit with his belief system. I don't think he likes you very much either."

"Yeah, I got that impression at breakfast," Decker replied. "Which is why I decided to start with a friendlier face."

Lauren put down the screwdriver she was using to remove the filter cover. She stood and heaved herself back up through the opening in the floor and sat on the edge with her legs dangling in the hole next to her toolbox. "All right then, you have five minutes. What do you want to know?"

"Well, to begin with, why don't you tell me what you've experienced?"

"A few weird things. Odd feelings that I'm being watched, or a glimpse of movement from the corner of my eye. It happens mostly when I'm over on the U-boat, in the engine room poking around. Nothing like what Mac experienced."

"What do you make of Mackenzie's claim?"

"You mean do I believe her?"

"Sure."

"I don't have any reason not to. She's always struck me as levelheaded." Lauren shrugged. "I can see how she got spooked over there on her own, though. Who wouldn't? It's dark and damp. It smells like old socks, especially in the crew accommodation. Plus, it's weird just thinking about why the German's built the sub and the people it killed."

"You agree with Patrick then?" Decker raised an eyebrow. "You think she might have scared herself and tripped in the dark?"

"No. I think something happened to her. Like I said, I felt things too. I was over there one afternoon in the engine room studying the diesels, and I could've sworn someone was moving about near the front of the boat. I could hear their footsteps. When I went to investigate, nobody was there. I was the only person over on the U-boat that afternoon. I asked around to see if anyone else had come over, but they all said no. It freaked me out at the time. I didn't go back on the sub for three days."

"I can imagine."

"A few days before you got here, I went looking for Pavel and Claudia on the U-boat. They were in the forward torpedo room with Thomas. I climbed down into the control room and noticed the aft pressure bulkhead hatch door standing open. Something made me glance through it, and there was a shadowy figure standing in the galley, watching me. It scared the hell out of me. I practically ran toward the torpedo room. When I looked back, it was gone. But I know what I saw."

"What did the figure look like?"

"I didn't get a good look. Male. Thickset. He was standing in the shadows and like I said, I only glimpsed him."

"Anything else?"

"No. Those are the only experiences I've had." Lauren shook her head. "I know that other members of the team have sensed things. Even Patrick, although he doesn't like to admit it. The most common feeling is one of being watched, but it's hard to quantify whether it's real or if we're just getting spooked. Even so, it's very unsettling."

"That begs the question, do you believe the sub is haunted?"

"I don't believe in ghosts. I've always thought of them as nothing more than superstitious mumbo-jumbo. Still, I don't have another explanation for what's going on, so I'm keeping an open mind."

Decker leaned against the wall and met Lauren's gaze. "An open mind is good."

"That's what I tell myself." Lauren dropped her gaze. "I'm not ready to join the ranks of the believers, but I don't have any better theories."

"Fair enough." Decker stepped toward the door. "I think I've taken up enough of your time. If I think of any more questions, I'll let you know."

Lauren nodded. She watched Decker turn and leave before lowering herself back down into the sub-level. She picked up a screwdriver and continued removing the panel covering the air filter. She was careful to remove each screw gently so that none of them dropped into the machinery. If that happened, she would never find them again. Worse, they might cause damage if they got stuck in the wrong place. At length, she pulled the panel away and set it aside. She was about to reach in and remove the filter when she heard footsteps crossing the floor above.

"Thought of another question, huh?" Lauren said over her shoulder, assuming Decker had returned to ask her something else.

She glanced up, expecting to see him looking down at her, but instead she saw a dark figure swinging an arm down in a blur of movement. She flinched and brought her hands up in self-defense, a frantic scream escaping her lips, just as the pipe wrench contacted the side of her head with a sickening crack.

Chapter 17

DECKER FOUND Patrick Marchant in his office on the second level of Annex D. The office door was ajar. When Decker knocked, Patrick glanced up, clearly irritated.

"I'm trying to work."

"If this isn't a good time, I can come back later," Decker said.

"You're here now." Patrick sank back into his chair and swiveled to face the door. "You might as well come in."

Decker stepped inside and looked around the cluttered office. A bookcase lined one wall, brimming with thick volumes, many of them in German. There were photographs of the U-boat's control room pinned to a large corkboard affixed to the wall opposite the door. Most of them were close-ups showing groups of valves or clusters of dials. Patrick's desk was so cluttered with paperwork that there wasn't one inch of the actual desktop showing. A laptop computer set to one side, a screensaver of looping patterns dancing across its screen.

"To what do I owe the pleasure of this unexpected visit?" The tone of the Frenchman's voice contradicted the assertion that Decker's arrival was a pleasure.

"I'm interviewing each member of the team individually

to get a handle on what everyone has experienced since coming down here."

"And how's that going?" Patrick asked. "Have you had your fill of supernatural claptrap yet?"

"I'm working on it," Decker replied with a disarming smile. He nodded toward the desk where a leather-bound volume sat open. Scratchy, untidy handwriting filled its yellowed pages. "Anything interesting?"

"If you must know, it's the logbook from the U-boat. I've been reading through it in an effort to learn more about how our submarine came to be where it is and what it was up to before it sank."

"Have you found any useful information?"

"I'm not sure yet. There are some facts I need to verify." Patrick closed the logbook and rested a hand upon it. "I'll be reporting to Claudia in due course. If she shares that information with you, that's up to her."

"I'm sorry, I didn't mean to pry."

"Yes, you did, but that's okay." Patrick fixed Decker with an icy stare. "If you have questions for me, you'd better ask them. I'm a busy man."

"I'll keep it short then," Decker said. "When we were talking at breakfast, you were quite unreceptive to the idea that Mackenzie had an experience on the U-boat. Why was that?"

"Why do you think? She's nothing but a child. A hysterical girl who let her imagination get the best of her."

"She's a very competent young woman according to her bio in the file that CUSP provided to me." Patrick's attitude was rankling Decker. "And I have seen no evidence that she's hysterical."

"Really?" Patrick snorted. "She's convinced a spook assaulted her, thinks there are ghosts haunting the U-boat. That sounds pretty hysterical to me."

"Something happened over there."

Patrick shrugged. "We only have her word for that."

"And the bruise on her arm."

"She could have gotten that anywhere. She probably banged it when she fell over. There're all sorts of hard edges on the U-boat, especially if you're fumbling around in the dark."

"So basically, you don't believe a word she says."

"All I'm saying is that there's probably a rational explanation for what people have been experiencing."

"Like?"

"Like we're all stuck down here on the ocean floor in cramped accommodations with no access to the outside world. Prolonged solitude and the thought that nothing lies between us and death except a thin layer of steel is enough to fray anyone's nerves. Not to mention that damned U-boat sitting over there taunting us. It's an enigma. There is no way it should be in the condition that it is. There's no rust, no decay. It still holds pressure, which is practically impossible given how long it's been down here and how old it is. It's as if the thing sank yesterday."

"So, you have had no experiences yourself?" Decker asked.

"Nothing that would make me believe in the supernatural." Patrick shook his head. "Sure, I've felt a little uncomfortable over on the sub. That's a natural reaction to the surroundings."

"Especially given your family history with the Nazis."

"Indeed. Before the occupation, my family owned a farm outside Limoges. The Germans took it from them."

"Which is why they joined the Resistance."

"They were already in the Resistance before that. Losing the farm just made them more determined to fight back." Patrick drummed absently on the logbook with his fingers. "If you have a file on me, you know this already."

"I'm just trying to understand where you're coming from,"

Decker said. "Why you are so willing to dismiss the experiences of your colleagues."

"I'm not dismissing them. I'm saying that we shouldn't jump to conclusions just because a couple of people got spooked. We're professionals. We should act like it."

"Sometimes there isn't a rational explanation." Decker nodded toward the logbook. "The submarine defies logic, according to you. It can't possibly be in perfect condition given the circumstances, and yet it is."

"Which is why we're here. That doesn't mean there's anything supernatural happening," Patrick said. "We'll get to the bottom of it, but not through half-baked woolly theories. Science will explain the U-boat's pristine condition, not superstition. If you're expecting me to tell you that an otherworldly force is at play, you're wasting your time."

"I'm not expecting anything," Decker replied. "I'm just looking for the truth."

"As am I," Patrick said. "I'm glad we agree on something, at least."

Decker was about to reply when he heard footsteps approaching. He turned around to see Mackenzie striding toward him. She looked harrowed.

"Claudia sent me to find you," she said. "There's been an incident. You need to get up to the crew quarters right now."

"Why? What's happened?"

"It's Lauren."

"What about her?"

"She's been hurt," Mackenzie replied, breathless. "She's in her bunk room. Please hurry."

Chapter 18

LAUREN WAS SITTING on the bed looking miserable when Decker arrived at her bunk room. When he entered, the first thing he saw was Thomas Barringer wiping blood from the side of her face with a wet cloth, while Claudia Landry looked on with a concerned expression.

"What happened?" Decker asked.

"She took a nasty blow to the head," Thomas said, glancing briefly in Decker's direction.

"I didn't just take a blow to the head," Lauren countered. "Someone attacked me."

"When?" Decker stepped into the room. "We only talked an hour ago."

"After you left." Lauren winced as Thomas touched the cloth to a nasty gash behind her left ear. "I thought you were coming back to talk to me again. But it wasn't you. I didn't get a good look, but whoever attacked me was heavier set. Not that I had long to realize what was going on. As I turned around, I got clobbered by a pipe wrench. Whoever attacked me must've taken it from my toolbox. It knocked me senseless. I came around not long after, but by then I was alone again." She winced and glared at Thomas. "Ouch, be gentle."

"Sorry, I'm going to have to clean this wound in order to see how bad it is," Thomas said apologetically.

"Just be careful, it stings like crazy." Lauren gritted her teeth as Thomas continued tending to her. She looked up at Decker. "I guess I got one up on Mackenzie. Whoever grabbed her when the lights went out didn't have a pipe wrench handy."

"I have to admit," Claudia said. "I was a little skeptical of Mackenzie's story. This certainly changes things."

"You can't identify your attacker?" Decker asked. "Think hard. No detail is too small."

"I've told you all I know." Lauren shook her head.

"Keep still," Thomas grumbled. "I'm trying to be gentle like you asked, but it's kind of hard with you moving around."

"My bad." Lauren gave Thomas a weak smile, then addressed Decker. "When I looked up, the light was in my eyes. I glimpsed a silhouetted figure looming over me and then saw the pipe wrench. I'm sorry I can't be more help, it all happened so fast."

"That's okay." Decker glanced toward Claudia. "Did anyone else see anything?"

"Once we patch Lauren up, I'll be speaking to the rest of the team. My first concern is making sure she's okay."

"Naturally," Decker said. "Who found her?"

This time it was Thomas who responded. "That would be me. I was on my way down to the umbilical when I heard a scream. I discovered Lauren in the mechanical room, looking dazed. I got her out and brought her up here, then notified Claudia."

"You noticed nothing out of the ordinary?"

"You mean other than finding one of my colleagues bleeding profusely from a head wound?"

"Yes, other than that. You didn't see anyone coming or going?"

"No. I was speaking to Pavel a few minutes before, but I didn't see anyone on my way down to the umbilical."

"And what about the umbilical hatches?"

"I don't follow."

"Were either of them open?" Decker asked. "You must've noticed. The mechanical room is right there."

"I don't recall either of them being open. As you said, I would've noticed if they were. Not that I was paying much attention. I was more concerned with Lauren."

"Of course."

Claudia looked at Decker. "Are you suggesting that Lauren's attacker came across from the U-boat?"

"I'm not suggesting anything, I'm just trying to rule out possibilities, and at the moment there are only two. Either an unknown party is coming and going from the U-boat or someone on your team is responsible for the attacks on Mackenzie and Lauren."

"I can't imagine that anyone on the team would have done this to me," Lauren said, a horrified look upon her face. "Honestly, I wish I'd gotten a better view of my attacker. All I can say for certain is that it was a man. I feel awful. What if they strike again?"

"That's another reason we're speaking to the rest of the team soon as we're done here," Claudia replied. "I want to look everyone in the eye and see if any of them are acting out of character."

"That's a good idea." Decker watched Thomas working on Lauren for a moment, then spoke again. "Is she going to need stitches?"

"I don't think so. It's a nasty cut, but it should heal up okay." Thomas picked up a fresh towel and wiped his hands on it before reaching for a tube of antiseptic. "I don't see any sign of a fractured skull either. The damage appears to be pretty superficial, considering." He looked down at Lauren. "You're one lucky woman."

"I don't feel lucky. I've got a raging headache, and it hurts like a bitch where I got whacked."

"I'm not surprised. The thing I'm most worried about is a concussion. I'd like you to stay here and rest for a while with the lights dimmed."

"I've got so much to do." Lauren glanced toward Claudia. "I don't have the time."

"Thomas is right. You need to stay off your feet for a little while," Claudia said. "I would rather not make it an order, but I will if I have to. Pavel can pick up your duties in the meantime."

"Fine. I'll stay here."

"Make sure that you do." Thomas motioned for her to lie down. "I'll check back in an hour and I expect you to be here."

"I said that I would." Lauren fluffed up her pillow and laid back. She pulled a blanket over herself.

Thomas reached out and dimmed the lights. "I'll say this, you have a hard head."

"Funny. That's what my father always used to say. I'm pretty sure he didn't mean it like this though." Lauren closed her eyes. "Now if you want me to get some rest, you'd all better scoot."

Chapter 19

THEY GATHERED in the mess on the lower level of the accommodation annex. Everyone except Lauren, who was still recovering from her ordeal in her bunk room. They gathered around the table and Bertram brought out steaming mugs of coffee, which he handed to everyone before Claudia addressed the group.

"I'm sure by now you've all heard what happened to Lauren."

A murmur rippled through the team.

"If anyone saw anything, or heard anything, now is the time to speak up."

"How is she?" Mackenzie asked.

"She has a nasty bump on her head, but she'll live." Thomas leaned back in his chair. "It could have been much worse."

"I don't understand who could have done this to her." Mackenzie looked around the group, her eyes wide.

Decker spoke up. "That's what we're here to find out. She said it was a man that attacked her."

"Wasn't me," Patrick said. "I was in my office the whole

time and I can prove it too. The government man was giving me the third degree."

"For the last time, I'm not a government man." Decker grimaced. "But yes, I was there."

"And I was with Thomas," Pavel said. "We were discussing running metallurgy tests on a sample we cut from the conning tower to see if the metal has any unusual properties. We're still trying to figure out why it hasn't corroded after so much time on the sea bottom."

"That's true." Thomas nodded in agreement.

"And we can rule out Claudia and Mackenzie since Lauren said her attacker was a man," Decker said.

"Not that you need to rule me out," Mackenzie said. "I would never do something like that."

"That makes me the only plausible suspect." Bertram didn't sound happy.

"No one said you're a suspect," Decker replied. "But it would be helpful to know what you were doing at the time of the attack."

"I was in the kitchen preparing chicken pot pie for dinner. After breakfast I went to the laundry room and put on a load of sheets. I was going to change the bed linens later. I went back to the kitchen after I finished. I've been here ever since. I didn't even know anything was happening until half an hour ago."

Mackenzie raised a hand. "I can vouch for Bertram, at least for part of the time. I came in here to get a can of soda and I heard him in the galley. He was singing Abba songs."

"That's disturbing in its own right," Patrick commented.

"I like to sing while I cook." Bertram shot Patrick a withering look. "It gets lonely being back there all day while everyone is off doing stuff on the submarine. Plus, I like Abba. It's happy music."

"So basically, everyone has an alibi," Decker said. "And no

one saw or heard anything out of the ordinary until Thomas responded to Lauren's scream."

"It would appear that way." Claudia didn't look happy. "So where does that leave us?"

"In the same place we were when I came aboard," Decker said. "Except that we now know there is a genuine threat here."

"We just don't know what or who it is." Thomas sighed. "Or how someone hit Lauren over the head when all of us appear to have alibis."

"Maybe it was two people working together," Patrick said. "They could cover for each other."

"Are you making a confession?" Mackenzie asked.

"Don't be stupid. I've already told you I was with the government man."

"And you also suggested it might be two people working together," Mackenzie countered. "Maybe you and Decker are in cahoots."

"What possible reason could I have for doing something like that?" Patrick asked.

"I don't know, you tell me."

"This isn't getting us anywhere," Decker said, raising his voice. "It wasn't me, and it wasn't Patrick. I've only been on Habitat One for twenty-four hours, but I'm a pretty good judge of character, and none of you strike me as the homicidal type."

"If none of us did it, that only leaves one option." Thomas looked around the group. "That someone else did it."

"And now we're back to ghosts." Patrick rolled his eyes.

"I never said it was a ghost," Thomas snapped. "But it doesn't take a genius to figure out that if none of us did it, there must be someone else on the habitat."

"That's not possible. How would they have gotten down here?" Claudia didn't look convinced.

"It's not out of the question. The submersible hasn't left

since Pavel brought Decker down, so we know they didn't get in that way, but there's the moon pool."

"That would be one hell of a dive." Now it was Pavel's turn to look skeptical.

"But not impossible."

"All right, genius," Patrick said. "Tell me this, where are they now?"

"That's a good question." Thomas glanced toward Decker. "Maybe we should find out."

"Aren't you forgetting something?" Mackenzie said.

"What's that?"

"Lauren's attack isn't the first. Someone tried to grab me days ago over on the U-boat." Her expression was one of vindication. "Not that any of you believed me."

"I did," Pavel said.

"And what about the alarm last night?" Bertram said. "None of us were missing when that happened either. It woke us all up. This latest incident would seem to prove that an intruder opened the umbilical hatch door."

"The evidence does point in that direction," Decker admitted. "If there is an intruder on the facility, they must have been here for a while."

"That's not possible. Where would they hide?"

"The obvious place is the U-boat," Claudia said. "At least at night."

"And in the day?"

"I don't know," Claudia said. "But I agree with Thomas, we should find out. And sooner rather than later. Lauren wasn't badly hurt, but we might not be so lucky next time."

"I agree." Thomas stood up. "If John is agreeable, the two of us will search the facility from top to bottom. If there's anyone hiding here, we'll find them."

"And what about us?" Mackenzie asked. "What should we do?"

"You should all go to your bunk rooms and stay there."

"What about my chicken pot pie?" Bertram looked dismayed. "I don't have time to sit around on my thumbs, at least if you all want to eat tonight."

"I'm sure we can stand to wait a little longer to eat." Now it was Claudia's turn to speak. "We will go to our rooms as suggested and wait for Thomas and John to conduct their search."

Chapter 20

MACKENZIE FOLLOWED CLAUDIA, Bertram, and the rest of her colleagues on Habitat One up to the bunk rooms on the second level of Annex B. Thomas Barringer and John Decker followed up the rear and lingered in the hatchway until they were all safely ensconced in their quarters, leading her to wonder if the two men didn't trust them. After that she heard them converse for a few minutes, but she couldn't make out what they were saying. Then they moved off to start their search of the facility and the U-boat beyond.

Alone in her quarters Mackenzie locked her door and paced back and forth. She felt nervous. No, it was more than that. She was actually afraid. Even though she was sure of her own experience on the U-boat, it was easier to dismiss it as an anomaly, perhaps even a figment of her own imagination like Patrick suggested, before Lauren had ended up on the wrong end of a pipe wrench. Her stomach clenched. She hated being confined like this, not knowing what was happening elsewhere. She hoped Barringer and Decker found what they were looking for. If they came across an intruder, it would prove that all the strange occurrences, the feelings of being watched, and of the two physical assaults that had occurred, were nothing more than a bad actor fulfilling an unknown agenda. If they found nothing, they were back at square one.

She was still pacing, wearing a groove in the floor as her mother would have said, when there was a light knock at her bunk room door.

"Hello?" She looked around, surprised.

"Mac. Can I come in?" She recognized Pavel's voice on the other side of the door.

"I don't know," Mackenzie replied. "We're supposed to be staying in our bunk rooms."

"That's not exactly what we were told to do."

"Fine." Mackenzie went to the door and unlocked it. She slid it back and stepped aside to let Pavel in. "To tell the truth, I wasn't doing too well all alone in here, anyway."

"Me either," Pavel admitted.

"If Claudia catches us, this was all your idea."

"I can't imagine she cares. Thomas and John Decker only wanted us here to keep us out of the way while they search the facility. We're not actually under house arrest."

"Oh. Right." Mackenzie flushed. "Of course not."

"Besides, Claudia is in with Lauren, making sure she's okay." Pavel slid the door closed again. "I think the bigger risk is Bertram sneaking off. I imagine he's itching to get back down to that chicken pot pie of his."

"I'm sure he is," Mackenzie replied. She tried to force a smile, but it wouldn't come. "I can't believe this is happening."

"Neither can I," Pavel said. He pulled the chair out from under Mackenzie's desk and sat on it backwards, with his legs straddling the seat and the backrest pressed against his chest. He watched Mackenzie for a moment. "You going to sit down? That constant pacing isn't helping ease my nerves."

"Sorry." Mackenzie forced herself to stop and climbed onto the bunk where she sat with her back against the wall. Even then, she couldn't stop her fingers from drumming against her leg. "Do you really think someone could've accessed the habitat through the moon pool?"

"Honestly, I don't. Even when we had the dive team down here to study the outside of the submarine and make sure that the pressure hull really was in good enough condition for us to go aboard, they were using hard suits. We're almost six hundred feet down. It's pretty inhospitable out there."

"Maybe an intruder used a hard suit to come down here. They could have launched off a surface vessel and made their way to the facility using the personal thrusters built into the suit."

"Unlikely. Even if someone *could* navigate all the way from the surface in a hard suit, which I'm not denying is possible if improbable, they certainly wouldn't be able to come aboard through the moon pool and then get out of the suit unaided. And even if they could, where would they hide the suit?"

"I guess you're right," Mackenzie admitted, but she wasn't entirely convinced.

"I am right. The only easy way on and off this facility is my submersible, and I sure as hell didn't bring any unauthorized folk down here."

"Your submersible?" Mackenzie couldn't help smiling at this, even through her discomfort. "That's funny, I thought it belonged to MERO."

"The Maritime Exploration and Recovery Organization might have their name on the title in the glove box, but while I'm piloting her, she's all mine."

"You almost make it sound like you're a couple."

"I'm not denying that there's a certain rapport between us." Pavel stood and pushed the chair aside. It rolled across the floor and came to rest near the wall. He scooted up onto the bunk next to Mackenzie. "I have a feeling I'm not doing much to reassure you."

"I'm not sure anyone can reassure me." Mackenzie inched closer to him. "I have no idea if there's some deranged intruder hiding themselves away, or if one of the team has gone stir crazy and started bashing people over the head. For all I know there's a pissed off ghost running around exacting revenge for some perceived slight. But whatever's going on, I'm afraid."

"I know you are."

"And it's made even worse by the knowledge that we're stuck down here. Even if we wanted to leave, we couldn't. There's bad weather up top and it won't let up for at least a day or two. The support ship can't even reach our position. I feel so alone."

"You're not alone." Pavel reached out and slipped an arm around Mackenzie's shoulder. He pulled her close. "You have me. I won't let anything happen to you."

"I believe that, if nothing else," Mackenzie replied. Somewhere deep within her, the fear eased, if only a little. She rested her head on his shoulder and for a while at least, she felt safe.

Chapter 21

Two hours after sequestering the residents of Habitat One in their quarters, Decker crossed the umbilical to the U-boat for the second time that day with Thomas Barringer at his side. They had already performed a systematic search of the entire facility. In order to speed the process, they had split up, searching the upper levels first. Having come up empty, they moved to the lower level and went room by room, leaving nothing to chance. As expected, the submersible that had brought Decker down to the habitat was still there, which eliminated the docking bay as a means of entry for an intruder. The moon pool in Annex A was also deserted, and there was no sign anyone had used it recently. When Decker checked the hyperbaric chamber next to the pool, it too was empty. Now, as they made their way to the submarine, Decker wondered if their search was in vain.

"It looks like we're not going to find proof of an intruder," he said as they reached the hatch leading to the conning tower and closed it behind them.

"It appears so," Thomas replied. "The alternative, however, is not pleasant."

"That a colleague scared the life out of Mackenzie and

assaulted Lauren." Decker followed Thomas up the metal steps to the U-boat hatch.

"For the life of me I can't figure out how any of them could have done it though." Thomas dropped into the hatch and climbed down into the sub's control room.

"I agree that it seems unlikely. Impossible even." Decker followed behind and soon found himself surrounded by antiquated control panels. "But if we search the submarine and it turns out to be empty, as I suspect it will, then we have eliminated the alternative."

"That's what I'm afraid of." Thomas ducked under a pipe and moved toward the front of the sub. "It also means that someone coming over here triggered the alarm last night."

"Which we already know is impossible because we accounted for everyone."

"I never said it made sense." Thomas grimaced. "Honestly, just thinking about it gives me a headache."

"There must be something we're overlooking."

"I agree. If you have any ideas, I'm all ears."

"Is there any way on or off the U-boat other than the main hatch?" Decker was grasping at straws and he knew it. "Could another submersible have somehow docked with it, and that's how our intruder is getting aboard and making their escape?"

"Absolutely not." Thomas shook his head. "I wish it were that simple. The only two ways aboard Habitat One are the docking bay, which our own submersible already occupies, and the moon pool. We've ruled both out as a means of entry."

"Which leads us right back to a member of the team." Decker sighed. "We're just talking in circles."

"I agree. But someone hit Lauren over the head, and I intend to find out who it was." They had reached the forward torpedo room now. They could go no further. Thomas turned and headed back in the other direction. "We'll check the crew compartment and engine room, but I already know it's going to be a waste of time."

"How well do you know the rest of the research team?" Decker asked. "Have you worked with any of them before?"

"I've been on two expeditions with MERO prior to this one. Both involved World War II vessels. Claudia was the team leader on one of those expeditions. Pavel and Lauren were on both of them."

"And the others?"

"I've never worked with any of them before. Patrick has done some work for MERO before, but this is his first time on site. The other times he acted as an advisor from his home in France. As for Mackenzie, she's barely out of college. This is her first real gig."

"Bertram?"

"The steward. He's been with MERO for a long time, but he normally runs the galley on the support ship. I haven't had much interaction with him before now. This is the first long-duration mission for Habitat One. Before this, it was in testing. The habitat's real purpose is to provide a base of operations for recovering artifacts from shipwrecks, without needing to descend from the surface. Instead, they can use hard suits pressurized to one atmosphere and work on the bottom for extended periods. The umbilical was retrofitted after we discovered the U-boat was still pressurized."

"I see," Decker said. The team were exactly what he would have expected. No one jumped out to him as a prime suspect.

They were passing through the galley now, on the other side of the aft crew accommodation. Thomas paused and opened a door to reveal a tight compartment beyond. He stuck his head in and looked around, then stepped aside for Decker to see. "Believe it or not, this room acted as the pantry, and once supplies got low enough, a second toilet."

"That's rather disturbing," Decker said. Claudia hadn't

mentioned this during their tour earlier that day. He peered within, noting that it still contained food items. Incredibly, he could easily read the labels after all this time. There was coffee in large cans. Boxes of dried potatoes. Tinned meats with names like Schmalzfleisch and Rinderbraten, the contents of which Decker had no clue. None of it looked very appealing, especially since it was all stacked above a crude-looking metal toilet. Clearly food hygiene was low on the German Navy's list of priorities. He pulled his head back out and closed the door, then followed Thomas, who was already moving off.

They continued on through the remaining compartments, which Decker recognized from his previous tour as the engine room where the diesels that powered the U-boat on the surface were located, and the electric motor room which powered the boat when submerged. Beyond this was one more small space containing an air compressor and the aft torpedo tube. None of them showed any sign of recent activity.

"Well, that's that," Thomas said evenly. "We've searched everywhere. If anyone's hiding, they're doing a smack up job of it." He took a step back toward the control room. "Might as well head back over and give Claudia the news."

Chapter 22

AT A QUARTER past three that afternoon, Decker and Barringer stood in Claudia Landry's office back on Habitat One. Decker glanced around. It was the same size as Patrick's office, which he had visited earlier in the day, although it was decidedly neater. The door was closed, making the tiny space feel even smaller. Too small, he thought, for three grown adults to occupy simultaneously, which was why the room contained just one chair, upon which Claudia presently sat.

She did not look pleased. "I presume your search was fruitless."

"We found nothing that would show an unauthorized presence aboard the habitat or submarine," Thomas said.

"Which leads us to the inescapable conclusion that one of our own perpetrated the recent acts of violence."

Decker stood uncomfortably near the closed door. "Except we know that's not—"

"I'm well aware of the problem with that assumption, Mr. Decker," Claudia said, interrupting him. "Everyone appears to be accounted for whenever there is an incident. They all have, as a detective would say, airtight alibis."

"Which means there must be another answer," Decker

replied. It hadn't escaped his attention that Claudia had returned to addressing him formally, rather than by his first name. This was, he speculated, an attempt to assert her authority as the team's leader and also to distance herself should it become clear that one of their own was indeed the perpetrator. He was, it appeared, not above suspicion even though he had not been present when Mackenzie was assaulted on the sub.

"If you have that answer, please enlighten me." Claudia glanced between the two men.

Thomas shook his head. "We've got nothing."

"Do you agree with that summation?" Claudia's gaze shifted to focus on Decker.

"On the face of it, yes I do." Decker couldn't help thinking there was more to what was going on than met the eye. If no unauthorized outsiders had come aboard the habitat, and they had all but ruled out one of their own, that left one conclusion, albeit far-fetched. They were being visited by someone or something that didn't adhere to the rules of the regular world. "I can't help thinking about the events reported by your team. Not just the two attacks, which obviously have a basis in fact, but the less tangible experiences. The feelings of being watched. Seeing shadowy figures. A general air of uncomfortableness. I'm sure that these are all part of the bigger picture, rather than being the product of overactive imaginations."

"Here we go," Thomas snorted. "I was wondering how long it would take to get to this."

"Would you like to explain what you mean by that?" Decker glanced sideways at the prickly munitions specialist.

"I know all about your past. I did some digging before you came down here. It seemed prudent to know who we were dealing with."

"And?"

"For one, I find it hard to trust the judgment of a man

who thinks he shot a werewolf." Thomas raised his hands in mock deference. "I respect the fact that you defended your town from what was obviously a vicious killer, but you do seem to have a knack for coming to outlandish conclusions. Word on the dark web is that you are employed as a monster hunter."

"I didn't think we had access to the internet down here," Decker said, as evenly as he could muster.

"We don't. I used the radio to contact an old friend who was in military intelligence before he retired. He knows how to find things out."

"He wouldn't have had to look very hard regarding what happened in Wolf Haven," Decker said. "The more sordid details were all over the press. I can't imagine he needed military intelligence training to find that out."

"That wasn't all he found out. There are rumors of an incident involving you in the Florida Woodlands. A bunch of people got killed. Something about a genetically engineered prehistoric alligator. It was all covered up, of course, but the breadcrumbs are there if you know how to follow them."

"Your friend might need to check his sources," Decker said. "You'll be telling me I know the true identity of Jack the Ripper next. He's a vampire if you can believe that."

"Very funny," Thomas replied, even though he didn't look amused.

Claudia rapped her fingers on the desk. "When you two are finished sparring like a pair of five-year-old's, can we get back to the problem at hand? I really don't care what Mr. Decker's background is so long as we resolve this situation before anyone else gets hurt."

"I was just trying to keep us grounded in reality." Thomas shrugged. "But hey, what do I know."

"Do you have a plan to get to the bottom of this, Mr. Decker?" Claudia asked, ignoring Thomas's barb.

"Actually, I do." Decker shifted his weight from one foot to the other. He was starting to feel uncomfortable standing in the cramped office. "As I see it, a member of the research team would know that opening the hatch sets off an alarm. It would be better to conduct their nefarious business prior to the habitat switching over to night mode. An intruder unfamiliar with the workings of the facility would have no such knowledge. Yet when we searched the habitat and U-boat, we found no evidence of an intruder. Our only clue so far is the faint footprint we discovered last night outside the hatch, and anyone could have left that. It wasn't even clear enough to compare against the soles of the team members' shoes. What we need is actual evidence."

"How do you propose we get that?" Claudia leaned forward.

"Simple. Whoever has been infiltrating the facility will most likely return. Most of the activity has taken place on the U-boat or near the umbilical hatches. Even Lauren's attack occurred in the mechanical room near the umbilical. I propose we set up a video recording device near that hatch and see what happens tonight."

"There's only one problem," Thomas said.

"What's that?" Decker asked.

"We don't have any video recording devices. There aren't even security cameras on the facility."

That's not entirely true," Claudia said. "There's the D-SLR we've been using to document the U-boat's interior. Don't those things have a video mode?"

"They absolutely do," Decker replied. "We used our digital camera back in Wolf Haven to take videos of crime scenes all the time."

"Then all we need to do is mount it on a tripod and let it record. Easy as pie."

"After that we go to bed as usual," Decker said. "By morning, we should have our answer."

"Good." Claudia looked pleased for the first time since the

meeting began. "Let's keep this among the three of us though. If our mysterious assailant is indeed one of the other team members, I don't want to tip them off."

"Unless it's one of us three," Thomas said. "In which case we already have."

"Then we'd better hope it isn't one of us," Claudia said, looking between the two men. "Or this whole exercise will be in vain."

Chapter 23

THAT EVENING, after a later than usual dinner in the mess hall, Decker left the researchers sitting around sharing a bottle of bourbon that Pavel had brought from his bunk room. Sinking shots, they swapped war stories of their experiences on other expeditions, each more far-fetched than the last. Claudia, it appeared, had completely given up on enforcing the no alcohol policy, perhaps realizing that tensions were running high and they needed a release. Decker wasn't sure that alcohol was the right approach, since they still had no answers regarding the events of the last twenty-four hours, or Mackenzie's encounter days before on the U-boat. But he wasn't about to dissuade them, since the impromptu gathering allowed him to go about setting up the surveillance of the umbilical hatch door unobserved. But before that, he wanted to check in on Lauren, who was still in her bunk room. After serving the rest of the team, Bertram had taken a slice of chicken pot pie up to her, but upon his return had reported that she was unenthusiastic.

Decker made his way to the second level accommodation and knocked on her door.

"Yes?" The response was immediate.

"It's John Decker. May I enter?"

"You can come in, I'm decent."

Decker slid the door open and stepped inside, then closed it behind him. Lauren was sitting propped up in her bunk wearing a baggy T-shirt. The covers were pulled up to her waist. She had a book propped on her bent knees.

"Are you sure you should be reading?" Decker asked. "It might not be the best thing if you have a concussion."

"I'm not sure there's a moratorium on reading if one has a bump on the head," Lauren replied. "Do you actually know anything about concussions?"

"Apparently not." Decker smiled. "I just wanted to stick my head in and see how you were doing."

"Physically I feel fine." Lauren closed the book and set it aside. "I'm sure I'll have a nice lump where the wrench got me, and I had a headache most of the afternoon. It's gone off now though."

"Good." Decker nodded.

"The pills Claudia gave me from the emergency medical kit helped with that." Lauren's voice faltered. "Did you have any luck with your search of the facility?"

"No, we didn't." Decker wished he had better news for her. "We're no closer to solving the mystery of who attacked you than before."

"Oh. That's a shame." Lauren paused for a moment, as if lost in thought. "I'm sorry I wasn't more help earlier. I've been racking my brain ever since the attack, wondering if there was some detail I forgot to mention, but there isn't. I can't believe I didn't see his face. It all happened so fast."

"Don't worry about it." Decker eyed the untouched chicken pot pie that sat on the desk with a fork next to it. "Have you eaten anything?"

"Not yet. I haven't been very hungry, to be honest. I know I should eat. I'll force some down, don't worry."

"Make sure that you do." Decker glanced toward the door.

"I should go. I'm sure you want to get back to reading your book."

"Okay," Lauren nodded. "Thank you for checking in on me."

"My pleasure," Decker replied. "I'll check on you again before bed, and I expect that pie to be gone."

"You don't need to fret over me," Lauren said, her cool blue eyes meeting his own. "I can take care of myself."

"The lump on your head would seem to contradict that."

"You make a valid point." Lauren laughed. "I'll do as I'm told and eat the pie."

"Perfect." Decker turned and stepped out into the corridor. From below he could hear raucous laughter. The residents of Habitat One were still busy demolishing Pavel's bottle of bourbon, which should distract them long enough for Decker to set up surveillance of the umbilical hatch without drawing attention. If they were lucky, they would know the identity of Lauren's attacker by morning.

Chapter 24

WHEN DECKER ARRIVED BACK on the lower level, Thomas was waiting for him. He had the camera in one hand and a tripod under his arm.

"Are you ready to set a trap for our mysterious visitor?" Thomas asked as Decker approached.

"Can't wait," Decker replied. Pavel's voice, full of excitement, drifted from the direction of the mess. The marine archaeologist was telling a tall tale, no doubt with a glass of bourbon in his hand. "I trust you didn't have any issues slipping away."

"Nah. They're all so engrossed in their stories that they barely noticed me leave. By the way they're acting, you would think everyone was having the time of their lives, but I think they're all just so wound up that they need an outlet. Besides, it won't take us long to set the camera up. If anyone asks where I went, I'll just say I was checking on Lauren." Thomas frowned. "How's she doing, by the way?"

"She's pretty chipper, considering. Hasn't eaten yet, but I think I talked her into it."

"She'd better eat his chicken pot pie, or else." Thomas chuckled. "Bertram was mad enough that dinner was delayed because he was confined to quarters earlier today, but if someone snubs his pie too... Let's just say I wouldn't want to be that person, head wound or not."

They were in the corridor leading to the umbilical hatch now. Decker looked around. "We should put it somewhere unobtrusive."

"There aren't many hiding places here," Thomas said. He glanced toward a door near the central hub. "How about there?"

"That might work." Decker opened the door. He flicked the light on and peered inside at the workshop beyond. Work surfaces lined the walls, with cabinets mounted above. What looked like pieces of the sub sat on a table in the center of the room. There were cowlings, engine parts, and what looked like a small fuel tank.

"I stripped a torpedo down after I disarmed it," Thomas explained. "It's one thing to read about these things in a book, but quite another to see one up close. It's actually quite fascinating."

"I bet."

Thomas pointed to an object that looked like part of a radio, with a copper pickup coil, and what looked like an old-fashioned bulb that Decker guessed was a vacuum tube. "That's part of the magnetic pistol. It's a proximity detonator. The torpedo had two ways to take out an enemy ship. It could either explode on impact, or it could go off as it passed under the ship's keel. U-boat commanders preferred the second method because it broke the vessel's back and sent it to the bottom quicker."

"Thanks for the history lesson," Decker said, stepping into the room and checking the line of sight from the door to the umbilical hatch.

"From the tone of your voice, I suspect you want me to stop prattling and get on with it."

"Fascinating as those torpedo parts are, I think we'd better focus on the job at hand," Decker replied. He was still irritated by their earlier conversation in Claudia's office, and Thomas's comments regarding his past. "We can set up the camera in the doorway, pointing toward the hatch. With the light off and the door almost closed, it won't be noticeable."

"Tell me something," Thomas said as he placed the camera on the ground and opened the tripod. "The incident in Wolf Haven that got you fired. Did you really believe there was a werewolf running around?"

"It wasn't a werewolf, not exactly. But yes, I did." Decker wondered if his confrontation with the Loup-Garou was going to haunt him for the rest of his days. It felt like everyone he encountered knew about it. "I came face to face with it. It's hard to dispute the evidence of your own eyes."

Thomas was extending the tripod legs. He shook his head. "I don't know, man. It sounds crazy."

"That's what the board of inquiry that fired me thought too."

"Which is why you're now working for CUSP, instead of the Sheriff's Department."

"It's better than being unemployed." Decker watched Thomas position the tripod inside the workshop on the doorway's threshold. "I don't expect people to believe what I encountered, but it doesn't make it any less true."

"And you think there's something similar going on here?" Thomas reached down and picked up the camera. He checked the media slot to make sure there was a card inserted and then attached the camera to the tripod shoe. "I don't mean a werewolf, obviously. But something supernatural."

"Honestly, I don't know what to think." Decker stood back and examined the setup. "Looks good. Not too noticeable."

"Shall we see if it works?"

"Sure." Thomas set the camera and stepped away. A red LED blinked above the lens. "Looks like were up and running."

"That red light won't work," Decker said. "It draws the eye. Too obvious."

"That's why I brought this." Thomas reached into his pocket and took out a roll of black electrical tape. He peeled a piece off and stuck it over the light. "Better?"

"If you weren't looking for it, you'd hardly know it was there," Decker said. "Especially once the habitat goes into night mode."

"We're done here, then." Thomas checked the camera one last time, then stepped away. "Might as well leave it running. I have a 256 GB SD card in there. We should get at least twenty hours of recording."

"We won't need more than half that."

"Better safe than sorry." Thomas rubbed his hands together. "I say we go back to the mess and see if Pavel has any of that bourbon left. I don't know about you, but I could use a nightcap before bed."

Decker glanced at his watch, surprised to see that it was past ten o'clock already. Only two more hours until Habitat One switched to night mode. He felt a tingle of anticipation. If anything happened tonight, they would capture it on video. In the meantime, a nightcap actually sounded good. He took one last look at the camera sitting on its tripod and turned to Thomas. "Come on. Let's get that drink before the rest of them polish off the entire bottle."

Chapter 25

Decker couldn't sleep. He lay on his narrow bunk and wondered if the camera they had set up would catch anything. More to the point, he wondered if it would reveal their intruder to be one of the team, despite being circumstantially improbable. Only himself, Thomas, and Claudia knew the hatch was being recorded. Either way, if an intruder visited tonight, the camera should catch it.

Decker rolled over onto his side and closed his eyes. The habitat was quiet. Everyone had retired to their bunk rooms a little over an hour ago. He lay that way for a while, his mind too active to grant his body the rest it craved. After another thirty minutes, he rolled back over and sat up, frustrated. He slipped out from under the covers and got dressed. The clock above bunk told him that it was a little before two in the morning. So far there has been no sign of an intruder. No alarms going off.

He went to his bunk room door and slid it open a little, then peered out. The corridor beyond was dark and empty. He pushed the door open further and stepped out, then made his way along to the central hub and down.

He had found that when he couldn't sleep, a cup of hot

tea often soothed him. He especially liked green tea. It was a remedy that surprised Nancy the first time he drank it in her presence. He was, she said, a constant surprise. Not someone she would've expected to enjoy such a dainty pleasure. He had laughed at this. He also allowed her to introduce him to other types of tea. Chamomile, peppermint, and lavender. But he still liked green tea the best, not that he held much hope of finding it here. If there was nothing else, he would settle for breakfast tea.

He crossed to the mess and stepped inside, making his way through the dimly lit room toward the galley at the rear. The bourbon bottle still sat on the table, but now it was empty. Their whisky glasses were gone, however. No doubt cleared away by Bertram before he headed up to bed. He turned his attention back toward the galley and noticed a thin sliver of light glowing through the space where the double doors met.

The galley lights were still on.

Either Bertram had neglected to switch them off before he left for the night, or he wasn't alone. Decker came to a halt and listened. At first, he heard nothing and thought that Bertram had indeed forgotten the lights. But then he heard muffled footsteps and the sound of someone opening a cabinet. Several seconds of running water followed.

Decker crept forward and pushed one door open enough to peer through the gap. A figure stood at the end of the galley, facing away from him. At the sound of the door, the figure turned, startled.

Decker relaxed. It was just Pavel.

"Heavens above, you nearly gave me a heart attack."

"Likewise," Decker said. "I wasn't expecting to find anyone down here."

"I was making myself a hot drink," Pavel replied. "Couldn't sleep."

"You too, huh?" Decker saw a kettle sitting on the stovetop, steam rising from its spout.

"I'd be surprised if anyone is sleeping, given the circumstances. Between that alarm going off last night and Lauren being attacked…"

"I know what you mean." Decker nodded toward the kettle. "What are you making?"

"Hot chocolate." He ripped open a single serve packet and deposited the contents into a mug. "It would be better with milk, but we have a limited supply and Bertram won't be happy if I squander it, so water will have to suffice."

"Here's hoping you have marshmallows at least."

"If only." Pavel chuckled and picked up the kettle. He poured boiling water into the mug. "That's me done. I'm outta here. There's still hot water if you want it."

"Thanks."

Pavel picked up the mug and started toward the door. "Our selection of beverages in the cabinet next to the microwave, although I can't vouch for the selection."

"I'm sure I'll find something," Decker replied.

As Pavel reached the door, he glanced back over his shoulder. "Here's hoping for a quiet night."

"Indeed." Decker watched Pavel leave and then went to the cabinet. As expected, there was no green tea, but he found a mostly empty box of oolong. He prepared his beverage and turned the galley lights off before exiting. When he reached the central hub, he paused. The corridor leading to the umbilical was bathed in a yellow half-light. Curious, he crossed to the corridor and looked toward at the camera in the workshop doorway. With the facility in night mode and the lights dimmed, the D-SLR was barely noticeable.

Satisfied the trap was still set, Decker turned and made his way back up to the second level and his bunk room. He sat on the bed and drank the tea, then climbed back under the covers and closed his eyes. This time, sleep found him.

Chapter 26

THE FIGURE STOOD CONCEALED in darkness on the other side of the hub, his body pressed into the shadows of the Annex A corridor leading from the moon pool. He watched John Decker exit the mess, clutching a mug from which steam rose. The hub was busier than he expected given the time of night. Pavel, one of the two marine archaeologists on the habitat, had emerged a few minutes earlier and made his way back up to the bunk rooms on the second level of Annex B. Decker did no such thing. Instead, he crossed to D and poked his head inside the corridor leading to the umbilical. He lingered there momentarily, then as if satisfied that all was in order, Decker finally headed back up to his own bunk room.

The man waited a while longer in the shadows, to make sure no one else was going to come down for a midnight snack or sleep-inducing beverage. Then, satisfied that all was quiet once more, he slipped from concealment and crept across the hub toward the lower level of Annex D. When he reached the threshold; the man stopped in almost the exact place Decker had stood moments ago.

There was a digital camera here, secreted inside the workshop doorway with a view of the umbilical hatch. It stood on a tripod tucked behind the doorframe and would be barely noticeable if you didn't know it was there. This was what the meddling CUSP operative had been attending to, no doubt checking that it was still recording.

He knew all about John Decker. He had done his homework. Decker's presence here was far from ideal. In fact, it was a rather large inconvenience. It increased his risk of being discovered before completing his mission. Regardless, he would keep going. He expected such obstacles, like the night alarm on the hatch door leading to the umbilical. It had taken him a while to figure out how to turn that off from the server room. Now there was this camera pointing at the umbilical hatch, waiting for an unsuspecting intruder to breeze by. It was a clever trap that might have worked under different circumstances. He felt a flicker of annoyance. The camera posed a dilemma. If he left it recording, they would surely see him. Turning it off was not ideal either, since it would create a noticeable break in the recording. The latter was, however, the more desirable of his options. The man reached out and turned the camera off. There was a piece of electrical tape covering the recording light. Just to be safe, he peeled back the tape. The light was not on. It was safe to proceed.

The man stepped further into the corridor and made his way to the hatch door. He gripped the release handle and turned it, then swung the door open. With one last look over his shoulder, the man stepped into the umbilical and pulled the hatch door closed again behind him. Then he made his way toward the waiting U-boat.

Chapter 27

THE NIGHT PASSED WITHOUT INCIDENT. Decker stirred a little before seven, surprised how rested he felt. He rose and dressed, then went to the washroom at the end of the corridor to freshen up. By the time he deposited his toiletry bag back in the bunk room, other members of the team were emerging from their own quarters.

Pavel nodded a greeting. "Did the tea work?"

"I think it might have," Decker replied. "How about you?"

"Slept like a baby."

"Which is much easier when there isn't an alarm blaring in the middle of the night," Patrick said, pushing past them in the direction of the central hub.

"He's happy this morning," Pavel said, watching him go.

"Is he ever?" Decker asked.

"Sometimes." Pavel ran a hand through his unbrushed morning hair. "He liked it the first day we were on the habitat, and Claudia opened a bottle of champagne to celebrate. Of course, he said it wasn't the good stuff. Still drank it though."

"I'd hate to be his wife," Decker commented.

"I can't imagine that he's married."

"You'd be wrong." Mackenzie was leaving her room with a

towel clutched in one hand and a makeup bag in the other. "He's been married three times. He's racked up just as many divorces. When the man's not gracing us with his presence on the ocean floor, he apparently lives in an apartment outside Paris with the mistress that broke up his third marriage."

"I find that improbable." Pavel shook his head. "Four different women found Patrick attractive?"

"Only telling you what he told me." Mackenzie started toward the washroom. "I'm going to take a shower. I wanted to take one before bed but the thought of being in there alone with the habitat in night mode was too much, especially after what happened to Lauren."

"Speaking of which," Decker said. "I wonder how Lauren is feeling this morning."

"You can ask her yourself at breakfast," Mackenzie called back over her shoulder. "She left her bunk room a while ago. I heard her talking to Bertram and Claudia."

"Are you going to be okay in there on your own?" Pavel asked as Mackenzie reached the washroom door.

"You volunteering to keep me company in the shower?" Mackenzie paused in the doorway and looked back.

"What? No... I was just..." Pavel looked flustered. "I didn't mean it like that."

"Oh. Then you don't want to keep me company?" Mackenzie sounded hurt.

"Yes, I do... I mean... This is coming out all wrong." Pavel said. "I was concerned, that's all. You've been so stressed. I wasn't asking if I could hop in the shower with you or anything."

"Shame. Sounds kind of fun, if a bit cramped. There's not much room in that cubicle, space being at a premium and all. Although that could have its upside too."

"Mac..."

"Relax." Mackenzie laughed. "I was just messing with you. I know what you meant."

"You can be evil. You know that?" Pavel couldn't help a tight smile. His cheeks were flushed red.

"Gotta keep things interesting," Mackenzie said, her eyes sparkling. And then she was gone, drawing the door closed behind her and locking it.

Decker patted the ruffled archaeologist and sub pilot on the back. "She sure got the better of you."

"Yes, indeed. I believe that she did." Pavel cleared his throat and turned toward the hub. "I'm going to get me some breakfast before this gets any more embarrassing."

Chapter 28

When Decker entered the mess, Claudia pulled him aside before he could join the others at the table.

"Have you taken care of the camera yet?" She asked in a low voice.

"Not yet." Decker's stomach rumbled. Bertram was clattering around in the galley and judging by the bottle of real Vermont maple syrup sitting on the table. It looked like pancakes were on the menu. "I'll get it after breakfast."

"Good. I'd rather not leave it there any longer than necessary. We may have to set it up again and I don't want anyone seeing it."

"I'm in full agreement," Decker said. "I find it hard to believe any of your team are responsible for what has been happening, but I'm certainly not ruling it out."

"My sentiments exactly." Claudia nodded. "Just because nothing happened last night doesn't mean there won't be more occurrences and I would like to rule out the members of my team once and for all."

"Not to mention solving the mystery of who is coming aboard," Decker replied. Bertram emerged from the galley with a piping hot carafe of coffee. He took a step toward the table, hoping Claudia would take the hint. He'd gotten a better night's sleep than expected, but he would still function better after an infusion of caffeine.

"That too." Claudia turned toward the table. "After breakfast then."

Decker nodded. He followed Claudia to the table, and they took their seats.

Bertram was pouring coffee into mugs, which he then passed around until everyone had one. He left one mug empty. "Since Mackenzie hasn't joined us yet."

"She's not far behind," Pavel said.

"I hope not. Ten minutes and the food will be ready." Bertram turned and ambled back toward the galley, wiping his hands on his apron as he went.

Decker took a packet of sugar, ripped it open, and dropped the contents into his coffee. He stirred it and watched the liquid swirl around for a moment, a curl of steam rising from the center. He blew on it and then took a sip. The coffee was strong, the way he liked it. A lot of folk back in his native Louisiana liked to put chicory in their brew. Not Decker. He found it gave the coffee a slightly bitter taste.

Lauren watched him over the rim of her own mug. "Are we allowed to ask how your investigation is going, John? Have you made any progress?"

"Not as much as I'd like," Decker admitted.

"Have you got any theories yet?" Pavel asked. "Mackenzie has been freaked out the last few days. I would sure love to put her mind at rest."

"I bet that's not all you'd love to do," Patrick mumbled under his breath.

"Excuse me?" Pavel turned to look at the Frenchman. "What's that supposed to mean?"

"I've seen the way you look at her." Patrick snorted. "Plus, I noticed you sneaking into her room yesterday afternoon while the facility was being searched."

"I wasn't sneaking into her room. I went over there to see if she was okay, that's all."

"If you say so." Patrick rubbed his chin. "You do know there's a rule against fraternizing with other team members, right?"

"I'm not fraternizing. Besides, my relationship with Mackenzie, platonic or not, is none of your business."

"For heaven's sake, you two," Claudia said, giving the table a sharp slap with her palm to get their attention. She glared at Patrick. "Why can't you play nice?"

Patrick shrugged.

"That's what I thought." Claudia sighed. She looked at Decker. "I swear, it's like being at summer camp with a bunch of unruly children."

"I wouldn't know," Decker said. "I never went to summer camp when I was a kid."

"You didn't miss much," Lauren said. "Lots of sitting around a campfire singing 'Kumbaya' and making friendship bracelets."

"Doesn't sound all that bad," Decker said.

"That's because you never went to summer camp," Lauren shot back.

"Touché." Decker took another long sip of his coffee.

"Thank you." Lauren sat back in her chair and smiled. "Summer camp aside, what's the deal with you?"

"You're going to have to elaborate on that," Decker said. "I'm not sure what you're asking."

"Well, for a start, what brings you down here?" Lauren waved a hand. "Not literally, of course. I know Pavel brought you down here. I mean, how did you end up working for CUSP? And what exactly do CUSP occupy themselves with when they're not financing obscure expeditions?"

Decker glanced toward Thomas, but the burly specialist remained silent and didn't return his gaze. If the man had engaged in scuttlebutt with anyone, it certainly wasn't Lauren.

"I'm curious about that myself," Claudia said.

Decker felt every pair of eyes turn upon him. "There's really not much to tell. I was in law enforcement for many years. NYPD for a while, and then as sheriff of a small Louisiana town. After that, CUSP approached me. They needed someone with my analytical skills. As for what we do, I'm not at liberty to say beyond the fact that we support a lot of archaeological and research expeditions."

"That was a lot of words to tell us nothing," Patrick said.

"All right. How about something easier?" Lauren said. "What about your personal life? Is there a Mrs. John Decker waiting somewhere out there?"

"Now that I can talk about." Decker sipped his coffee. "There is. Or at least, there will be as soon as we set a date."

"Ah. You're engaged."

"Her name's Nancy. High school sweetheart. We reconnected last year."

"Now this is interesting." Lauren leaned forward.

"I don't find it very interesting," Patrick said with a grimace.

Lauren glanced toward him. "Not surprising." She turned back to Decker. "And Nancy doesn't mind you taking off and putting yourself in danger like this?"

"I wouldn't go that far," Decker replied. "I think she'd rather I was at home with her."

Pavel glanced toward the door. "Speaking of people being with us, Mackenzie should be here by now. I wonder if I should go and check on her."

"See," Patrick said. "This is what I was talking about."

"I'm sure she's fine," Claudia said.

A moment later, as if to prove her wrong, a terrified scream pierced the air from the level above.

Chapter 29

WHILE THE REST of the team retreated downstairs to get started on breakfast, Mackenzie stepped into the washroom and closed the door, then locked it. The chamber was small, containing nothing but a sink with a vanity mirror installed above it, and a single shower stall. The only other object of note in the room was a sign affixed to the wall next to the mirror, reminding everyone to limit their showers to less than five minutes. Water was at a premium, as was the electricity needed to heat it.

Mackenzie was looking forward to hers.

She placed her towel on a hook next to the shower and brushed her teeth. That done, she reached into the stall and turned the water on. Then she stripped off her flannel pajamas and folded them neatly, depositing them next to the towel, before checking the water temperature with her hand. Satisfied, she stepped into the stall and pulled the curtain across.

The piping hot water felt good on her naked skin, even though the pressure wasn't great. She squeezed body wash from a dispenser mounted on the wall and lathered it. It was nice to be clean again. At home, she showered every night before bed. Sometimes, if she had been jogging or exercising at the gym, she showered twice a day. On Habitat One she was reduced to twice weekly showers. The facility boasted its own workout room, albeit more the size of a closet, with a stationary bicycle and an elliptical trainer. Mackenzie didn't make use of it though, partly because long days at the research team's beck and call had left her exhausted, but mostly because she had no desire to work up a sweat without the ability to shower afterwards. She suspected that everyone else avoided the exercise room on the second level of Annex C for the same reason. Except for Patrick, who she doubted had done more than five minutes of exercise in his entire life. He wasn't exactly overweight, but he wasn't in the peak of fitness either. Not to mention the slight but ever-present stink of the Gitanes he'd chained-smoked on the deck of the research ship that brought them out here. Given the strict smoking ban aboard the habitat, Mackenzie was sure he had not smoked a cigarette in weeks, yet the odor remained. She wondered if he even knew the exercise room was there.

She rinsed off the body wash and held her head under the shower jet, running her hands through her hair to wet it, then squeezed shampoo from a second dispenser and massaged it into her scalp. She let out a murmur of pleasure and closed her eyes, relishing the tingle as the hot water rinsed the shampoo away, and lingered under the cascading stream. She was loath to step out into the chilly air beyond the shower cubicle and put an end to one of the few luxuries she looked forward to. She knew her five minutes had surely elapsed, but everyone else was down in the mess. No one would know if she eked out a few extra minutes of bliss.

Then, from beyond the curtain, she heard a faint but perceivable shuffling sound.

Mackenzie's eyes flew open. She tensed involuntarily. Held her breath. Listened.

She felt an overwhelming conviction that someone was

standing on the other side of the shower curtain. Unmoving. Listening right back at her.

Had one of the other researchers come back up to the bunk rooms to look for her? But that didn't make sense. She had locked the washroom door. Besides, they would surely hear the shower and leave her in peace.

Breathing out slowly, so that whoever was there would not hear the exhalation, she reached out and touched the shower curtain, but then withdrew her hand. If she really wasn't alone in the washroom, she wanted to know. At the same time, a part of her didn't want to know. But standing there naked and trembling under the water would do her no good. Scared or not, she had to find out.

Stealing herself, Mackenzie pinched the edge of the shower curtain between her thumb and forefinger and inched it back just enough to view the room beyond. Her heart pounded against her ribs. She felt blood rushing in her ears.

But nobody was there.

What she did see was a pile of crumpled white fabric on the floor below the sink. The towel had fallen, that was all. She almost laughed out loud, giddy with relief.

She stepped back under the shower and stood there a moment longer, even though she was way over her allotted time by now. Then, reluctantly, she pulled the curtain back and stepped out, turning the water off as she did so.

The air was chilly on her skin. Actually, it was freezing. The ambient temperature on the habitat was always kept lower than she found comfortable, and while the act of showering itself was pleasurable, the moments after were not. She felt goosebumps rise on her skin. She shivered and bent down to pick up the towel.

When she stood again, her eyes aligned with the vanity mirror and what she saw there sent a jab of terror coursing through her.

Mackenzie dropped the towel and screamed.

Chapter 30

MACKENZIE'S SCREAM split the air. Decker was the first on his feet, jumping up and almost toppling his chair as he sprinted toward the central hub. Pavel was close behind. Even Bertram had run from the galley to see what the commotion was about.

They sprinted through the hub toward the metal steps leading to the second level. Decker took them two at a time and raced around the upper gantry. He reached the accommodation block, where the bunk rooms were located, and skidded around the corner to see Mackenzie at the far end of the corridor, standing in the washroom doorway wrapped in a towel.

She was dripping wet, her hair plastered down over her shoulders. When she saw him, she made a move forward, relief flooding her face.

"What happened?" Decker gasped as he reached her. "Are you hurt?"

"I'm not hurt." Mackenzie's voice trembled when she spoke.

The rest of the team were crowding behind Decker now. Pavel pushed his way forward. "What happened? Did someone attack you again?"

"No. I wasn't attacked." Mackenzie looked like she was on the verge of tears. She cast an uneasy glance back over her shoulder into the washroom. "But there was someone in there with me."

"How?" Pavel shook his head. "That's impossible. We were all down in the mess."

Mackenzie nodded. "The door was locked too."

"Then how do you know someone was there? Did you see them?" Decker asked hopefully. If Mackenzie had gotten a good look at the intruder that disturbed her shower, it would go a long way to figuring out what was happening on Habitat One.

"I didn't *see* a soul." Mackenzie hugged the towel tight to herself. Water dripped from her body onto the metal floor, making a tap, tap, tapping sound. "That's not how I know I wasn't alone. I'll show you." She hesitated a moment, then stepped back into the washroom and pointed.

Decker followed her in, with Pavel at his heel. The room was too small for everyone to crowd inside, so the others lingered in the doorway with craning necks to see what had so frightened their coworker.

At first Decker noticed nothing. The room looked just like it had earlier. Then he realized what Mackenzie was pointing at. There, upon the steamed-up mirror, someone had written five words in a shaky hand.

Können Sie mir bitte helfen?

Decker stared at the phrase. His eyes narrowed as he recognized the word construction, even if he couldn't decipher it. "That's German."

"Let me see." Pavel's voice rose in pitch as he nudged forward to peer over Decker's shoulder. "What does it say?"

"That's a good question." Decker glanced backwards, looking for Patrick, who was already pushing his way past the group to gain access to the washroom.

Pavel stepped aside and allowed the Frenchman to enter.

"Well?" Decker asked.

Patrick scratched his chin, a puzzled expression crossing his face. "This makes absolutely no sense."

Pavel let out a frustrated huff. "Just tell us what it means."

"Very well," Patrick said. "Roughly translated, it reads, *can you please help me?*"

Chapter 31

THE MESSAGE WAS ALREADY FADING as the steam dissipated. Decker pushed back through the gathered researchers toward his bunk room. "I should get my phone and photograph this, before it's too late."

"Good idea." Claudia poked her head inside the washroom to look at the cryptic message. She turned to Mackenzie. "Are you sure you didn't see anything?"

"If I had, I would've told you." Mackenzie was shivering.

Lauren stepped forward. She put an arm around Mackenzie's shoulder. "We should get you back to your room. You'll feel better once you're dressed."

"I'm not sure I'll feel better until we're done down here and off this facility." Mackenzie's bottom lip trembled. "But I would like to put some clothes on. It feels kind of weird standing here in nothing but a towel with everyone crowding around me."

"Of course." Lauren steered the frightened research assistant back toward her bunk room.

"You won't leave me alone, will you?" Mackenzie asked, her brow furrowing.

"Absolutely not." Lauren gave her a sympathetic smile.

"I'll stay with you the whole time. I won't let you out of my sight."

Mackenzie nodded, obviously relieved.

Decker let them pass and then ducked into his own bunk room and scooped up his phone from the desk. It was the first time he'd thought about it since arriving on the habitat. There was no cell service or internet, so he hadn't needed it until now. He hurried back to the washroom and squeezed his way inside, then snapped off several fast photos of the quickly disappearing message. When he was done, he checked the phone's screen to make sure the pictures were clear, then pushed the phone into his pocket. He wished he could email them to Adam Hunt. He also wanted to send his boss a report on the strange occurrences and his progress so far, but it would all have to wait until the bad weather eased overhead and Pavel could take him to the surface in the submersible. He didn't need to worry about being in range of a cell tower so long as he had a view of the sky. While he could not place or receive calls this far out to sea, the specially built CUSP phone could connect to the internet via a highly classified military satellite network. How his employer had gained access to such technology Decker did not know, and he suspected that any inquiries regarding the matter would fall on deaf ears.

With Mackenzie absent and the message all but gone, the rest of the team were drifting away now. Bertram cleared his throat and started toward the central hub. "I'm going down to finish making breakfast. We might be through the looking glass, but we still need to eat."

"I second that," Pavel said. "I'd like to sort this out as much as anyone, but we'll think better if we aren't hungry."

As the corridor emptied, Decker pulled Claudia and Thomas aside. "I'm going to retrieve the footage from the camera right now. I don't think it would be wise to leave that camera unattended a moment longer."

"My thoughts exactly," Claudia said, nodding.

"What's the big rush?" Thomas asked. "I'm sure it can wait until after we eat."

"I'm not so sure about that," Decker replied. "With all that has been going on around here, I'd like to make sure it's secure as soon as possible."

"I agree with John," Claudia said, finally reverting to using Decker's first name. "Assuming there are no more surprises, we'll review it in my office immediately after breakfast."

"What's the point? It won't show much," Thomas said. "The alarm didn't go off last night, so we know the umbilical hatch remained closed."

"We don't know that for sure," Decker replied, although he suspected Thomas was right. The recording probably wouldn't show much since the night hours had passed uneventfully. But they couldn't rely on assumptions, especially since one or more unknown persons appeared to be moving around the habitat at will. "Given what has occurred, it would be prudent to verify one way or the other if the camera recorded any unusual events last night."

"You're absolutely right, of course," Thomas said. "I'll retrieve the SD card and return the camera to the server room equipment locker."

"I'd prefer to remove the card personally, if you don't mind," Decker replied. "And let's keep the camera where it is for now. I'd like to record again tonight. Just because we haven't yet caught anything, doesn't mean we won't. Eventually, the intruder will reveal themselves."

"And when they do, we'll get to the bottom of this," Claudia said.

"Or it will deepen the mystery," Decker replied thoughtfully as Mackenzie's bunk room door opened, and the two women emerged. "I have a feeling that we are, as Bertram so succinctly phrased it, through the looking glass."

Chapter 32

DECKER DESCENDED from the upper level and hurried across the central hub toward Annex D. The camera was exactly where he and Thomas had left it the evening before, concealed inside a workshop doorway.

He peeled the electrical tape from the front of the camera, satisfied to see the red indicator light blinking. It was still recording. He fumbled with the buttons on top and turned it off, then opened the cover protecting the SD slot. He depressed the card and released it, letting it click out, and pulled it free. That done, Decker lifted the tripod with the camera still attached, and pushed the workshop door open. He placed the camera and tripod inside, and pulled the door gently closed. It was unlikely anyone would go in there except Thomas, who had been tinkering with the innards of a torpedo which now lay scattered in pieces across a table in the center of the room. Satisfied, Decker slipped the card into the back pocket of his jeans and retreated across the hub to the mess.

When he stepped inside, the team had gathered around the table. As usual, there was a carafe of hot coffee, now half empty. Decker took his seat and helped himself to a mug just as the galley door swung open and Bertram emerged with plates and flatware. These he deposited on the table before returning to the galley and reappearing moments later carrying a platter piled high with fluffy pancakes. He went back and forth twice more, bringing a tray of bacon and a serving dish of scrambled eggs.

"You'll have to forgive me," Bertram said as he laid the dish down. "The eggs are overcooked. I was in the middle of making them when our morning's excitement happened. I would have remade them, but that would have been wasteful, not to mention depleting supplies to an unacceptable level."

"It's quite all right," Claudia reassured him. "The eggs look perfect, as always."

"You're too kind." Bertram moved off back toward the galley. "I'll put some fresh coffee on before I join you."

Mackenzie watched Bertram leave, then turned her attention to the food. "I'm not sure that I'm hungry. To be honest, I feel kind of sick."

"Understandable. You had quite a scare," Pavel said. He was sitting to her right, and now reached out and took her hand in his, giving it a reassuring squeeze. "But try to eat, anyway."

Mackenzie pursed her lips and nodded. "I'll do my best."

"I've been thinking about the writing on the mirror, and how it could have gotten there," Thomas said, spearing two pancakes with a fork and dragging them across onto his plate before dousing them in a liberal helping of maple syrup. He turned his attention to the bacon and piled several rashers on top of the pancakes, but ignored the eggs. He cut into the pancakes and lifted a mouthful on his fork before speaking again. "There's only one person on the habitat who speaks German."

"I don't like what you're implying," Patrick said, giving Thomas a withering look. "I would never do such a mean thing to Mackenzie."

"I'm not saying you did it." Thomas popped the food into his mouth and chewed noisily. After swallowing, he continued. "I'm merely pointing out the obvious."

"I locked the door before I undressed and got into the shower," Mackenzie said, coming to Patrick's defense.

"Then those words must have been there before you took your shower." Thomas continued to dig into his plate of food, even though no one else was eating yet. "It's only logical."

"You saw them. Those words were written in condensation on the mirror," Mackenzie objected. "I know they weren't there before. Besides, I heard a noise while I was showering. When I pulled the curtain back, my towel had fallen onto the floor. I assumed that was what I heard. But I'm not so sure now." She shuddered. Her face drained of color. "There was someone else in there with me, even though I locked the door."

"And it certainly wasn't me," Patrick said. "Apart from the obvious complication of the locked door, I was here with all of you when Mackenzie screamed."

"I'm sure none of us wrote that message on the mirror," Claudia said. "Just like we didn't assault Lauren with a wrench or turn the lights off and grab Mackenzie in the U-boat."

The color drained further from Mackenzie's face. "Thanks for reminding me of that. I've had my fill of unexplained phenomena. Next time it's someone else's turn."

"I wasn't trying to scare you further," Claudia replied. "I was just trying to make the point that we shouldn't start accusing each other."

"Who else does it leave?" Thomas asked. He glanced toward Decker. "And I don't want to hear anything about ghosts or monsters. There's a perfectly reasonable explanation for everything that has happened. We just need to find it."

"I agree we shouldn't jump to conclusions," Decker replied. Thomas's attitude irritated him. "But I agree with Claudia, it was none of us."

"Why don't you do your job and figure out who it was so we can all get back to work and be done with this nonsense." Thomas mopped up a puddle of maple syrup with the last of his pancake. "Isn't that why you came down here?"

"I intend to," Decker said. He noticed Mackenzie was sitting with her hands clenched so tight her knuckles were turning white. The conversation was doing nothing to ease her shattered nerves. "In the meantime, I suggest we talk about something else."

"Fine." Thomas licked his lips. "What would you like to discuss?"

At that moment, the galley door opened, and Bertram emerged carrying a fresh carafe of coffee. He looked down at the barely touched spread with dismay. "How about we talk about why nobody except Thomas is eating the breakfast I made for y'all."

Chapter 33

ONE HOUR later Decker stood beside Thomas in Claudia's office and looked over her shoulder as she inserted the SD card into her laptop. When the icon appeared on her desktop, Claudia clicked it. A new window opened, displaying a folder created by the camera. Claudia clicked again to open it, and Decker was surprised to see two files contained within. The card had been blank when they started recording. Decker had checked it himself to make sure there was enough space. Both recordings had been made the previous night.

"That's odd," Decker said.

"I agree." Claudia peered at the screen. "There should only be one video file."

"Unless an unknown person stopped the recording and then restarted it. That would create two files." Decker leaned close. "Setting up the camera was not a futile exercise, after all."

Claudia clicked on the first file. "Let's play it and see what we got."

The spinning wheel icon appeared while the computer processed the file, then a video player opened up. A view of the corridor that ended in the umbilical hatch door appeared on the screen. It showed Decker discussing the placement of the camera with Thomas. He stepped out of view as the conversation continued, then a few minutes later, silence. The recording continued this way for a while, with only an occasional distant murmur of conversation breaking the silence. Decker knew this to be the sound of the team polishing off the bottle of bourbon. Eventually even the conversation faded away as the lights dimmed, and the habitat transitioned into night mode. Soon the recording was still and quiet.

"Can we pick up the pace?" Decker asked. "The recording is several hours long, and I don't want to stand here all day."

"Right you are," Claudia said. She clicked her mouse, and the recording sped up, first to four and then eight times the speed. Soon they were zipping along at sixteen.

When a figure stepped into frame again, Decker instructed her to return to regular speed. "That's me. I came down to make a mug of tea around two in the morning."

"We're almost at the end of the first recording," Claudia said, pointing to the nearly completed time bar. "Can't be more than a minute or two left."

"This will be interesting," Decker said. He focused his attention on the screen as the remaining time on the recording expired. With a couple of seconds left, a long shadow appeared on the floor, but its owner remained hidden. Then the recording ended.

"Well, that was anticlimactic," Thomas said. "We're no better off than we were before."

"That's not true," Decker replied. "The shadow on the floor confirms that it wasn't a camera glitch or some other malfunction. The recording was turned off deliberately and then restarted sometime later."

Claudia nodded slowly. "The question is *how much* time later."

"That's easy to find out." Decker motioned toward the

files. "Select the second file and view its properties. The time-stamp will tell you when the recording resumed."

"Of course," Claudia said. She clicked on the file to bring up the properties window.

Decker studied the screen. "The recording resumed at five in the morning and then stopped again just before eight. The latter was me when I retrieved the SD card."

"A window of about three hours." Claudia furrowed her brow in thought. "I wonder what they were up to?"

"It's impossible to know, but it clearly involved the U-boat," Decker said.

"Pure speculation," Thomas said. "There are two work-shops on that level. They might have been after something in one of those."

"I can't imagine," Claudia replied. "There's nothing of any value there. Certainly not worth skulking around in the dead of night for. I agree with John. Whoever turned that recording off wanted to access the U-boat, and they wanted to do it clandestinely."

"Only the three of us knew the camera was there," Decker pointed out.

"They probably just stumbled across it," Thomas said. "Blind luck. Or maybe they were being cautious and checked around before entering the corridor and saw the camera. It was hidden but not invisible."

"A good point," Decker agreed. "But the hatch alarm did not sound."

"Which brings us back around to where we started." Thomas said. "No one accessed the U-boat. Whoever turned the camera off was interested in the workshops."

"Or they knew how to turn the alarm off prior to accessing the umbilical."

"That can only be done from the server room," Claudia said.

"And who would have that knowledge?"

"Lauren," Claudia replied. "I know how to turn it off too. I don't know if anyone else on the team does. It's not exactly a closely guarded secret since it's not meant for security. The alarm is a safety feature, that's all."

"We're not getting anywhere with this," Thomas said. He eyed the door. "It's a dead end and I have a butt load of work to do. I'm going to excuse myself unless anyone has any objections."

"I don't think there's much more we can glean from these recordings." Claudia sounded disappointed. "You might as well get back to your work."

"That's what I thought." Thomas turned and strode from the room.

Decker watched him go and then turned back to Claudia. "I don't buy Thomas's theory that our intruder wanted access to the workshops rather than the U-boat."

"Neither do I," Claudia said.

"I still think someone disabled the alarm. There's no way to prove it though."

"That's not strictly true," Claudia replied. "Opening the outer umbilical hatch door creates a log entry in our system. Lauren can tell you if anyone opened that door last night, even if she can't tell you who it was. We already know the alarm didn't sound, so if the hatch was opened it proves that the intruder knew how to turn it off."

"It also proves they went over to the U-boat and spent roughly three hours onboard," Decker said. "I think I'd better go find Lauren and check those logs."

Chapter 34

PATRICK MARCHANT WAS NOT in a good mood. The squabble with Thomas at the breakfast table had left him irritable and wondering, not for the first time, why he'd even taken this job. Life aboard Habitat One was less than ideal at the best of times. The food was passable but hardly haute cuisine. Despite several team members sneaking alcohol aboard, there wasn't a decent bottle of wine to be found. Or any wine at all, for that matter. And worst of all, he couldn't even smoke a cigarette. Now he was being accused of God knew what. Sneaking into a washroom and scribbling ridiculous phrases on the mirror in German. Like he would bother engaging in such childish activity. Sure, Thomas had claimed the comment wasn't directed at him, but Patrick knew better. He also knew he wasn't well liked by the rest of the team. They viewed him as elitist and a little obnoxious. Not that he cared. God, how he'd like to light up one of those Gitanes he'd been forced to leave on the research ship and blow the sweet, calming smoke in their faces.

Instead, he was returning to his office with a mug of steaming black coffee. No milk or sugar, just as he liked it. This would be his fourth beverage of the morning, but Patrick didn't care. In the absence of his other usual vices, a steady stream of coffee was all that kept him from murdering his colleagues, if not literally then figuratively.

He was almost at his door when the government man, Decker, came waltzing out of Claudia's office. He nodded a curt greeting to Patrick as they passed. Patrick glanced back to watch him leave, wondering briefly what Decker and Claudia had been discussing. Deciding that he didn't really care, Patrick continued on to his office and opened his door, stepping inside. Then he came to an abrupt halt. He wasn't alone in the office. Thomas Barringer was standing at his desk, examining hard copies of the photographs Mackenzie had taken in the sub several days before. He felt a sharp flash of anger.

"What do you think you're doing in here?" He asked, not bothering to hide the fury in his voice. "This is my private workspace. My sanctuary."

"Doesn't say private on the door." Thomas kept on rifling through the stack of photographs without bothering to look at the Frenchman. "Maybe you should get a plaque made and put it up there, so we know not to come in."

"You haven't answered my question." Patrick felt a vein throb above his right eye. His hand was shaking. Coffee slopped over the rim of the mug and splashed onto the floor. This only infuriated him all the more. "Are you looking for something or are you just ransacking my desk for the hell of it?"

Thomas stopped what he was doing and dropped the photos onto the desk. Now he turned to look at Patrick. "You're not much of a team player, are you?"

"That depends if the team's worth playing with." Patrick stepped forward and put his mug down atop a pile of books sitting near the edge of his desk. "Well?"

"Very well. I'm looking for a technical diagram of the G7e torpedo and I thought you might have one."

"You won't find it in those photographs."

"My curiosity got the better of me." Thomas held his hands up in submission. "I can always go ask Claudia if she knows where there's one."

"Shouldn't you already have a technical diagram?" Patrick set his feet and folded his arms in the most defiant stance he could muster. "You've been taking those torpedoes apart for weeks."

Thomas looked sheepish. "You're right. I had one, and it got damaged. I wasn't minding what I was doing and spilled a can of Coke. It was careless, I know, but hey, I'm clumsy."

"It still doesn't give you the right to go snooping through my desk."

"You're right, I'm sorry."

"You could try being nicer to people, especially if you want something from them." Patrick glanced past Thomas toward his empty chair. He wanted the man gone so that he could get back to work. "You can be rather rude."

"Me?" Thomas raised an eyebrow. "Has anyone ever told you you're about as friendly as a cactus and twice as prickly."

"I don't believe they have." Patrick pushed past Thomas. "I'll find that schematic so you can get out of my hair."

"You know what, you look busy. You can drop it down to the workshop whenever you have a free minute." Thomas stepped into the corridor. "No hurry. I've got plenty to be going on with for now."

"Suits me," Patrick replied. Anything to get the uncouth American the hell out of his domain.

"Great." Thomas tapped the doorframe on his way out. "You're a lifesaver."

Patrick watched him leave. He kicked the door closed, relishing the hard-earned solitude, then picked up the stack of photographs that Thomas had been perusing. They depicted the equipment in the control room. A mass of gauges, valves, levers, and pipes that covered the curved inner hull from floor to ceiling. He'd been careful to keep the photos arranged in the order in which Mackenzie had shot them. That way he could lay them out in a grid and see the controls as they appeared on the U-boat. Thomas had mixed them all up. Sighing, Patrick set them aside. Now he would have to put them back in the correct order. But not right now. First, Patrick wanted coffee. And a cigarette, come to that. Once again, his mind drifted to the Gitanes going to waste in his locker on the research ship docked seventy-five miles away in French Guiana. He mumbled a curse, then picked up the coffee, which was already going cold, and took a gulp. If he couldn't get any nicotine into his system, a healthy dose of caffeine would have to suffice.

Chapter 35

DECKER FOUND Lauren in the mechanical room on the lower level, finishing up the air filter replacement interrupted the previous day. As before, she was down in the crawlspace under the floor with her head bent over the machinery when Decker entered, but upon his approach her head snapped around.

"Only me," he blurted, not wishing to frighten her. The memory of her attack was still raw, and the brief look that flashed across her face before recognition dawned confirmed her unease.

"I hate being down here alone after what happened, but I wanted to get this finished and out of the way." Lauren stood and wiped her hands on her jeans, then heaved herself up and out of the hole. She clambered to her feet and dropped the socket wrench she had been using back into a yellow plastic toolbox that sat nearby.

"Am I disturbing you?" Decker asked.

"I'm about done." She took hold of a square metal panel sitting to one side of the hole and slid it back over the opening until it dropped into place, then engaged latches on both sides of the panel to keep it secured. "I can't tell you how happy I am to have that job over with. Just being down there was giving me the creeps after yesterday. I would have finished in half the time if I hadn't kept looking over my shoulder."

"You could have asked someone to stand watch while you worked," Decker said. "I would happily have done it. It would have been no trouble."

"That's sweet, but I'm a big girl. I can handle myself."

"No doubt." Decker said, his gaze coming to rest upon the chunky utility knife handle poking out of her trouser pocket. "Are you carrying that for work or protection?"

"A little of both." Lauren pushed the knife deeper into her pocket to conceal it. "But mostly protection. I know it's silly, but the knife makes me feel better."

"Nothing wrong with taking precautions."

"My thoughts exactly. Although I'm not sure how much use it would actually be. I'm not exactly a ninja warrior in case you hadn't noticed. I'd probably end up dropping it at the first sign of trouble." She cocked her head to one side. "But I'm sure you didn't come down here to talk about my knife fighting skills."

"No."

"Then what can I do for you?"

"Claudia suggested I check the logs to see if anyone opened the umbilical hatch door last night."

"Why?" Lauren closed the toolbox and picked it up. "The alarm didn't sound and checking the logs won't tell us anything about who left that message on the mirror this morning."

"True." Decker nodded. "But I have a hunch, and I'd like to satisfy it."

"Sure. Why not?" Lauren shrugged and started toward the door. "We'll have to visit the server room. That's where the computer that monitors the habitat is located."

Decker followed behind, allowing her to lead him up to the second level. When they arrived at the server room,

Lauren dropped the toolbox on the floor and went straight to a desk with a laptop on it.

"That tiny little computer controls the entire facility?" Decker asked, incredulous.

"What were you expecting, a mainframe with magnetic tape reels and lots of blinking green lights?"

"No. Not exactly." Decker wasn't entirely sure what he was expecting to see, but he'd thought it would be beefier than a slim little silver laptop. "I just thought the facility would be more high tech."

"This is high tech." Lauren patted the machine. "It's only a couple of months old. But we have to be careful not to let the battery run out of juice, otherwise the entire facility stops running. Air filtration. All the sensors on the doors. The lights. Trust me, if the battery runs down, it would be terrible."

"You don't even have a backup system?" Decker was aghast. "Why would you use a laptop for that?"

"What else would we use?"

"I don't know…" Decker struggled to find the words to express his unease. "That mainframe sounds like a good idea right now."

"Relax." A giggle escaped Lauren's mouth despite her best efforts to suppress it. "We don't run the facility on this laptop. Why do you think we call this the server room?"

"You were pulling my leg." Decker felt a rush of relief.

"It was so easy," Lauren said. "You should have seen your face."

"All right, you got me." Decker glanced around the server room. It was small, like most of the other spaces within the habitat. Floor to ceiling cabinets with perforated panels set into the doors took up one wall. Next to these was a workstation with a large black box sitting upon it. There were dials and buttons on the front, and a handheld mic attached to the side. Decker assumed this was the VLF radio. The desk containing the laptop sat against the opposite wall below what looked like a row of fuse boxes, although he guessed their contents were much more sophisticated. A low-level hum told him that unseen fans were working somewhere in the room. He nodded toward the row of sleek cabinets. "The real computer is in there, isn't it?"

"Enlightenment dawns," Lauren said good-naturedly. "Those are the rack servers. They're kind of like the beating heart of Habitat One. We use the laptop to access them."

"They still depend on electricity though, right?" Decker asked. "What happens if the facility loses power?"

"There's a three phase multi-megawatt UPS behind the server racks."

"Huh?" Lauren had lost him. She might as well have been speaking Greek.

"An uninterruptible power supply. It's basically a big-ass battery system. If the main electrical supply goes down, it can run the entire facility on emergency power for six hours."

"That's good to know."

"And now that I've given you a crash course on our computer systems, perhaps you'd like to look at those logs?"

"That would probably be a good idea," Decker said. "I'm taking up far too much of your time."

"Nonsense." Lauren took a seat in front of the laptop and typed, her eyes on the screen. A minute later she looked up. "I think I have what you're looking for."

"And?"

"You were right." Lauren glanced back over her shoulder at Decker. She pointed to the screen, and a line of text in a terminal window. "I checked the log files, and the hatch door opened briefly a little after two in the morning. It opened again approximately three hours later for less than one minute."

"Someone coming and going from the U-boat," Decker said.

"That would appear to be the case." Lauren frowned.

"Which means they came in here and turned off the hatch alarm first, or we would've heard it go off."

"And there are only a few people who know how to do that."

"Mainly myself, and Claudia, and I know I didn't do it." Lauren looked upset now. "And Claudia would have no reason to be surreptitious. She's in charge. She can go to the U-boat whenever she wants. Technically, any of us can. It's not off-limits or anything. As I've said before, the alarm is a safety feature, not a security device."

"Understood." Decker stared at the laptop screen and the mysterious log entries a while longer, then he thanked Lauren for her time and left the server room. There was only one reason to circumvent the hatch alarm and sneak over to the sub in the dead of night. The perpetrator did not wish to draw attention to themselves and their reason for being there. Or perhaps they wanted to avoid detection because they weren't a member of the research team at all. Everyone aboard the facility had alibis for the most egregious incidents of the last few days. It appeared to be impossible for a member of the team to have attacked Lauren or written the message on the mirror when Mackenzie was showering. But then again, Decker could not see how anyone else could get aboard the facility unnoticed. Still, in the back of his mind the loose strands of a theory were weaving themselves together, but he wasn't ready to acknowledge it. Not quite yet...

Chapter 36

AT A LITTLE BEFORE one in the afternoon, Decker left Lauren in the server room, intending to visit the mess and grab a light snack. There was no official lunch break on the habitat, so Bertram made himself available in between his other duties to whip up sandwiches or reheat leftovers for any hungry souls looking to tide themselves over until he served dinner. Decker had barely taken ten steps, however, when Patrick's office door opened, and the Frenchman flagged him down.

"If you aren't busy Mister Decker, I would very much appreciate a few moments of your time."

"I was about to track down a ham sandwich," Decker said, glancing wistfully toward the central hub. "But I've got time. What can I do for you?"

"It's more what I can do for you." Patrick stepped aside to allow Decker into his domain. "After this morning's unfortunate incident, I got to thinking. I can't tell you how that message got on the mirror, but there are anomalies regarding the U-boat I think you should know about given the circumstances."

"Like what?" Decker asked, his interest immediately peaked.

Patrick reached behind Decker and pushed the door closed, then returned to his desk and sat down. As usual, there was only one chair, which left Decker once again standing. He wondered if the facility had a suggestion box, because if it did, he would like to suggest that they invest in some extra office chairs.

Patrick tapped a finger on a worn book that Decker recognized from his last visit with the Frenchman. The U-boat's log, a running journal of the boat's activities penned by the captain.

"As you know, I have been going through the various written records and logs recovered from the U-boat."

Decker nodded.

Patrick continued. "From these documents I discovered the names of the commander, the first watch officer, and a smattering of the crew. I discovered the names of other crew members from personal effects still aboard the U-boat. In all, I've identified twenty-six officers and crew. I've also made a tentative identification of the U-boat itself, although I haven't yet confirmed its hull number."

"It sounds like you've been busy," Decker commented.

"I'm always busy." Patrick tapped on the logbook again. "The U-boat currently sitting at the other end of our umbilical is the U-909."

Decker waited for Patrick to expand upon this nugget of information, but the Frenchman appeared to be expecting a reaction from him. "I'm not sure how this helps us."

"Nor I. However, it is an inconsistency, and given the events of the last few days, it may or may not prove significant."

"Why is it an inconsistency?" Decker asked. "Weren't all U-boats numbered?"

"They were indeed. There were seven hundred and three Type VII U-boats constructed by the Germans, making them the most produced submarine design ever. Only one still remains intact. The U-995 on display in Laboe, Germany. Then there's our boat which brings the total produced number to seven hundred and four. It also means the Laboe vessel is no longer the only preserved example."

"Are you trying to tell me we have an unknown, never documented U-boat sitting out there?"

"That's exactly what I'm saying," Patrick stood and went to his shelves. He pulled out a thick volume and returned to the desk, then opened it. "This book is a history of the Kriegsmarine, and specifically the U-boat service. There is an appendix at the back that lists every U-boat produced. The problem with our boat is that it never was. The Kriegsmarine ordered U-909 built on September 22, 1942. Construction began sometime later at the Hamburg shipyard. Then for reasons unknown work halted in September 1943. The German navy officially canceled construction almost a year later in July 1944 without explanation."

"Maybe they just decided not to build any more submarines. It sounds like they had an awful lot of them."

"Except that wasn't the case. They built and commissioned many more U-boats after that time. The Germans needed a constant supply of new submarines, especially in the latter years of the war, because the Allies got so good at sinking them."

"There's more, too. I've been going through the log, and there are entries that make no sense. According to the logbook, the U-909 took part in at least four war patrols. The commander kept meticulous records of his movements and unless he was making navigation mistakes, which seems unlikely, he could not possibly have covered the distances written into the log within the time frames he recorded."

"How big a discrepancy are we talking?" Decker asked.

"Large." Patrick leafed through the logbook and pointed at a faded entry. "See here. It says that they left Trondheim for their third war patrol and then less than eight hours later they were in the middle of the Atlantic, six hundred miles west of the Irish coast. No U-boat could have moved that fast. It's impossible. And that isn't the only such entry. The book's riddled with them. If you believe what the commander wrote in his log, the U-boat was pinging back and forth all over the ocean. It's no wonder he recorded so many kills. He appeared to just show up wherever there was an Allied convoy and then disappear again."

"Are you sure about this?" Decker asked.

"I'm absolutely sure. There's more too. A second logbook full of calculations. At first, I wasn't sure what it was, but many of the coordinates cited in the commander's log appear to match numbers in the other log. I'm not sure that the second book is actually a log at all. I think it was used to make on-the-fly calculations by a navigator or helmsman."

"If I understand what you're telling me," Decker said. "A U-boat that never existed, and which is now lying empty in perfect condition on the ocean floor right outside of this habitat, could somehow move around at incredible speed, mount assaults on Allied shipping, and then escape as if they were never there."

"That's exactly what I'm saying," Patrick said. "It sounds crazy, even to me, and I don't have an explanation for it, but my research is sound."

"Why didn't you mention this before?"

"Interesting as the anomalies are, I didn't think they bore any relevance to the investigation you are conducting. Until that phrase in German showed up on the mirror today, I viewed this as nothing more than a historical mystery, but it's become increasingly clear that the U-boat lies at the center of what is occurring. If that's the case, the past may hold the key to the present."

"Are you saying you finally believe in ghosts?" Decker asked.

"Not by a long shot," Patrick replied. "But I think the

anomalies I've uncovered are now relevant, which is why I'm sharing this information with you."

"I appreciate it," Decker said. For the first time since coming aboard the habitat, he found the Frenchman tolerable.

"I've written up a report of my findings so far," Patrick said, handing Decker two sheets of laser printed paper. "It's not exhaustive by any means, and I skipped the more boring aspects of my research, but you will find all the information I've relayed to you is there. I've also listed the names of as many crew members and officers as I can."

Decker accepted the sheets and glanced down at them. "Thank you for this. It will be a great help, I'm sure."

"You're welcome, Mr. Government Man. You can thank me by figuring out what is going on so everyone will stop distracting me with their dramas." Patrick made a shooing motion with one hand. "Now if you don't mind, I have a lot of work to catch up on."

"Not at all." Decker stepped out into the corridor. He glanced down at the papers in his hand for a second time and knew what must happen next. Difficult as it might be, because of his location so far beneath the waves, Decker needed to speak with Adam Hunt.

Chapter 37

AFTER LEAVING PATRICK, Decker went in search of Claudia. The only way to contact the outside world was the radio in the server room, which was apparently off-limits without authorization. He checked her office but found it empty. He retraced his steps back to the central hub and descended to the lower level, wondering if she was working over on the U-boat. As it happened, he encountered her exiting the mess alongside Pavel. They both carried sandwiches and cans of soda, which reminded Decker of how hungry he was. But once again, that would have to wait.

"Did you speak to Lauren?" Claudia asked as Decker closed the gap between them.

"I did," Decker replied. "I also just left Patrick. He relayed to me some rather interesting information. I think it might have relevance to the strange incidents that have been occurring."

"You're making progress then?" Claudia looked pleased.

"I believe I am." Decker kept silent about the theory that had been fermenting in the back of his mind since speaking to Lauren. His conversation with Patrick had only brought it into sharper focus. He was not, however, willing to voice his suspicions until he could confirm their validity. With that in mind, he got straight to the point. "I know you limit use of the radio due to the amount of power required to transmit, but I need to contact CUSP and speak with my boss, Adam Hunt."

"Can it wait?" Claudia asked. "There's still a storm topside, but it should blow through by tomorrow. We have a satellite phone that will work from the surface. I can have Pavel bring you up in the submersible as soon as weather permits."

"My own phone will also work from the surface, but I'd really rather not wait that long." Decker wondered if he should fill her in on his theory after all, but still he hesitated. Partly because he had no proof to back it up, and also because he had a suspicion Adam Hunt would want to control the narrative. If Decker was correct, CUSP had bankrolled this expedition for the same reason they funded the dig to find Grendel's bones in Ireland. His employer suspected the submarine was more than it appeared, beyond the obvious mystery of its pristine condition. And speaking of funding, it wouldn't hurt to remind Claudia where the money for her little jaunt to the seabed had come from. "I'm sure that CUSP would be grateful for your cooperation."

"Very well, then. If it's that urgent…" Claudia turned to Pavel. "Can I leave this in your hands?"

Pavel nodded. He turned to Decker. "We won't be able to call CUSP directly. The radio doesn't work in the same way a phone does. I have to contact the support ship and have them reach out to Adam Hunt. Once they have him on the line, they can patch him through to us and then you can talk to him directly."

"That would be acceptable," Decker replied. "How long do you think it will take?"

"I'll head up to the server room right away, but I don't know how long it will take to get your boss on the line."

"I can provide a contact number if you need it," Decker offered.

"That won't be necessary. CUSP assigned us a liaison as part of the funding terms. They've been aboard Sheena since the expedition started."

"Really?" Decker didn't realize that another CUSP operative was already working with MERO. As usual, Hunt had been tightlipped, providing only the information Decker needed to perform his job.

Pavel nodded. "I'll let you know as soon as I have Adam Hunt on the horn."

"Thank you."

"All in a day's work," Pavel said, starting off toward the second level, and the server room, with Claudia at his side.

Decker watched them go. He hoped it wouldn't take too long to get in touch with Hunt. He was eager to see if his theory had legs.

His stomach growled, reminding him where he was going before Patrick waylaid him. He now had a few minutes, so he might as well grab that sandwich. Besides, he could use the time to read through the pages Patrick had given him. Maybe he would spot something in there that would bolster his theory, and even if he didn't, Decker still felt that he was on the right track.

Chapter 38

AFTER JOHN DECKER departed his office, Patrick closed the door and sat back at his desk. His day had been nothing but one distraction after another. First there was Mackenzie's incident in the washroom. Then there was the run in with Thomas at breakfast. And then, as if to add insult to injury, he found Thomas rifling through his desk not one hour later. Patrick was not a neat person by any stretch, but there was a method to his mess. He knew where everything was. Thomas had upset that gentle equilibrium and now it needed righting. He would start with the stack of photos Thomas had gotten out of order in his haste to paw through them. Patrick would much rather be getting on with some proper work, but he wouldn't relax until he did this. That was part of the problem with being both messy and obsessive-compulsive. Clutter was only fine if it was the right clutter. A single item carelessly shifted out of place would taunt him until he fixed it. Now his entire desk was out of place, including the stack of photographs. Patrick grumbled a curse word and picked them up. He laid them out one by one on his desk, over the top of other papers that he would also need to reorganize thanks to the annoying munitions specialist. He placed them in a grid pattern, trying to match each photo with its relevant location in the U-boat's control room. It took a while at first, but soon he was moving at a good clip, piecing them together in the correct configuration, one by one. Then he noticed something. An anomaly he might have missed had Thomas not shuffled the photos and forced him to study each one.

A gray metal box adorned with small gauges that sat near the attack periscope and to the left of the steering controls. It looked inconspicuous, yet wrong, both at the same time. The U-boat's control room contained a dizzying array of equipment that packed every available surface. More valves and gauges than he'd seen in any other oceangoing vessel. Yet this particular box loaded with gauges gave him pause. It was clearly retrofitted. He could see empty screw holes on the wall above, as if the Germans had removed one piece of equipment, and then added this one.

He stood and went to the bookshelf and selected a hefty volume. He opened it on the desk, leafing through until he found what he was looking for. A set of glossy plates in the book's center that showed sections of a typical U-boat type VII control room. The photographs were black and white, but they served their purpose. When he compared the vintage photos to his own copies of the photos Mackenzie had taken aboard the U-boat sitting at the other end of the umbilical, they didn't match. At least, not entirely. He was lucky to find one photo of the area around the attack periscope taken from a similar angle as Mackenzie's photo. The bulky periscope hid much of the section that interested him, but it showed enough for Patrick to confirm the difference between the U-909 and the U-boat in the book illustrations. In the old photos, there was a much taller and narrower box in that position, and it had no dials. It also had wiring emerging from it and sneaking up over the U-boat's ceiling. The box in Mackenzie's photo was wider and shorter. It also stuck out further into the room. Also, there was a narrow seat under the box, identical to the seat used by the helmsman. This wasn't in the vintage photograph either. The box appeared to have been a manned station, which was odd because there were no controls beyond a row of dials.

Patrick could feel the curiosity welling up inside of him. They had been down here for weeks trying to unlock the U-boat's secrets. Like why it was in such good condition. Not to mention the lack of crew, which was also baffling. He didn't believe Claudia's theory that the submariners had flooded the ballast tanks and abandoned the vessel. It made no sense. The crew had access to scuttling charges. Not only that, they could open a valve in the control room to flood the boat and send it to the bottom quicker. And if the crew abandoned the U-boat in the middle of the ocean, then where had they gone? The life rafts were still in their compartments under the deck, and it seemed unlikely an allied vessel would have picked them up, and then allowed the U-boat to slip beneath the waves unhindered. There was valuable information inside. An Enigma Machine complete with its accompanying codebook, for a start. The British and Americans had captured several other U-boats and deciphered German codes because of it, at least until the Germans realized and changed them. But not before the code breakers saved hundreds, if not thousands, of Allied lives.

Patrick felt a tingle of excitement. Whatever that box contained, it appeared to be unique to this submarine. Maybe it would even answer some of their questions. He dropped the rest of the photographs on the desk in an untidy pile, his need to put right what Thomas had disturbed overwhelmed by a burning desire to know what was in that box. He took one last look at the anomalous photo, holding it up once again against the vintage picture of the same location. Then, sure of his conviction that he had stumbled across something important, Patrick hurried from his office toward the umbilical.

Chapter 39

Pavel returned quicker than Decker expected. Bertram had barely brought his sandwich out when the submersible pilot and marine archaeologist entered the mess to inform him that Adam Hunt was waiting on the other end of the VLF radio. Unwilling to delay his lunch any longer, but eager to talk to Hunt, Decker took the sandwich with him. He followed Pavel back to the facility's room and then asked for privacy. Once he was alone, he picked up the handheld mic and pressed the talk button.

Hunt responded immediately. "John. It's good to hear your voice, even if it is faint."

"Not much I can do about that, I'm afraid. Radio waves don't travel well in water apparently, which is why they have to use low frequency. If it's any consolation, I don't think it's any better on my end."

"It's a wonder we can talk at all. We'd better make this quick, just in case. What can I…" A sudden burst of static obscured the rest of Hunt's response.

Decker guessed what Hunt had said. "I'd like you to do some research for me."

"What type of research?"

"I have a designation for the U-boat. It's the U–909. According to our resident historian, the German Navy canceled U-909 before they finished construction, yet here it is. I also have a partial crew list. I'd like you to look up the U-boat and crew names and see what you can find out."

"Sure. Normally I would request that you email the information over, but that obviously will not work in this case, so you'll have to read it to me instead."

Decker obliged. He started with the commander and the first watch officer, and then gave Hunt the names of several other crew members, including the helmsman and a couple of petty officers. That done, he filled Hunt in on recent events, including the attack on Lauren and the message written in German on the mirror.

"That's troubling," Hunt said when Decker finished. "Do you have any theories?"

"Nothing solid," Decker admitted. "But I have a hunch."

"I'd love to hear it. But first, are you alone?"

"Yes," Decker replied. "No one will overhear us."

"Good. Begin when you're ready."

Decker took a deep breath. This was when his theory would either come into focus, or Hunt would laugh. "What would you say if I told you I think the sub and habitat really are being visited by apparitions?"

"I'd say it sounds crazy," Hunt replied. "But no crazier than your encounter with Jack the Ripper in London. Are you implying we have a haunted sub?"

"No. I don't think so." Decker believed there was a more scientific explanation than the disgruntled spirits of dead sailors passing over from the other side, although no less strange. "I think the crew might still be alive. Don't ask me how because I haven't gotten that far yet. I also don't know why we only encounter them sporadically. They seem to appear and disappear out of thin air. Regardless, that message was an unmistakable cry for help."

"Interesting." There was a pause at the other end of the line. "You say the logs showed this U-boat traveling vast distances in an impossible timeframe?"

"That's what the historian tells me," Decker said. "He's not the most pleasant man, but he seems to know what he's talking about."

"And the U-boat doesn't officially exist."

"That also appears to be the case."

"Most intriguing, especially when you consider that the submarine looks like they built it yesterday."

"I can attest to that," Decker said. "It's kind of eerie going over to that sub. Like going back in time."

"While I'm sure it does not involve time travel, I think you're onto something," Hunt said. "I have a theory of my own that aligns nicely with what you've told me, but I would like to do some digging."

"Would you like to share?" Decker asked hopefully.

"Not yet. But I think you may be correct about the crew of that U-boat. Why don't you give me…" Another squawk of static erupted from the radio. Adam Hunt's voice faded into the background momentarily. "… I have some answers I will call you back. In the meantime, I would like you to go over to the U-boat and have a look around. Pay special attention to the machinery and controls. See if anything looks unusual or out of place."

"I'll do that," Decker agreed. "Is there anything in particular I should look for?"

The question went unanswered. Decker's only response was another blast of static and then crackling silence. He had lost his tenuous connection to the outside world, at least for now. Decker would do as Hunt asked and take another tour of the submarine. Then he would wait for his enigmatic boss to make contact again. But before that he was going to eat. Decker picked up his sandwich and bit into it with satisfaction.

Chapter 40

PATRICK HURRIED across the umbilical and into the watertight chamber surrounding the U-boat's conning tower. He was about to climb the steps to the bridge, and the hatch leading inside the sub, when Mackenzie appeared above him, camera in hand.

"Hey there," she said, peering over the side of the conning tower. "You want access to the sub?"

"Unless I will be in your way," Patrick replied. "I don't want to mess up your photographs."

"No worries, I'm done. I've been trying to finish up the photography for days. To be honest, I was loath to come back across here after the lights went out and someone grabbed me. Then I thought I might as well just get it over with." Mackenzie moved onto the steps and started down. "To be honest, I kind of wish you'd come here earlier. I hate being in the sub by myself."

"Why didn't you ask someone to accompany you."

"Pavel was busy. I thought about asking Thomas, but he was in the workshop playing with his beloved torpedo parts."

"Well, sorry I didn't get here earlier." Truthfully, Patrick was not sorry. He was eager to examine the panel in the control room and would rather not have prying eyes watching while he did so. If there really was something important hiding behind that panel, he wanted to keep credit for the discovery all for himself. It would make for a fantastic chapter or two in the book he was planning to write about the mysteries of the U-909. That was his principal reason for agreeing to be part of the expedition. The thought of spending weeks at a time on the ocean floor in cramped surroundings with a bunch of people he didn't like was hardly appealing. But the thought of writing a critically acclaimed book and being held as an expert by the world at large did appeal. Sure, he already had kudos in the tight-knit historical community, was even a minor celebrity, but no one cared what dusty old historians thought. A sensationalized book about the strangely intact submarine would appeal to a broader spectrum. It might even get him on the nonfiction best-selling charts. That thought made him smile, albeit internally. His outward demeanor did not change. He merely watched Mackenzie descend the steps and squeeze past him into the umbilical.

"Holler if you need anything," she said, even though no one would hear him from within the submarine even if he did. Then she swung the submarine-side umbilical door closed, leaving him alone with his thoughts, and the ominous, hulking U-boat.

Chapter 41

THE SUBMARINE'S interior was cold and full of long shadows. Patrick climbed tentatively down into the control room, careful not to slip on the metal ladder's smooth rungs. When he reached the bottom, he stopped and looked around. It was hard to believe that almost four dozen men worked and lived in this claustrophobic and inhospitable space for weeks and sometimes months at a time.

Patrick shuddered.

Mackenzie was right. It was creepy being on the submarine alone. He glanced toward the open forward pressure bulkhead hatch, and the narrow corridor that ran the length of the sub, past the three tight cabins that would have been home to the commanding officer, second-in-command, and chief petty officer. Beyond this, falling away into gloom was the torpedo room. He wondered how many people had died because of the weapons launched from the tubes within that room. More than he wished to count, no doubt.

From somewhere deep within the bowels of the vessel, there was a groaning creak. This was usual. The immense pressure of water pressing on the hull made the submarine moan and complain, as if all it wanted to do was leave its dark and rigid grave and see the surface once more.

Patrick shook off the feeling of unease that had wormed its way into the back of his mind and turned his attention to the valves and gauges lining the control room walls. In particular, he was looking for one set of gauges, and the unusual box that held them. The box that had given him pause when he was studying Mackenzie's photos taken several days before. He quickly located it on the wall near the attack periscope, to the left of the aft and forward planesman's stations. He stepped close to study it.

Now that he saw the box up close, he realized that his initial instinct had been correct. This was not original to the submarine. He could see the screw holes where a box of different dimensions had once attached to the inner hull. He suspected they made this modification in the shipyard prior to the U-boat's completion and launch. He wondered if there was a connection between the installation of this box and the German naval records that falsely listed U-909's construction as suspended and eventually canceled. There was only one way to find out. He needed to figure out why the box was there and what its purpose was.

Patrick examined the gauges adorning the front of the box. There were six. None were labeled. He tapped on the nearest gauge and watched the needle jump in response. He ran his hands around the outside of the box, feeling a slight ridge under his fingers. He wondered if the front panel was a separate piece. Then his finger touched a hidden depression on the left-hand side of the box and within it what felt like a release button. His breath quickened. He pressed down.

For a moment nothing happened, and Patrick felt a tug of disappointment. But then, just as he was about to lift his finger away, there was a click and the front panel swung open.

Patrick stepped back in surprise.

Inside the box was a control panel constructed of smooth

polished metal with six dials attached in two rows. It was unlike anything he had ever seen in a U-boat. Intervals from zero to sixty ringed the circumference of each. Printed above the top row of dials was a single word. Breiten. Above the second row, another word. Längengrad.

Patrick stared in disbelief. He knew what these dials were for. To set latitude and longitude by degrees, minutes, and seconds. He reached out and touched a dial. The panel felt warm, as if something were running deep within it. Then he his gaze shifted above the dials, to a second panel roughly twelve inches long on each side and held in place by four clips. There was a bold warning in German. Do not remove. With shaking hands, he reached out and unlatched each of the clips one by one, ignoring the decades-old notice, then lifted the panel away and peered within. What he saw made him gasp with shock.

Sitting within a steel enclosure beneath the panel was a round orb set into a metal clamp with wires leading off from each side. The surface was smooth and colored gunmetal gray. Strangely, it appeared both reflective and flat simultaneously, which Patrick knew to be impossible. No material could be in two states at the same time. Yet he could not discount the evidence of his own eyes, and the reflection that looked back at him from a surface that reflected nothing else in the room. He felt a chill creep up his spine. Then he noticed the symbols etched around the circumference of the orb. They looked almost Egyptian, but they were not. There were squares and rectangles and strange curving shapes strung together in a way that reminded him of writing, employing both syllabic and logographic elements. Yet he knew no such writing system existed. At least on Earth.

He stared at the strange symbols for a long while, both fascinated and troubled. Then he noticed a low hum that filled the air like an electronic fog. There was only one place such a sound might come from. Patrick reached out his hand, and as his fingers grew close to the orb, the hum increased. He hesitated, his fingers an inch above the strange metal surface. Then, just as he was about to touch the orb, he heard another sound from his rear.

Footsteps.

He drew his fingers back and was about to turn around when a powerful hand slipped over his mouth and pressed down. Then he felt a strange sensation under his rib cage that soon flared into searing agony.

Despite the hand restraining him, Patrick glanced down at his chest in time to see his attacker withdraw a sleek steel blade now stained crimson.

His eyes flew wide with alarm. He tried to summon a breath, but his chest felt tight and unresponsive. Then, as his thoracic cavity filled with blood, Patrick felt himself being gently lowered to the floor. His last earthly image was of his attacker standing over him, knife in hand, looking toward the recently discovered orb with a smile.

Chapter 42

AFTER SPEAKING TO ADAM HUNT, Decker went in search of Lauren. He was eager to follow Hunt's advice and return to the U-boat to see what jumped out at him. He sensed that, as usual, Hunt knew more than he was letting on. Did his boss expect Decker to find something on the sub? There was only one way to find out. Go over there and look. But he didn't want to do it alone. He didn't know enough about U-boats, which was where Lauren came in. He found her sitting in front of a laptop in the mess, with what appeared to be a cup of cocoa in one hand. With the other, she typed furiously on the laptop's keyboard.

"Hey." She looked up as he entered. "Are you done with the radio?"

"For now," Decker said.

"Good. I've been hanging out here to give you some privacy, but there are a few chores I can only do from the server room terminal."

"It's all yours," Decker replied, stepping into the room. "But first, do you fancy little jaunt?"

"Ooh. Road trip." Lauren grinned. "I love road trips. You got anywhere exotic in mind?"

"How about the U-boat?"

"That's not much of a road trip." Lauren feigned disappointment.

"I think you might have been setting your expectations a little high," Decker replied.

"That's me, always optimistic." Lauren halted her work on the laptop, closed the screen, and stood up. "What's the purpose of this foray? Have you got a hot lead on the mysterious doings around here?"

"Not exactly."

"Well now, that's a shame." Lauren's expression turned serious. "I'd rather hoped we could put all the strangeness behind us before bed tonight. I'm not exactly sleeping well. I worry that someone's going to sneak into my room. I feel like I'm being watched all the time."

"Whatever happened to always optimistic?" Decker asked.

"It's there, just diluted with a healthy dose of self-preservation." She walked toward the door. "So, if we're not following a lead, why are we going over on the sub?"

"I want to see if anything looks like it shouldn't be there."

"Pavel or Claudia would be better for that, surely. They've been studying the submarine for weeks, examining it stem to stern. All I've been doing is crawling around in the sub levels under the habitat, switching out air filters and unclogging pipes."

"That's exactly why I want you. The others are too close to it. They've been over there so much they know the sub like the back of their hands. If they haven't discovered an anomaly by now, they probably aren't going to. Plus, you have a mechanical background. You know how things work. I'm hoping that you'll spot something the others missed."

"I know squat about World War II submarines. That's not my job."

"I disagree. You might not be an expert on the second world war, but you know a lot about the inner workings of subs," Decker replied. "Isn't the habitat nothing more than a submarine bolted to the ocean floor? And anyway, a little ignorance might go a long way. You won't be blinded by what you expect to see."

"All right. You've convinced me. I was kinda bored anyway." Lauren started toward Annex D, and the umbilical. "Come along then. Let's see what we can see."

"Excellent." Decker tagged along behind.

"But you still owe me that jaunt. This doesn't count." She turned the handle to open the umbilical hatch door and heaved it back then stepped through and waited for Decker before closing it behind them.

"Where would you like to go?"

"I don't know. Anywhere but the seabed. I didn't mind it down here at first, but after a while it gets wearing. The conversation has become banal. The food is all the same, not that Bertram doesn't try. Even the habitat switching between night and day mode grates, eventually. It isn't real. You can't see the sky, watch the sunset. We're living in an artificial, windowless world with no idea what's happening above us. For all we know, the zombie apocalypse has broken out and we're the last humans left."

"If it makes you feel any better, the zombies hadn't taken over a few days ago when I came down here," Decker said with a laugh. "And if it happens, they'll probably ask me to take care of it."

"See, your job is way more interesting than mine. The only time they'd come and get me is if a zombie had trouble starting their Humvee."

"It could happen."

They were at the hatch on the other side of the umbilical now. They let themselves through and climbed the steps up to the U-boat's bridge.

"After you," Decker said, reaching down and opening the hatch leading into the conning tower.

"What a gentleman," Lauren said, accepting his offer and stepping onto the ladder leading down into the sub. She climbed down, her footfalls ringing on the metal rungs. Decker waited for her to reach the bottom and then started down himself. He'd barely made it halfway when Lauren let out a terrified screech.

"What's wrong." Decker swung his feet away from the rungs and slid down the last few feet into the sub with his hands gripping the ladder's outside rails. He landed heavily in the control room and raced to join her. Lauren was standing near the ladder, next to the attack periscope. Her eyes were wide. "You wanted me to find something out of place," she said in a trembling voice. "Well, I think I did."

Decker came up behind her and stopped short. He gazed down in horror at the still spreading pool of blood, and the man who lay sprawled within it.

"Is that…" Lauren started to ask before she became too choked up to continue.

"Yes," Decker replied. "It's Patrick."

Lauren took a step back and bumped into the periscope. "Is he dead?"

Decker kneeled, careful to avoid the blood. He leaned over and placed two fingers against the Frenchman's neck. Then he looked up toward Lauren. "Very much so."

Chapter 43

EVERYONE GATHERED IN THE MESS, their faces gaunt. Mackenzie had been crying, and now she wiped the salty wetness from her cheeks. Pavel paced back and forth; hands pushed deep into his pockets. After a few minutes, Claudia glared at him.

"For the love of God, please quit that."

"Sorry." Pavel came to a halt, but still his left leg jiggled a nervous rhythm. "This is beyond dreadful."

"I can't believe Patrick is dead. How is it even possible?" Mackenzie asked between sobs. She looked around, studying each person one by one. "Someone in this room must be a murderer."

"Let's not jump to conclusions," Thomas said. "We don't know who killed Patrick."

"Oh, get real." Pavel shook his head in disgust. "There are only eight people on the habitat. We've already discussed this. It's not possible for an intruder to get on board without us seeing them."

"Seven," Mackenzie said.

"What?" Pavel looked at her.

"There's only seven of us now. Patrick is gone."

"Oh. Yes." Pavel dropped his head and studied his feet. "It doesn't alter the fact that one of us must be the killer."

"I agree with Thomas," Lauren said. "We shouldn't jump to conclusions. I glimpsed the man who hit me with that wrench. It was brief. All I saw was his outline. But I didn't recognize him. I'm sure I would've if it had been one of us."

"I don't care who it was," Mackenzie said. "I don't want to stay down here one minute longer. It was bad enough when we were seeing shadows, but now a man is dead. And whoever the killer is, he probably won't stop with Patrick. I don't want to die next."

"We can't leave. Not yet." Pavel was still staring at the floor.

"I don't see why not? We'll just call the support ship on the VLF and then we can get the hell out of here."

"That's my point," Pavel replied. "The support ship can't come and get us, even if we radio them. The storm is still raging up top. Is not due to ease until morning. They won't put out to sea until it's safe."

"It's not safe down here either," Mackenzie replied. "Who cares if there's a storm? It's a big ship. We should make them come."

"Even if they could get to us, it wouldn't do any good. They wouldn't be able to bring the submersible aboard in this weather. The waves are too high. We'd get tossed around like a cork."

"Face it, Mackenzie. No one's coming for us until tomorrow at the earliest." Thomas glanced toward her. "We're stuck here until then, and you might as well suck it up and get used to it."

"Ease up on her, okay?" Pavel took a step forward.

"Or what?" Now it was Thomas's turn to take a step forward.

"Stop it, both of you." Claudia positioned herself between them. "We'll call the support ship on the VLF and tell them to get here as soon as weather permits. I hate to abandon our work, but I don't see any other option."

"Finally, some sense," Lauren said. "I really don't care about the stupid U-boat anymore. All I want to do is put this mess behind me. I have no intention of ever coming back down here."

"Me either," Mackenzie said.

"We'll worry about that later." Claudia cast her eyes around the group. "We make the call first, then we need to move Patrick out of the sub."

"Shouldn't we leave him where he is?" Mackenzie asked. "The authorities will want to investigate. Someone murdered him, after all."

"I'm aware of that," Claudia replied. "But who knows how long it will take them to get down here to examine the crime scene. I'm not willing to leave him over there that long. He deserves better than that. Besides which, he's going to start to…"

"Decompose." Thomas finished her sentence. "If we don't move him, Patrick will get pretty rank."

"Gross." Lauren turned away. The color had drained from her face. She looked queasy.

"We're agreed then?" Claudia asked, although it sounded more like a statement than a question.

"You can count me out," Pavel said taking a step backwards. "I'm not paid to lug corpses around."

"Me either," Bertram said. "And anyway, I have to make dinner tonight and I'm sure you'd all feel better if I hadn't been handling a dead body right beforehand."

"For heaven's sake," Thomas snorted. "What a bunch of sissies. John and I will do it." He turned to Decker. "If that's agreeable to you?"

"It really isn't," Decker said. He'd seen his share of dead bodies, had handled several of them, but the idea of lugging

Patrick up and out of the U-boat held no appeal. "But I'm in."

"That's settled then," Claudia said. "We'll bring Patrick over from the U-boat and put him in the galley walk-in. If the authorities want to examine the corpse, they can do it in there."

"You are *not* putting Patrick in my freezer," Bertram said with a horrified look on his face. "There's food in there. It's not sanitary. Besides which, there isn't room."

"Then make room. I'm in charge of this expedition, and I'm telling you that Patrick is being put in the freezer whether or not you like it."

"Fine." Bertram shrugged. "But don't expect fries from here on out. We have three boxes and I'll have to remove all of them to make room. Same goes for the bags of vegetables. They're stacked in crates against the back wall. The meat can stay. I don't want it turning rancid in my kitchen. Not that I think anyone's going to want to eat a steak if it's been sharing the freezer with a corpse."

"We'll worry about the food later," Thomas said. "Right now, we have more urgent matters to attend to."

"Like calling the support ship and getting them out here to rescue us," Mackenzie said between sniffs.

"Precisely. Which is why I'm going to radio them right now," Thomas said. "The rest of you should stay here. I don't want anyone walking around the habitat. When I'm done with the radio, I'll come back for John and we'll take care of Patrick."

"Thank you," Claudia said. She looked relieved. "We'll stay here and look after each other."

Thomas nodded and started toward the central hub.

As he was about to leave the mess, Lauren called out after him. "Please be careful out there."

"Oh, I will. Have no fear," Thomas said without looking back, and then he stepped into the hub, and was gone.

Chapter 44

An hour after the gathering in the mess, Thomas and Decker set out for the U-boat. The rest of the team, except for Bertram who insisted on staying in his kitchen, had retired to their bunk rooms. No one wished to see the body being brought aboard the habitat and stowed.

In the U-boat's control room, Thomas stood and looked down at the splayed corpse of Patrick with a pained expression on his face. "Holy hell. That is quite a mess."

"Let's just get this over with," Decker said. He stepped around Thomas. The halo of blood had grown no larger. Decker guessed this was due to lividity. Whatever blood remained in Patrick had settled toward his back and extremities because he was lying face up. The wound that had killed Patrick was obvious. Below a gash in his shirt, Decker could see the thin unmistakable slit of a knife wound. He glanced up at Thomas. "Patrick's attacker probably had military training."

Thomas furrowed his brow. "What makes you say that?"

"The wound. It's right below the rib cage. Judging from the amount of blood, one or more arteries leading to the heart were severed. I'll bet an autopsy will show a long blade pushed upwards under the ribs and through his lung into the heart. Whoever did this must've been strong. It takes a lot of power to push a knife that deeply into a person's chest. I can't imagine many of the crew aboard the habitat would have either the skill or bodily strength to do such a thing."

"We're looking at an intruder then," Thomas said. "Even though Patrick was a cantankerous old fellow, but I can't imagine any of the crew hated the man enough to kill him."

"His killer might have been protecting something."

"Then again, he could've just been in the wrong place at the wrong time. Maybe he came across our intruder and disturbed them."

"Maybe." Decker glanced around, paying careful attention to the immediate vicinity of the body. The control room was a dizzying mess of valves and dials. There were large boxes mounted to the walls, some of which had their own dials. These, he surmised, might be fuse or junction boxes. Or they might not be. Irrespective of their function, Decker saw nothing that struck him as odd, and he didn't want to spend too long investigating right now. If there was something concealed on the U-boat, perhaps worth killing for, he must alert no one else to its presence. He didn't know who he could trust. Besides, CUSP had provided the financing for this expedition, and they would only do that for one reason. The submarine hid a secret. Despite his curiosity, Decker forced his attention back to the job at hand. He would return later to conduct a more detailed search. He looked at Thomas. "You want the head or the feet?"

"Does it matter?" Thomas was standing with his arms folded, studying the corpse. "He's going to bleed on us the minute we move him either way."

"In that case, you take the head." Decker positioned himself at the lower end of the corpse. "You're bigger than me. I'm sure you have better upper body strength. You can go up the ladder first and I'll support Patrick from below."

"I don't know why he couldn't have gotten himself murdered somewhere easier," Thomas grumbled as he looped his arms under Patrick's shoulders. He lifted with a grunt. "Oof, he's heavy. How does such a small man weigh so much?"

"He's French," Decker said. "Eating is a national pastime."

"Good point." Thomas half dragged and half carried Patrick toward the ladder while Decker struggled to lift the dead man's legs.

By a combination of luck and brute force, they got him up the control room ladder and through the conning tower hatch. On the bridge they caught their breath, before lifting him down the steps and off the submarine into the umbilical.

"We should've brought something to wrap him in," Decker said as they lumbered through the umbilical with their grisly cargo.

Thomas glanced behind them at the floor. "He's not dripping blood anywhere, so I think we're okay."

"I guess." Decker tried not to look at Patrick's pallid face, and the pair of milky dead eyes that stared back at him. He wondered if the Frenchman had suffered much. He hoped not. Then he thought of the woman waiting back in Paris. She surely wouldn't expect something like this to happen to him on such a routine expedition. Patrick might have been a scoundrel with a trail of ex-wives, but he didn't deserve this. And neither did his current partner. Decker was glad he wouldn't be the one to break the news to her.

They were at the hatch leading into the habitat now. Normally it would be closed, but on this one occasion it was standing open to allow them easier passage. They heaved the body across the central hub and into the now empty mess. When they got to the galley Bertram was there, looking less than pleased.

"I made space in the freezer," he said. "You'd better hurry

up and get him in there. I'm making dinner soon. Although I can't imagine anyone is going to want to eat after this."

"Get the door for us?" Thomas asked, motioning toward the walk-in.

Bertram hurried across the galley and opened the door. He watched the two men struggle into the freezer with Patrick and sit him against the back wall. When they stepped back out, he slammed the door closed.

"That should keep him nice and fresh," Thomas said.

Bertram turned away, shaking his head.

"What?" Thomas asked.

Decker almost told him to be more respectful, but he realized it was pointless. Thomas was brusque. Ex-military. He'd probably seen his fair share of death. If this was how he coped with the emotion, so be it. Instead, he followed Thomas back out into the mess, just as Pavel entered from the opposite direction.

"John. Good, you're finished. You need to come up to the server room." He waited for Decker to reach the door and held it open for him. "Adam Hunt is back on the line, and he's itching to speak with you."

Chapter 45

DECKER FOLLOWED Pavel to the server room and took a seat in front of the radio. He waited until the marine archaeologist had left and closed the door before picking up the mic.

"What on earth has been going on down there?" Hunt asked as soon as he knew Decker was there. "Pavel told me there has been an incident."

"That's an understatement," Decker said. The connection to the surface was better than it had been during their last conversation. The static had eased, possibly because the storm raging above them was abating. "The historian, Patrick Marchant has been murdered."

There was a moment of silence on the other end as Hunt absorbed this information. "How?"

"A knife to the chest."

"Tell me everything," Hunt instructed.

Decker complied, filling Hunt in on his discovery of the body, and his theory that the killer possessed military training.

"It sounds like the situation has gotten out of hand down there," Hunt said after Decker finished. "You'd better watch your back."

"I always do," Decker replied. "But it would help if I knew

what I was dealing with. Did you find any information on the sub or its crew?"

"Nothing on the sub. At least, nothing official. The crew is another matter. It appears there was a cover-up, probably to explain their disappearance. The official records list both the captain and first watch officer as going down on a completely different submarine two months after the last entry in the U-909's log. All the other crew names you gave me show the same fate, but spread over at least six other lost submarines. There's no mention of this crew ever serving together, and certainly not on the U-909, which the Germans never officially built."

"Interesting," Decker said. "That proves the Kriegsmarine went to great lengths to hide the existence of the U-909. But it doesn't tell us why."

"I have a theory on that, and it ties in with your hypothesis that at least some Germans are still somehow alive."

"I'm listening," Decker said.

"Before I get into the specifics, let me ask you a question. Have you ever heard of the Philadelphia Experiment?"

"Sure. It's a mostly debunked conspiracy theory regarding a Second World War attempt to make a Navy ship invisible. It grew out of a real experiment the navy carried out to degauss a ship's hull to render magnetically fused mines useless against it."

"Precisely. The ship in question was the USS Eldridge. The degaussing didn't take place on the Eldridge, though. That was the USS Engstrom. But I'm sure the powers that be were more than happy to propagate the myth that it was nothing more than a misunderstanding of fairly mundane technology. Both the British and Canadian Navies used it, and some vessels still use it even today."

"Are you telling me that the military used a conspiracy theory to cover up a real experiment?"

"That's exactly what I'm telling you. The navy never fitted

the Eldridge with degaussing equipment, but they *did* briefly install an unrelated technology of more exotic origins. A propulsion system so advanced that they couldn't even replicate it."

"When you say exotic—"

"I mean non-earthly. Roswell was not the first time an alien spacecraft was captured. A similar incident occurred six years earlier in the Mohave Desert near Death Valley. The terrain is so remote and rugged that the military could remove the craft without drawing attention. It was the propulsion system from that craft that ended up on the Eldridge. It allowed the destroyer to move incredible distances in brief spans of time. But the technology was never fully understood. It still isn't. There were some accidents. A couple of fatalities. After that, the navy removed it."

"I've heard the stories," Decker said. "You're talking about teleportation."

"That's probably a close analogy," Hunt said. "I'm told the device manipulates time and space using Einstein's unified field theory and quantum mechanics. I'm sure a physicist could explain it better than me, but we don't have the time for that."

"You think the Germans possessed similar technology?"

"The Nazis became obsessed with exotic technologies. They even had a name for it. Wunderwaffe, or miracle weapon."

"But where did this technology come from?"

"If the intelligence reports of the time are true, they got their propulsion device from a foo fighter."

"What the hell is that?" Decker asked. "I've never heard of it."

"Foo fighters were unusual balls of light that shadowed and interacted with Allied aircraft during the war. The British and Americans speculated they were some sort of German secret weapon, but the Germans saw them too, and assumed they were an Allied secret weapon.

"They were neither. Several years after the war, the Pentagon brought a Nazi scientist to the United States. This was a common occurrence. Our space program built on advancements made by men such as Wernher Vonn Braun, who helped design the V2 rocket and later worked for NASA. But this scientist didn't work on rockets. He was part of a special project to reverse engineer a device recovered at the site of a crashed Allied bomber after it collided with a foo fighter near the Belgian border in Germany. A farmer discovered the craft in his field. The SS then showed up and confiscated it."

"Sounds like the plot of a science fiction B-Movie," Decker said.

"I agree. But it happened. Just like us, the Germans couldn't replicate the technology. Rumor was they then took the original device and fitted it into a submarine which gave it with the ability to travel vast distances in the blink of an eye and attack completely unsuspecting Allied convoys, then escape before being detected. There was never any proof of this. The scientist in question had nothing to do with actually rigging the device into the vessel. After they failed to reverse engineer it, the original team of scientists got reassigned and sworn to secrecy. He never knew for sure what happened to the device after that."

"But we know what happened to it," Decker said. "Or at least, we suspect. It's somewhere on the U-909."

"That would be my guess. I assume there was an accident, just like with the Eldridge. They tried to use the device, and it didn't work properly."

"That doesn't explain why the U-boat is in such immaculate condition," Decker said. "Or how any of the German submariners could still be alive."

"It does if the device never fully disengaged. It might have left the U-boat caught between our reality and wherever it goes when it teleports, maybe even existing outside of normal time and space. Time is not passing for that U-boat."

"The device may have similarly affected the crew, stranding them between dimensions only to appear briefly if the circumstances are right."

"That would explain the odd occurrences," Hunt said.

"And the attacks on the researchers."

"Yes."

"The writing on the mirror really is a cry for help."

"It would appear so."

"It would also explain Patrick's murder if one of the crew reappeared to find a stranger poking around on their vessel."

"For them, the war has never ended. They are merely protecting their territory."

"What a dreadful thought." Decker shuddered. "Do you think they know what happened?"

"Hard to say. They certainly know they're trapped. The message on the mirror confirms that," Hunt said. "You need to find the device on that sub. It won't be big. They installed the one on the Eldridge in an enclosure less than two feet wide."

"Do you have any idea what the device looks like?"

"Not a clue. I'm sure you'll know when you see it."

"I hope so," Decker said. "I'll do what I can."

"Good," Hunt replied. "Get back in touch with me when you do. And be discreet. Make sure you're not observed. I don't want anyone else knowing about this unless there's no other choice."

"I understand." Decker waited for Hunt to sign off, then placed the mic on its hook next to the radio. If Hunt was right, the situation was even more dangerous than he previously thought. There wasn't just one intruder. The U-boat had a crew of forty-five, which meant he could be dealing with dozens of terrified men who thought they were still at war.

Chapter 46

THEY GATHERED in the mess earlier than usual for dinner. Bertram's previous assessment proved prescient. Nobody was hungry, except for Thomas, who ate with hearty abandon. The rest of them picked at their food, which turned out to be hamburgers and fries, mostly because Bertram wanted to use up as many of the supplies removed from the freezer as possible before it spoiled.

After Bertram cleared away the barely touched meals, they sat around the table and discussed their predicament.

"How long will it be before the storm lets up and the support ship can come for us?" Mackenzie asked.

"Ten hours. Twelve at the outside," Pavel said. He glanced toward Thomas. "I assume you reached the support ship on the radio?"

"Yes." Thomas nodded. "The support ship will leave when weather permits. They'll contact us when they get here."

"What are we going to do until then?"

"We do the same as always," Claudia said. "We go to bed. In the morning we can get off this rig and then the body in the freezer, and that wretched U-boat over there, will be someone else's problem."

"You want us to just go to sleep as if nothing happened?" Lauren looked horrified. "I don't think I can do that."

"It won't be easy, and that's a fact," Bertram said.

"We don't have any choice," Decker replied. "It's that or we huddle in the mess all night."

"I'm not sure that's the best idea," Claudia said. "I want everyone rested and thinking clearly."

"We'll be perfectly safe," Thomas said.

"Are you kidding me?" Mackenzie shook her head in disbelief. "What makes you think we'll be safe? Patrick was murdered, for heaven's sake. How do we know the murderer won't come back to kill someone else?"

"Come to that, how do we know the murderer isn't sitting at this very table," Pavel said.

"I agree with Claudia." Decker looked around the group. "It's unlikely the murderer is in our midst. We've already determined that most of the people gathered here would not have the strength to kill Patrick with a knife like that."

"Most of us, but not all of us," Mackenzie said, looking between Thomas and Decker.

"That's true," Thomas replied. "But many of the recent incidents occurred at times when none of us could have been the perpetrators, including two of the most egregious ones."

"I'm sure we will be safe in the bunk rooms tonight," Decker said. He wished he could tell the rest of the group about his conversation with Adam Hunt, and their theory that a member of the U-boat crew attacked Lauren and Mackenzie and killed Patrick. But Hunt had made it clear that he did not want to share that information unless absolutely necessary. "I do think we should be on the alert, however. Someone should be awake at all times to keep watch. Thomas and I can split guard duty between us in shifts."

"Sounds good," Thomas said. "There won't be any crazed killers getting past me, I can assure you of that."

"I still don't think I'll sleep," Mackenzie said. "But I'll feel better knowing someone is awake and watching over us."

"It's settled then," Decker said.

"You can take the first shift." Thomas glanced toward Decker. "I'll swap with you halfway through the night and keep a lookout until morning."

"And after that, we can meet the support ship and leave this hellish place behind," Mackenzie said.

This elicited a murmur of agreement from the entire group. Mackenzie, it appeared, was not the only one eager to escape Habitat One.

Chapter 47

A LITTLE BEFORE MIDNIGHT, Decker and Thomas escorted everyone up to their bunk rooms. Then they retreated to the central hub and closed the hatch door leading to the accommodation, before searching the entire facility, room by room. This was Claudia's suggestion. She thought everyone would sleep easier knowing the habitat was safe.

After checking the upper level, they descended and checked the moon pool, submersible docking bay, and the workshops. They also checked the watertight bulkhead doors on both sides of the umbilical.

"I sure wish we could lock these hatch doors," Decker said.

"It would make for a less stressful night," Thomas agreed. "Unfortunately, there's no way to secure them."

"Maybe you could have that feature added to the next undersea habitat MERO builds."

"I have a feeling I'll be parting ways with Maritime Exploration and Recovery after this gig is up."

"Not too keen on people trying to kill you, huh?"

"Not so much." Thomas turned and started back to the

central hub. "What did your man Adam Hunt want? He seemed mighty keen to talk to you."

"He was looking into a few things for me. Following some leads regarding the submarine."

"Anything you want to share?"

"There's not much to tell." Decker had no intention of explaining his theory to Thomas, not only because Hunt wanted to keep it on the down low but also because he didn't yet see the need to share. Not that he distrusted Thomas per se, but because he'd learned from bitter experience not to trust people just because they appeared to be friendly. Especially those who hadn't proven themselves. Working for CUSP had only heightened that instinct. With that in mind, Decker invented a plausible answer that was at least partly honest but avoided the bulk of their conversation. "Patrick gave me a list of crew names before he died. Hunt was checking on some of them, seeing if any of the crew made it off the submarine alive, and if so, where they might have gone afterwards. I thought it might explain the absence of human remains on the submarine."

"Did he find anything?"

"Not yet," Decker lied, then added, "I'll keep you posted."

"I'd appreciate that," Thomas said as they reached the central hub and started back up to the second level. When they arrived at the crew quarters, he opened the hatch. "I guess this is where I bid you adieu. I'll be back in a few hours to relieve you. Be careful. Just because we searched the facility doesn't mean that we are safe."

"I agree with you on that," Decker replied.

Without another word, Thomas turned and stepped through the hatchway into the accommodation block. He made his way to a bunk room door halfway down the corridor and disappeared inside, drawing it closed behind him.

Silence descended upon the habitat.

Decker stood there for a few moments, leaning on the

railing and looking down to the lower level. Everything was still and quiet. He took comfort knowing that anyone crossing over the umbilical from the U-boat would set off the hatch door alarm, just as they had done the first night he was on the facility.

He had no explanation for what had occurred the second night, when they had caught someone turning the camera off. He found it hard to believe that German sailors from the first half of the last century would have knowledge of such technology. It also concerned him that whoever turned off the camera was already on Habitat One. They had not come over from the sub, but rather were going the other way. This was troubling. It was a piece of the puzzle that didn't fit his theory. It bothered him.

He stood there a while longer, pondering this, then put the strange inconsistency aside. It would come to him. It always did. In the meantime, it was his job to make sure that the people huddling in their bunk rooms remained safe.

He turned away from the railing and hurried to his own bunk room. He ducked inside and took the office chair from under the small desk near the bed. He also grabbed his Kindle, a gift from Nancy so that he would have something to do on the long and lonely nights when he was on assignment. E-reader in hand, he wheeled the chair along the corridor and lifted it out through the hatch, positioning it on the gantry that ran around the upper level of the central hub. Then he sat down, found a book to read, and settled in for the long night ahead.

Chapter 48

MACKENZIE STOOD in her bunk room door and watched John Decker and Thomas depart to search the facility, closing the hatch separating the accommodation block from the central hub. Afterward, she turned and entered her bunk room. She couldn't imagine sleep would come easily, if at all. She picked up her toiletry bag and stepped back into the corridor. The washroom was already occupied, so she lingered outside until the lock drew back, and Pavel stepped out.

"It's all yours," he said as he passed her on his way back to his own bunk room.

"Thank you," Mackenzie said, stepping inside. She went to the sink and put her toiletry bag down, unzipped it, and took out her toothpaste and toothbrush. She looked up, remembering the words written on the mirror. There was no sign of the message now. She felt a shiver of unease and hurried about her business. When she was done, Mackenzie dropped her toothbrush and toothpaste back into the toiletry bag and hurried to her bunk room, where she locked the door.

She changed into a pair of flannel pajamas and got into bed, propping the pillow up behind her and sitting there with the light on. After a while she heard Decker and Thomas return. They had a brief conversation, after which the habitat fell silent. She reached out and dimmed the lights, but not all the way, which would plunge the room into absolute darkness. That was the last thing she wanted. She was about to settle down under the covers when there was a light knock at her door.

"Mac. It's me."

Mackenzie recognized Pavel's voice. She slipped back out from under the covers and unlocked the door, pulling it back to let him in. "This is becoming a habit."

"Sorry." Pavel stepped into the room. "I just wanted to see how you're doing. I couldn't stand the thought of you over here on your own, feeling nervous."

"I'm okay," Mackenzie said, even though she wasn't sure she believed it. "But I'm glad that you're here."

"Yeah?" Pavel's eyes twinkled in the soft lighting. "I'm glad I'm here, too."

A strange silence fell between them, neither one knowing quite how to proceed. Eventually Pavel cleared his throat and glanced toward the door. "I can leave if you want, now that I know you're okay."

"I think you should stay." Mackenzie took Pavel's hand. "I really don't want to be alone. Not tonight."

"Me either." He glanced toward the office chair. "If you'd like to go to sleep, I can sit in the chair and keep you company. I won't go anywhere, I promise."

"That would be nice." Mackenzie returned to her bunk and climbed back in. She watched Pavel pull the office chair out and settle down upon it.

She closed her eyes, more relaxed now that she wasn't alone. But still sleep eluded her. After ten minutes she opened her eyes again to find Pavel sitting there watching her.

"How's the chair?" She asked in a low and drowsy voice.

"Not bad," he replied.

"You sure about that? It doesn't look too comfortable."

"Don't you worry about me. You just settle down and get some sleep."

"I'm not sure that I can. It's kind of weird with you sitting there like that."

"I can go if you want me to."

"Don't leave." Mackenzie pushed over toward the wall, making room in the narrow bunk, then she slipped the sheets back and tapped the bed. "Come over here instead. If you're going to keep me company, you might as well do the job properly."

Pavel observed her for a few moments, possibly trying to judge if the offer was serious, then he stood and pushed the chair back under the desk before approaching the bunk bed and crawling in next to her.

"See. Isn't that better?" Mackenzie asked. She nuzzled up and wrapped an arm around him.

"I guess."

"That's all you have to say?" Mackenzie could sense Pavel's nervousness. But she didn't care. She liked him, and more importantly she felt safe.

"It is better," Pavel said, relaxing a little. He slipped an arm around her shoulder and held her.

Mackenzie rested her head on his chest and listened to the faint beat of his heart. "Good night," she said.

"Good night," Pavel replied. His hand slipped under her pajama top and gently stroked her back.

For a while they lay like that, locked in each other's embrace, and then she looked up and met his gaze.

"What's going to happen when we leave here," she asked.

"We'll move on to other gigs, I guess. There's a First World War troopship they just found in the Mediterranean. It might be a fun distraction."

"I don't mean work," Mackenzie said. "What will happen to us. Me and you. Are we going to see each other again?"

"Do you want to?" Pavel asked.

"What do you think?"

"Yes. We'll see each other again. Try to stop me."

"Good." Mackenzie glanced toward the light switch. "Why don't you dim the lights, just a little more."

"Why?" Pavel asked. "I thought you didn't like the dark."

"I don't, but I'm also shy. I'd rather not have it so bright for what's about to happen."

For a moment Pavel looked confused, but then Mackenzie lifted her lips to his and kissed him. An hour later they fell asleep in each other's arms, with the lights still low.

Chapter 49

A LITTLE AFTER three thirty in the morning Thomas showed up to take over from Decker, who had spent the last several hours dividing his time between reading and walking the gantry, peering down into the gloomy lower level for any sign of movement. There had been no incidents. The habitat remained dark and silent. A couple of times early in his watch, one or other of the team had appeared, either to visit the bathroom, or check on their colleagues. Pavel snuck into Mackenzie's room and was still there. Since that time there had been no activity from the direction of the bunk rooms. Everyone was either asleep or laying nervously awake waiting for what might happen next.

"You ready to catch some shuteye?" Thomas asked, stepping out onto the gantry.

"I'm not sure how much sleep I'll get," Decker replied. "But my bunk will be a hell of a lot more comfortable than sitting in this chair staring into the darkness."

"Better than the alternative," Thomas replied.

Decker agreed with that. In the morning Pavel would start shuttling the team up to the surface and the waiting support ship. No one else would get hurt.

He bade Thomas good night and left him settling in for the second watch. Back in his bunk room, Decker climbed onto the bed and lay there, listening to the ever-present hum of the air filtration system that was as close to silent as the habitat ever came. The evacuation of the facility, while necessary considering recent events, presented a problem. Hunt wanted to inspect the U-boat for unusual technology. He also wanted to keep that search under wraps. Since the abandonment of Habitat One was imminent, there was precious little time left to do it. Decker had already considered sneaking across to the U-boat during his hours guarding the accommodation. But he was reluctant to leave his post. If anything happened in the interim, he would never forgive himself. So instead, he remained where he was until Thomas showed up. Now, though, he was free to follow Hunt's orders. Except there was only one way out of the accommodation block, and Thomas was guarding the hatch. Anticipating this problem, and with many hours at his disposal while keeping guard, Decker had already come up with a plan. At 5 AM with two hours left until the habitat entered day mode, Decker put it in action.

He slipped from his bunk room and padded along the corridor toward the central hub. He would tell Thomas that he could not relax and wanted to search the facility one more time to make sure they were still alone. It was a plausible cover story and gave him a reason to cross the umbilical. Once he convinced Thomas to disengage the hatch alarm, that was. But when he stepped out into the central hub, the office chair was empty. Thomas was not there.

Decker came to a halt, alarmed.

A flicker of unease pulsed at the back of his mind.

He glanced back toward the bunk rooms, wondering if Thomas was answering the call of nature, but he wasn't. The restroom was unoccupied, door ajar.

Decker hurried back along the corridor and poked his

head into Thomas's bunk room. This too was empty. With a growing sense of alarm, he rushed back to the central hub and conducted a thorough search of the upper level, racing through the offices and storage rooms, moving through each annex. But it was to no avail. Returning to the central hub, he hurried to the stairs and descended. He paused in the middle of the hub's lower level and turned a complete three sixty, peering into each dim and lonely corridor, praying he would see his colleague. But he saw something else instead. Something that made his blood run cold.

The umbilical hatch door was standing open.

Chapter 50

DECKER APPROACHED the hatch with trepidation. Only a few minutes ago he had been hoping to convince Thomas to turn off the hatch alarm so that he could cross over to the submarine without waking up the entire facility. Now the door was open, which meant someone had disabled the hatch alarm. There was only one person who could have done that. But why? Had Thomas seen or heard something that convinced him to investigate the U-boat? Or was there a more sinister motive? Had Thomas waited for everyone to be safely out of the way and in their bunk rooms before sneaking off to board the U-boat unobserved? That thought did not sit well with Decker, especially since he still hadn't resolved the question of who turned the camera off the previous night.

Beyond the outer hatch, the umbilical lay swathed in a yellow half-light. Decker stepped over the threshold and started toward the other end. When he reached the hatch leading to the U-boat, he paused and listened.

Silence.

An image of Patrick laying in a pool of his own blood pushed its way into Decker's mind. He hoped he would not discover Thomas the same way. He also hoped there was a reasonable explanation for the man's absence.

Decker approached the steps leading up to the bridge. He climbed them, moving with a stealth honed by years of putting his life on the line as a police officer. Either Thomas was investigating an unauthorized presence, or Thomas was not who he seemed. Either way, Decker didn't want to signal his own approach.

When Decker reached the bridge, he saw that the submarine's access hatch was open. Again, he listened, hoping for some clue regarding Thomas's location, but again heard nothing. There was nothing else for it. Decker would have to enter the sub. He peered down into the U-boat's interior and felt his gut twist with apprehension. Climbing down the ladder would leave him exposed. But he couldn't help that. With a deep breath, Decker stepped onto the ladder.

Now he moved quickly, turning to scan his surroundings as he climbed down. The work lights strung throughout the submarine's interior cut a path of illumination through the vessel, but weren't enough to push the shadows back entirely. Decker waited for a frantic submariner to come tearing out of the gloom, knife in hand. None came. Decker reached the bottom of the ladder without incident.

He looked to his left, then to his right, but saw no sign of Thomas or anyone else. That didn't mean Decker was alone. The sub was full of bulky equipment and tight spaces, any one of which could be hiding someone.

Decker stepped around the attack periscope and moved to the center of the control room. And then he saw it. A box mounted to the wall near the steering controls. It was much like several other boxes mounted in between the valves and gauges. Painted a matte gray and sitting above what looked like a helmsman's position, it would not have garnered a second look except that someone had removed the front panel.

Adorned with fake dials, no doubt meant to disguise the box's true purpose, the panel now rested on the deck. But it was what the box contained that drew Decker's attention. A control panel with six dials mounted upon it, and above this a recessed space containing a dull gray metallic orb connected to a pair of wiring harnesses. Strangely, the orb appeared to glow with a faint inner radiance even though the metal looked solid.

Decker drew in a sharp breath.

This was what Hunt wanted him to find.

He glanced around one more time to make sure that he was still alone and approached the newly revealed control panel. Now that he was closer, Decker could feel a vibration in the air. The hairs on the back of his arms stood up as if reacting to a static charge. Even though the rest of the U-boat appeared to be dead in the water, the orb was clearly running on some kind of internal power. He wondered what else it was doing. According to Hunt, the device installed on the Eldridge had manipulated time and space, possibly even break the barrier between dimensions. This was how they'd achieved what appeared to be teleportation. Decker found it incredible that such a small device could have such capabilities, yet it made sense. With the device damaged but still running, the sub had become trapped in some sort of temporal bubble. That was how it could withstand the ravages of so many decades on the seabed. He wondered about the crew. Were they also here, trapped and invisible on some other plain, only to reappear briefly when the circumstances were right? Were they watching him right now, aware of his presence?

Decker felt a chill run through him.

He took one more look at the orb and then tore his eyes away. The mysterious device could wait. First, he needed to find Thomas. He backed up, intending to search the rest of the sub, but he never got that far. From his rear came the unmistakable sound of footsteps. He turned, surprised, just in time to see a heavy wrench whizzing through the air toward his head.

Chapter 51

DECKER DUCKED AND PIVOTED SIDEWAYS. The wrench sailed past the spot his head occupied mere seconds before and smacked into the periscope with a metallic clang.

Thomas grunted and raised the wrench again. "What are you doing down here?"

"I could ask you the same question." Decker stepped sideways to put the periscope between himself and his attacker. "But that open panel on the wall answers my question."

"Then why don't you stand aside and let me take what I came here for. Then I'll leave and those researchers can have their precious sub all to themselves."

"Sorry. Can't do that," Decker replied.

"I don't want to hurt you, John."

"The same way you didn't want to hurt Patrick, Lauren, and Mackenzie?" Decker glanced toward the ladder, wondering if he could make it up to the sub's bridge before Thomas could react. He decided he couldn't.

"I didn't touch Lauren or Mackenzie. That wasn't me. What kind of man do you think I am?"

"You tell me."

"I don't hurt women."

"What about Patrick?" The events of the past few days were clearer now. There wasn't just one threat on the habitat. There were two. "Do you deny killing him, too?"

"He found the device." Thomas was making his way around the periscope, inching closer to Decker. "He should have stuck to translating the logs and pawing through dusty old history books."

"Who are you working for?" Decker asked, backing away. "There's no way you're operating on your own."

"Wouldn't you like to know." Thomas lunged forward with the wrench held high.

Decker twisted sideways to avoid the clumsy assault. He scrambled away, reaching the control room pressure bulkhead, and climbed through the circular hatchway into the galley area. He looked around frantically for a weapon with which to defend himself. Thomas had deftly cut off his only escape route and trapped him. There was nowhere to go beyond here except the engine rooms.

"Give it up," Thomas said as he reached the bulkhead hatch. "I have you trapped. You're only delaying the inevitable. Might as well let me finish you now, without all the drama. I promise I'll make it painless."

"I don't think so." Decker picked up a cast iron frying pan that was sitting on the submarine's small hot plate. It wasn't much, but it was better than nothing.

"Suit yourself." Thomas stepped through the hatch, keeping pace with Decker as he retreated through the U-boat.

When they reached the diesel engine room, Decker realized he must make a stand while there was still enough space left to do so. He raised the frying pan and waited for Thomas to make the first move.

But Thomas was looking past him, eyes wide. "What the hell?"

Decker turned to see a figure standing at the other end of

the engine room. A man dressed in dark pants and a thick grimy sweater. On his head was a peaked cap sporting a heraldic eagle with wings spread. A scraggly beard covered much of his face. He observed them with an expression of startled surprise.

For a moment, no one moved.

The U-boat's hull groaned against the immense pressure of water pressing down upon it.

The overhead lights flickered.

Then the submariner lifted his hand and Decker saw he was carrying a gun. He recognized it as a Luger.

The man's mouth moved as if he were giving orders, but no sound came out.

Decker held his breath, aware that he stood between two disparate but equally dangerous enemies.

Then the submariner charged, waving the gun ahead of him as he closed in. Decker saw the man's finger flex on the trigger. He waited for the boom, wondered if the submariner was aiming at him or Thomas.

The Luger's muzzle flashed.

The bullet's impact lifted Decker off his feet and sent him sprawling between the diesel engines. He raised his head, tried to stand, but his chest felt like a freight train had hit it. The last thing he saw before the blackness closed in was the air ripping itself apart around the German, crackles of blue lightning dancing at its edges, before the tear collapsed in upon itself, taking the startled submariner along with it.

Chapter 52

THE FIRST THING Decker registered was pain. He swam back to consciousness slowly and with no idea where he was, or why it felt like he'd gone twelve rounds with a gorilla. But then little by little it all clicked back into place. The memories returned in fragments at first, but then they rushed back with a roar. One realization stood out among all the others.

The German had shot him.

Decker lifted his head, discovered that he was still in the U-boat, lying on the metal gantry between two large diesel engines. The overhead lights were dazzling. He squinted against them and lifted an arm, gingerly probing his chest. It hurt, but he didn't appear to be bleeding. His head throbbed too. He must've cracked it against the deck.

He sat up, afraid of what he might find, but other than a sore chest and the bump on his head, there didn't appear to be any other damage.

But how was that possible? The submariner had clearly fired the Luger at him. Then he glanced sideways and saw the cast iron frying pan he'd grabbed in the galley to fend off Thomas's attack. It had a large crack down the middle now. Then he understood. He was still holding it when the gun went off. The bullet must have hit the frying pan and slammed it into his chest, the force of which threw him backwards and knocked him unconscious. But it had not penetrated the pan's thick iron surface, which had saved him. Thomas had presumably fled, thinking Decker was dead, killed by the submariner.

He struggled to his feet, wincing as a fresh wave of pain hit him. He lifted his shirt and examined his chest. It was bruising already, but he could see no other external injuries. It was possible the frying pan had cracked a rib or two, but Decker didn't think so. He was lucky.

Decker glanced around, nervous, but he was alone. Whatever force had allowed the German to appear briefly had swallowed him up again, and no other members of the submarine crew had materialized in the time since, at least so far as he could tell.

Decker made his way back to the control room, and the box containing the orb. The strange gray sphere that had hummed with power and radiated a faint inner light was now missing. The clamps holding it in place were empty. The wiring harnesses connecting it to the sub dangled freely.

Thomas had taken what he came for.

Decker returned to the ladder and climbed up. With each rung he winced. The submariner's bullet might not have done any permanent damage, but it sure left him sore. When he exited the hatch and emerged onto the U-boat's bridge, he caught his breath and let the pain in his chest subside. Then he descended the exterior steps and made his way along the umbilical.

The outer hatch leading into Habitat One was closed, and Decker felt a brief flash of anxiety. What if Thomas had disabled the release mechanism and trapped him outside the habitat? But when he turned the wheel to disengage the hatch locks, they drew back with a satisfying clunk. Thomas hadn't needed to sabotage the hatch because he thought Decker was already dead, killed by a decades-old German bullet.

Decker pushed the hatch open and hurried through into the habitat, then closed it again behind him. Thomas surely wouldn't want to hang around after stealing the orb from the U-boat. He would look for a way to escape the facility. The submersible was the only obvious choice. It was already six in the morning. Decker had been out cold for at least half an hour. This gave Thomas a good head start. Even so, Decker clung to a slim hope that he wasn't too late to recover the orb. Maybe it had taken Thomas a while to disengage it, and Decker could still catch up with him before he had time to prep the compact sub for an ascent. He hurried to the central hub and made his way along the Annex C corridor leading to the docking bay as quickly as his aching chest would allow. But when he got there, the docking bay was empty, the submersible gone. Thomas had made his escape.

Chapter 53

AN HOUR LATER, the remaining crew of Habitat One gathered once more in the mess hall. After discovering that Thomas had taken the submersible and fled, Decker returned to the bunk rooms, where he woke Claudia and brought her up to speed on the night's events. She was horrified, not least because Thomas was a trusted member of her team. She was skeptical of Decker's explanation regarding the U-boat and trapped submariners, but grudgingly admitted that it explained the unusual occurrences plaguing them since their arrival upon the habitat. After waking everyone, they regrouped in the mess, and Decker filled them in. He left nothing out, telling them about the alien device installed on the sub, and how it had been keeping the U-boat preserved through the decades. He explained his theory that at least some German submariners had survived, caught between dimensions and only able to step back into the real world for short periods when the circumstances were right. He hypothesized that the researchers themselves were responsible for this. They had run cables over to the sub to operate the work lights and it was possible the device had been feeding off that new power source, leaching energy and briefly pulling the sailors back. His own encounter with the Luger wielding German amidst his confrontation with Thomas confirmed this. Adam Hunt had instructed him not to share information about the true nature of the U-boat unless absolutely necessary, but Decker deemed this situation to fall within those parameters. He could also see no way to explain Thomas's actions without revealing the man's true motives for being on the habitat.

"I can't believe that Thomas murdered Patrick," Lauren said once Decker had finished. "It makes no sense."

"It makes perfect sense to me," Bertram said. "I never liked the man. I couldn't put my finger on it until now, but he always made me uncomfortable."

"Poor Patrick. He was in the wrong place at the wrong time," Claudia said. "I wish he'd came to me regarding whatever he thought was on the U-boat instead of going over there on his own to check it out."

"If he had, he might still be alive," Mackenzie said. She paused for a moment, lost in thought, and then glanced toward Decker. "You really don't believe Thomas attacked Lauren and me?"

Decker shook his head. "No, I don't, and not because he denied perpetrating them, but because it wouldn't be in his best interests to assault other members of the team without good reason. He was trying to keep a low profile until he could find the navigation device on the U-boat and steal it, which was his real purpose for being here. He only killed Patrick because he discovered the device and had no choice."

"Then we really were attacked by ghosts," Mackenzie said. "I still don't understand how that's possible."

"They aren't ghosts," Decker said. "They are living people just like us. It's not surprising that their first instinct was to attack. Think about it from their point of view. Those men don't realize how much time has passed. For them, the war hasn't ended. All they know is that interlopers are coming aboard their submarine. They must have been reappearing for long enough durations to cross the umbilical and make their way aboard the habitat. That's why the alarm went off that night."

"They were exploring," Pavel said.

"Precisely." Decker nodded in agreement. "It must've been quite a shock for them to find the submarine stranded on the seafloor and connected to this facility."

"I bet that's where my loaf of bread went. They stole it. I knew I'd taken one out of the freezer to defrost in time for breakfast," Bertram said. "I thought I was going crazy."

"It makes sense that they would take food," Decker replied. "They must know their device malfunctioned and trapped them, but they would still follow their instincts. Who knows what they experience when they're not corporeal, or even if they're aware of the passage of time, but during the brief periods when they step back into the real world, they still have needs."

"Those poor men must be terrified," Claudia said.

"I wonder why they didn't repair the sub and free themselves?" Bertram asked.

"Maybe they tried," Decker said. "We don't know how many of them survived the initial accident that stranded the sub here. The U-boat had a crew complement of forty-five. If only one or two submariners could appear simultaneously, it would be incredibly difficult to make repairs and rescue themselves."

"Especially if they were only materializing for brief periods of time," Pavel said.

"Which is why one of them left a message on the bathroom mirror asking for help," Lauren said. "It must've taken a lot of courage to do that if they viewed us as the enemy."

"Exactly." Decker nodded.

"Not all of them are so benign." Claudia glanced around the group. "Let's not forget, the one Decker encountered tried to shoot him."

"And now we're trapped down here with them."
Mackenzie looked uneasy.

"I don't think that's the case. At least, not anymore."
Decker shook his head. "Thomas disconnected the technology
protecting the sub from the ravages of time. The same device
was also allowing the German sailors to cross back over.
Without it they won't be able to do that anymore."

"They'll be stuck for eternity on whatever plain the orb
imprisoned them in when it malfunctioned," Pavel said.

"How awful." Lauren shuddered. "Imagine being trapped
for eternity."

"We don't need to," Mackenzie said. "Thomas stole the
submersible. We're trapped too."

Chapter 54

"WE ARE NOT TRAPPED HERE," said Pavel, looking around the group. "At least, not for long. Thomas already radioed the support ship, remember?"

"Yeah, sure." Mackenzie snorted. "You really think he actually did that?"

"Someone should have gone with him to make sure he made the call," Bertram said.

"Why?" Claudia asked. "We had no reason to distrust him."

"Mackenzie is right though," Decker said. "Thomas didn't radio the surface. He only volunteered to prevent one of us doing it. He lied."

"We don't actually know that for sure," Pavel said, hopefully.

"Get real," Lauren replied. "No one but us knows Patrick is dead, just like they don't know we're trapped."

"Then I'll radio the support ship myself," Pavel said. "The storm should have blown itself out by now, so they'll be able to put to sea."

"How's that going to help?" Lauren asked. "We don't have a submersible, remember? That murdering bastard Thomas took it. Even after they arrive, we still won't be able to get up to the surface."

"Which is why I'll have them bring another submersible. Bela isn't the only sub available to MERO. There's an older model on loan to NOAA. If they can borrow it back and get it here fast enough, we'll use that. If not, I'm sure they can find one somewhere else. Plenty of private companies have submersibles, not to mention the U.S. Navy."

"That will take so long," Mackenzie said, her voice trembling. "What are we going to do in the meantime?"

Claudia shrugged. "We carry on as normal. The support ship wasn't due back with supplies for over a week, anyway. We have more than enough food to see us through and even if we can't get another submersible here, there are always the SEIE suits."

"What are SEIE suits?" Decker asked. "And how will they get us off the habitat?"

"SEIE stands for Submarine Escape Immersion Equipment," Claudia replied. "They're waterproof full-body escape apparatus pressurized to one atmosphere. There's a special airlock, the trunk, that will eject us from the facility one by one. Once we're on the surface, life rafts built into each suit will deploy to keep us buoyant and protected from the elements. There's also a GPS locator beacon in each one, along with a strobing light to aid nighttime rescue. The SEIE suit is a last resort option. I'd rather wait for a submersible to come get us, but I will use the suits if I have to. Either way, the situation is not as bleak as it would at first appear."

"I still don't like it," Mackenzie said. "I don't want to stay down here for one more minute."

"Me either," Lauren said. "I've had it with this place."

"I'm afraid we don't have any choice but to stick it out for now." Claudia folded her arms. "Whatever happens, help won't be coming for many hours, and probably days."

"I don't believe this." Mackenzie looked close to tears. Her eyes were wide with fear.

"Let's all just to keep calm, okay? There's no need to panic. Nothing has really changed. We're as safe now as we were yesterday."

"I don't feel very safe."

"Which is why we should radio the support ship without further delay," Claudia said.

"I agree," Pavel said.

"What about Thomas?" Lauren asked. "If we report him quick enough, maybe the authorities can get here and apprehend him while he's still in possession of the sub, then we won't need to find another way off the habitat."

"It won't do any good." Decker shook his head. "He'll be long gone by the time the authorities mobilize."

"What makes you so sure?"

"Because his presence on Habitat One was not circumstantial. His employers inserted him on this team without arousing suspicion. That took sophistication and planning. My guess is that a friendly vessel will meet him on the surface. At that point, they'll probably scuttle the submersible to cover their tracks."

"All the more reason to get off this facility quickly," Lauren said. "I don't want to be here if Thomas and whoever he works for, decide to come back. They might kill us all next time."

"I don't think that's likely," Decker said. "But I would like to alert Adam Hunt and CUSP to our predicament. The longer we wait, the further away Thomas gets with the orb."

"I think Mr. Decker's right," Claudia said. "Thomas probably won't return, but I'd rather not get caught spinning our wheels if he does." She looked at Pavel. "You and John should head up to the server room and radio the support ship immediately. We'll all rest easier knowing help is on the way, even if we have to wait awhile."

"Sounds like a plan." Pavel glanced toward Decker. "Ready?"

"Sure." Decker started off with Pavel at his heel. They made their way through the central hub and climbed to the second level. When they reached the Annex D corridor, he saw that the server room door was standing open.

"That isn't right," Pavel said, a worried expression crossing his face. "The server room is a climate-controlled environment. That door should be closed at all times."

"Maybe Lauren left it open accidentally," Decker replied as they approached the room, but deep down he had a bad feeling.

"I doubt it. She knows better. We all do." Pavel sounded nervous. "Something isn't right."

"Then let's find out what," Decker said as they reached the door. He stepped inside and stopped short.

Thomas had trashed the room.

"No, no, no," Pavel wailed and ran to the radio, which was sitting on its side with the case pried off. Wiring and circuit boards, ripped from their casing, now littered the desk. He stared in horror. "It's completely ruined. We can't use this."

"That might be the least of our problems," Decker said, his gaze resting on the server cabinets. The front panels had been removed and the blade servers within removed from their bays. They now lay on the floor, broken and buckled. Thomas had obviously taken a boot to them.

"That tears it," Pavel said, turning his attention to the server rack. "We're done for."

"What you mean?" Decker asked with a growing sense of alarm.

"Those servers control the facility's entire life support system. Air circulation, oxygen generators, even the heating." Pavel looked at Decker, his face a mask of fear. "Without them, we're dead men walking."

Chapter 55

WHEN DECKER and Pavel arrived back at the mess, Bertram had made hot cocoa for everyone. They were sitting in the lounge area next to the foosball table, lost in their own thoughts as they sipped their drinks and contemplated recent events.

When Decker stepped into the mess, Claudia looked up hopefully. "How did it go?"

"Not so good." Decker accepted a mug of cocoa from Bertram and held it with both hands, happy for the warmth. The habitat was always on the chilly side, but now it felt decidedly frigid to Decker, even though he knew it hadn't been long enough for Habitat One to lose its heat yet.

"Thomas destroyed the server room," Pavel said, his voice grim. "The radio was smashed."

"What?" Mackenzie jumped up. "Does that mean we can't call for help?"

"That's exactly what it means." Pavel rounded the sofa and sat down dejectedly. "It gets worse. Thomas pulled all the blade servers out and wrecked them."

"Those servers control our environment." There was a

frantic look in Lauren's eyes. "Without them, the habitat will stop circulating oxygenated air and we'll be asphyxiated."

"How long will that take?" Bertram asked. "Surely we'll have enough air to get us through until the support ship realizes there's something wrong."

"Nowhere close. We're looking at three, maybe four days at most," Lauren said. "And there will be more carbon dioxide buildup the longer we go."

"Don't you have a way of producing more oxygen?" Decker asked.

"Yes. Oxygen generators located underneath the habitat, pull water in and separate out the oxygen by electrolysis and send it to storage tanks. The computer constantly monitors the atmosphere in the habitat and releases oxygen as needed. There's always much more in the tanks than we need. This acts as a failsafe if there's an issue with the system. But the computer runs the oxygen generators, and without it they won't work. Neither will the system that monitors the habitat's atmosphere. We can release oxygen from the tanks manually if we need to, but once that's depleted there won't be any more."

"Why wasn't there a failsafe built in?"

"There was," Lauren looked sick to her stomach. "We have four rack server cabinets. Two of them run as an independent backup system. If any of the servers in the main cabinets go down, the backup servers take over."

"But Thomas destroyed *all* the servers," Pavel said. "Even the backup units."

"And it gets worse," Lauren said. "As I'm sure you've all noticed, the temperature has dropped a degree or two since we've been sitting here. That's because the computer also controls our ambient temperature. Now that it's not doing that, we have no way to generate heat."

"And what heat we do have is slowly bleeding into the ocean." Pavel leaned forward and put his head in his hands.

"It's going to get mighty cold in here long before we asphyxiate."

"Why would Thomas do this?" Bertram asked. "He took what he wanted."

"Because he can't let us live," Decker replied. "With us dead, no one will ever know he removed the orb from the submarine."

"So that's it then." Mackenzie wiped a tear from her cheek. "There's nothing to do but sit here until we die."

"We do have one option left," Claudia said. "The SEIE suits."

"What good are those?" Mackenzie shook her head. "Even if we reach the surface, we don't have any way to call for help. We'll be adrift in the ocean and no one will know we're there."

"It's better than becoming oxygen-starved popsicles," Bertram said. "At least we stand a chance if we get off the habitat."

"Claudia's right." Decker was still gripping his mug of cocoa. The drop in temperature hadn't been his imagination after all. He wondered how long before it would become uncomfortable. "Staying here is a death sentence. I saw those servers. There's no way to repair them. Same goes for the radio."

"It's settled then," Claudia said. "We use the SEIE suits."

"We'd better not leave it too long," Lauren said. "Every moment we stay here is using up more oxygen."

"Just great." Mackenzie choked back a sob.

Pavel moved seats so that he was next to her. He put his arm around her shoulders. "Hey, we'll get out of this. And if we don't, I can't think of anyone better to share the last of my oxygen with."

"Not funny." Mackenzie forced a weak smile.

"I'm going to check on the suits," Claudia said, standing up. "Who's with me?"

"I'll go," Decker said.

Pavel looked up. "I'm going to stay here with Mackenzie until it's time to leave."

"I'll go up to the server room," Lauren said. "You never know, something might be salvageable."

"And I'll make us something to eat," Bertram said. "If we're stranding ourselves in the ocean, we might as well do it on a full stomach."

"It's just the two of us then." Claudia turned to Decker. "Are you ready?"

"Lead on," Decker said. He followed Claudia out of the mess and back up to the second level. They entered Annex A and soon arrived at a room identified on a plaque next to the door as the Trunk Access Chamber. A large storage bay with sliding doors covered one wall. A metal ladder occupied the center of the room. Above it was a hatch door leading into the escape airlock itself, known as the trunk.

Claudia hurried to the storage bay and pulled the doors open. Then she stepped back with a gasp.

Inside, hanging from special hooks in the ceiling, were ten bright orange SEIE suits. But they would be of no help to the stranded crew, because Thomas had slashed each of them, rendering the suits useless.

Chapter 56

DECKER AND CLAUDIA RETURNED, dejected, to the mess hall to give everyone else the bad news. When they entered, Bertram was in the galley, but he soon came out when he heard their voices.

"Thomas destroyed the SEIE suits," Claudia said. "He took a knife to them. They're useless now."

"Are you serious?" Pavel jumped up. "Where does that leave us?"

"It leaves us stranded down here." Decker was mad at himself for not seeing the threat Thomas posed sooner. He should have suspected him the minute they found Patrick's body on the sub. He was one of the few people aboard the habitat who possessed the strength and knowledge to kill Patrick. But Decker had assumed a German had committed the crime. It was a stupid mistake. Decker knew better than to rely on assumptions, but there was no reason to believe that Thomas was anything but what he appeared to be. Worse, Decker had failed to handle the situation when he found Thomas on the sub in the early hours of the morning trying to remove the orb. It was Decker's fault that they were now in this situation.

"What about the hard suits?" Mackenzie asked. "The ones the technical divers used to inspect the U-boats outer hull when we first arrived on the habitat?"

"They won't do us any good," Pavel said. "Even if Thomas didn't destroy them, we only have two and there are six of us."

"It's better than nothing. If two of us can make it to the surface, they can summon help."

"Not likely." Pavel shook his head. "Even if we could use the hard suits to get to the surface, they don't have radios in them. There will be no way to contact anyone."

"And that would mean almost certain death," Claudia said. "The hard suits aren't buoyant like the SEIE's. They would sink and drown their occupants when the battery packs that run them expired, and even if they didn't, their users would end up swept further out to sea. Either way, they aren't a survival option."

"That's it then," Mackenzie said, burying her head in her hands. "We're going to die."

"The temperature is dropping faster now," Lauren said. "It's going to get pretty cold in here before we choke to death."

"We can go into the galley if the temperature dips too much," Bertram said. "I can turn the hot plates on full to heat the air. It's only a small room so it should keep us toasty for a while, at least."

"We're just delaying the inevitable," Mackenzie said. "Even if we crowd in there and run the hot plates, it won't make a difference. We'll still die before anyone topside even knows there's an issue. Like Pavel said, the support ship isn't due to make another supply run for over a week. And even if the cold doesn't get us, we'll run out of oxygen anyway, and there's nothing we can do about that."

"I'm not sure which is worse," Pavel said. "Dying from hypothermia or asphyxiation."

"Cut it out right now," Claudia said, looking around the group. "We're not dead yet, and I refuse to give up."

"Me either," Decker said. "In fact, I have an idea."

"Well, don't keep us in suspense," Lauren said. "I'm up for trying anything at this point, no matter how minuscule the chance of success."

Decker rubbed his hands together for warmth and then hugged them to his chest. "Isn't there a radio room on the U-boat? Why don't we use that?"

"It won't do any good," Pavel said, his voice laced with disappointment. "Even if the radio still works, it doesn't broadcast at a low enough frequency to transmit a signal this far underwater. If we were on the surface, perhaps, but not down here."

"I wasn't suggesting we use the radio on the U-boat to send a message," Decker replied. "But maybe we can cannibalize it."

"Of course. That might just work," Lauren said. "Depending on how badly Thomas wrecked the VLF. It's a long shot for sure, but there's a slim possibility I can strip parts from the submarine's radio and jury rig them into our own and get it working again, at least long enough to relay our predicament to the support ship."

"I don't know." Pavel didn't look convinced. "The VLF was pretty well trashed. You'll be lucky to even power it on, let alone transmit. Thomas really wanted to make sure we couldn't repair it."

"Does anyone have a better plan?" Claudia asked, glancing around.

No one did.

"It's settled then," she said. "Lauren will go over to the U-boat and take whatever parts she needs from the radio there. Mister Decker can go with her to assist. Everyone else will stay here to conserve oxygen and body heat, and if it gets too cold while we're waiting, we'll follow Bertram's advice and use the galley hot plates."

Decker glanced at Lauren. "Ready for an adventure?"

"Always." Lauren tried to smile but failed.

"Good luck," Claudia said as they made their way toward the door. "We're relying on you, guys. If this doesn't work, I'm not sure we'll still be alive come tomorrow."

Chapter 57

THEY CROSSED over the umbilical to the submarine and climbed up onto the conning tower. Lauren went first, swinging a toolbox in one hand, followed by Decker. He winced as he ascended the steps and made it to the U-boat's bridge with a relieved grunt.

"Are you okay?" Lauren asked. "You look like you're in pain."

"Getting shot in the frying pan will do that for you," Decker replied, trying to ignore his throbbing chest. Not for the first time that day, he wondered if he actually *had* cracked some ribs.

"Huh?" Lauren looked confused. "I don't get it."

"Never mind. Let's focus on the job at hand." Decker stepped around her and climbed onto the ladder leading down into the U-boat. He took it gently, going slow to minimize the pain in his bruised torso. Once he reached the bottom, Lauren stepped onto the ladder and followed him down.

In the control room she paused, approaching the panel from which Thomas had removed the orb.

"Is this where it was hiding?" She asked, peering at the empty clamps and disconnected wiring harnesses. "I can't believe there was alien technology right here on this sub and I never got to see it."

"If it's any consolation, neither did I until a few minutes before I got shot by a German," Decker said. "And I was actually trying to find it."

"That doesn't make me feel a lot better." Lauren looked disappointed. "I mean, come on. The propulsion system from a UFO? And it was right here under my nose the entire time. Dang it."

"Don't beat yourself up," Decker said. "The Germans hid it well."

Lauren reached out and touched the control panel with the six dials. "This must have been how they set the coordinates that allowed them to jump between two distant points. Longitude and latitude arranged by degrees, minutes, and seconds. Just dial them where they want to go, and poof. I wonder how long it took the Germans to figure out how to control the orb?"

"Who knows," Decker replied. He was eager to get on with the job at hand. The more time they wasted, the less time they would have to get the radio working and call for help before they froze to death. "How about we take a look at that radio?"

"Sure." Lauren pulled herself away from the control panel, but even so couldn't help glancing back at it as they made their way toward the radio room. "Just think how that technology could revolutionize travel if we replicated it. London to New York in ten seconds. Hell, New York to the planet Mars for that matter."

"That last one might be a tough sell," Decker said as they stepped through the pressure bulkhead hatch into the area that contained the officer's quarters and the radio room. "It's not high on most people's must-see list."

"Perhaps," Lauren agreed. "I sure wish we had that orb

device right now, though. We could fire it up and get the hell out of here in the blink of an eye."

"If the orb was still here, we wouldn't need to," Decker said. "Because Thomas wouldn't have felt the need to kill us."

"I'd rather not think about that," Lauren said, sliding the radio room door open and stepping inside. She placed the toolbox on the floor and opened it, removing a screwdriver, then went to work on the radio's case.

Decker watched in silence as she removed several screws and lifted the casing off. She turned and placed it on a narrow bench—presumably where the radio operator sat while operating the unit—and then turned her attention back to the exposed workings of the radio and leaned close to study it.

"Crap. This stuff is ancient." She let out a disappointed tut. "There might be some useful parts, but it will not be easy to cobble this stuff together with our radio, that's for sure."

"Just do the best you can," Decker said. He glanced around, looking along the U-boat's length toward the engine room. There was no sign of any German sailors now. He hoped he was right, and the orb's removal had shuttered their ability to appear. The last thing he wanted was another fight, especially in his current condition. One bullet a day was about all he could take.

"I always do my best," Lauren replied. She switched screwdrivers, selecting a longer flat head, which she pushed deep inside the radio. "If I can just reach the screws at the back of this thing, I can start taking it apart."

"We could just take the whole radio back with us," Decker said.

"Except that it's bolted to the bulkhead. Easier just to take what we need." Lauren withdrew the screwdriver. "I can't get to the screws from this angle." She repositioned the screwdriver and pushed it back inside the radio. Then, without warning, a spark jumped with a crackle.

Lauren cursed and pulled her hand away, letting go of the screwdriver.

"Yikes." She rubbed her palm. "Stupid radio's got juice."

"You mean it has a current?" Decker asked.

"Does it ever. That smarted." Lauren returned to the screwdriver and gingerly withdrew it. "It's completely impossible. We would've noticed before now if any of the electrics were hot. Except for our own work lights, which run off the habitat's power supply, there should be no electricity on this boat. The batteries must be long dead."

"It would appear they are anything but," Decker said. "And there's a simple way to verify it." He reached inside the radio room, to a switch mounted on the wall. When he flicked it, an overhead light snapped on, bathing the room in a cool yellow glow.

"Whoa." Lauren looked up in awe. "This just keeps getting weirder and weirder."

"Weird or not," Decker said. "We have power."

Chapter 58

IT HAD BEEN forty minutes since Decker and Lauren departed to scavenge radio parts from the U-boat. In that time, the air inside the mess had become noticeably cooler. Mackenzie sat on the sofa; her body pressed against Pavel's. She rested her head on his shoulder. Claudia sat at the other end of the sofa, while Bertram occupied a chair and occasionally rubbed his hands together for warmth. No one spoke. The thought of slowly asphyxiating to death had rendered them mute. Talking used up oxygen, so they didn't talk, at least until Decker and Lauren returned.

Mackenzie had her eyes closed when she heard their footsteps in the central hub. She looked up as they entered, hoping for some glimmer of good news. "Can we get the radio working?"

"I don't think so," Lauren said, shaking her head. "The VLF looks like a truck ran it over, and the equipment on that sub is rudimentary. I pride myself on thinking outside the box, but I'm not sure even I can Frankenstein a working rig from what's available."

"That's it then," Mackenzie said. She blinked away tears. "I don't want to die down here."

"We may not have to," Decker said. "This is going to sound crazy, but I think I have a way to get us all out of here and back to the surface."

"How?" Claudia jumped up. "The SEIE suits are ruined, it sounds like the radio repair is a no go, and we don't have a submersible. We can't exactly jump in the moon pool and just swim up in our skivvies."

"We don't need to. I have a better way." Decker glanced at Pavel. "It's all going to rest on you though. I hope you're as good a submersible pilot as you make out you are."

"I have a feeling I won't like the sound of this," Pavel said. He pulled his arm from around Mackenzie's shoulder and stood up, facing Decker. "You want to tell us what you have in mind?"

"Sure." Decker paused for dramatic effect before speaking again. "We're going to use the U-boat."

There was a moment of stunned silence.

It was Claudia who spoke first. "You can't be serious. The U-boat?"

"It's been sitting on the ocean floor for almost eight decades," Pavel said. "It's a wreck. A remarkably well-preserved one for sure, but still a wreck."

"That's where you're wrong." Decker smiled. "The U-boat is good as new. Remember what I told you about the alien device? It was running for all those years, keeping the sub in a protective bubble, effectively removing it from the passage of time. That submarine is as good now as it was in the 1940s. It only started aging again after Thomas removed the orb."

"That still doesn't help us," Claudia said. "Your plan won't work. Even if everything you've told this is true, and quite frankly I'm struggling to believe it, we can't use the submarine. Relic or not, it's dead in the water."

Lauren grinned. "Actually, it's not. Somehow, there's power over there. The sub has fully charged batteries."

"That's impossible," Pavel said. "We would have noticed. I've spent hours on that U-boat studying it, so have Claudia and Mackenzie."

"I can explain that too," Decker said. "Or at least I have a theory. Electricity is nothing more than a stream of electrons. If the orb kept the sub in some form of temporal stasis, effectively removed from time, then those electrons would not flow. Think of it like a river. If the water freezes, it stops running."

"But we saw no sign of electricity on the submarine," Pavel objected. "All the equipment was dead."

"Yes, and no. Since there was no flow of electricity, the equipment acted like it was not operational."

"Mr. Decker is right," Lauren said. "I can't speak for his theory of frozen electrons, but I'm not sure it even matters. That sub currently has power, and it appears to be in operational condition. We can absolutely ride it to the surface."

"Even if the U-boat could make it to the surface, we still have a problem," Pavel said. "That submarine had a crew complement of forty-five. I don't know how many of those it required to operate it, but I'm pretty sure they numbered more than we do. Not only that, but they knew what they were doing."

"That's where you come in." Decker fixed Pavel with a stern gaze. "I know we can't operate the sub in the traditional sense, but we don't need to. If we purge the water from the ballast tanks, the sub will rise on its own."

"An uncontrolled ascent?" Pavel shook his head. "Even if we can get the sub off the seafloor, it will be a hell of a ride."

"It's that or we stay down here until the air runs out," Mackenzie said. "I don't see that we've got any other choice."

"Neither do I," Claudia said. "We're going to do as Mr. Decker suggests and use the U-boat. If it really has power, we can use the radio to call for help once we're on the surface."

"It won't work," Pavel said. "The sub is almost eighty

years old. It'll shake itself apart and drown us before we even get halfway up."

"That's a chance we have to take," Claudia said. "This is not up for discussion. We're going to ride that U-boat to the safety, or we'll die trying."

Chapter 59

CLAUDIA GAVE them fifteen minutes to prepare and collect whatever belongings they wished to take with them. Decker possessed little, and most of it was still in the bag he'd brought with him. A few minutes after they dispersed, he found himself back in the central hub where they had all agreed to regroup prior to boarding the U-boat.

Moments later, Pavel descended the steps from the upper level, his own bag slung over one shoulder. In his hand, he carried a thick black ring binder.

"I'm going over to the U-boat," he said. "If Y'all expect me to pilot that thing to the surface, I'm going to have to get up to speed on the controls pretty dang quick." He raised the ring binder. "Luckily, I came prepared."

"You got step-by-step instructions on how to do a World War II submarine emergency tank blow in that folder?" Decker asked.

"Not quite," Pavel replied. "But it's almost as good. This is the operations manual for a type VII U-boat. Translated, of course. I downloaded it from the internet before we came down here. I thought it might be useful."

"I guess you were right," Decker said.

"It won't allow me to pilot the sub, but I will be able to find the correct controls to blow the tanks. I'm not sure what we'd do if I hadn't brought this."

"It's a good thing you did then," Decker said.

"Damn straight." Pavel moved off toward the umbilical. "I'll see you in the U-boat."

"Just as soon as the others return," Decker agreed. "Good luck in there."

"We're going to need more than luck." Pavel hesitated at the Annex D bulkhead. He turned and glanced back, his eyes roaming up and around the habitat. "I'm not going to miss this place, that's for sure." Then he turned and was gone.

Decker stood alone in the central hub. It was eerily quiet without the constant hum of the air circulation units. He wondered if the turbines on the outside of the facility that generated power were still running, and if not, how long before everything went dark. He shivered. If it wasn't for the U-boat, there would be no way to escape the habitat. The thought of sitting and waiting while it grew colder, and their air ran out, was bad enough. Doing it in the pitch black because the power had failed was worse. If it weren't for the orb keeping the U-boat protected from the ravages of time, Habitat One would have become a frigid and dark grave, just like Thomas intended. Even now, there was no guarantee they would live. The thought of barreling to the surface in a thin metal tube they had no control over made his gut clench. Their chances appeared slim at best.

He was still contemplating this, and wishing there was another way, when he heard footsteps approaching. He glanced around to see Claudia and the others descending from the second level, clutching whatever they didn't wish to leave behind. For better or worse, they were about to find out if the U-boat still had what it took to reach the surface.

Chapter 60

WHEN EVERYONE HAD GATHERED in the central hub, Claudia led them along the Annex D corridor to the umbilical. They stepped through and closed the inner and outer watertight bulkhead hatches behind them and then made their way across the umbilical to the U-boat. After stepping into the enclosure, circling the conning tower and securing one final hatch door, they climbed silently up the steps to the U-boat's bridge. Pavel had already disconnected the thick orange cable that had previously provided power to the sub and the work lights within. It lay coiled at the foot of the steps. Unless Pavel was working in the dark, the U-boat was now operating on its own power.

One by one, they descended into the sub, traversing the ladder down into the control room. Decker held back, allowing the others to go first, then he lowered himself through the hatch and pulled the door closed above him, turning the hatch wheel to lock it in place and seal them inside the aging U-boat. That done, he scrambled down the ladder to join the rest of the group.

The U-boat was indeed operating on its batteries. The

interior was lit by recessed bulbs in cages that spanned the length of the boat. More lights glowed over workstations.

The tension in the air was palpable. Decker could sense the group's combined nervousness. No one spoke because there was only one thing worth discussing. Their chances of survival. Yet there was one obvious problem with their escape plan that no one had yet broached. It wasn't until they stood in the control room that Mackenzie finally voiced what they were all thinking.

"I don't want to throw a wrench in our plan, but how are we going to get the sub off the bottom with the umbilical still attached?"

"I was wondering the same thing," Bertram said. "Won't it hold us down?"

"That's a very good question," Pavel said. He was standing at the map table with the binder open, studying what appeared to be diagrams of the U-boat's valve layout. "In theory, the positive buoyancy should be enough to break us free. The stilts supporting the umbilical are freestanding. They just rest on the seabed to provide extra stability. The umbilical's own rigidity and the connections between the habitat and U-boat keep it in place. It's actually designed to move with the currents. That flexibility reduces stress on the tube."

"And what happens if we can't break free?" There was a tremble in Mackenzie's voice.

"I'd rather not think about that," Pavel said. "If it's all the same with you."

"How long before we make our attempt?" Decker asked.

"No time like the present," Pavel said. "I've figured out about as much as I'm going to. At this point, we're just delaying the inevitable."

"Is there anything we can do to help?" Lauren asked.

"Absolutely," Pavel led her to a set of valves attached to thick pipes that disappeared into the pressure hull. "These operate the bow buoyancy tank vents. They will need to be open in order to purge water from the tanks. Don't open them until I tell you to."

"Are you sure you know what you're doing?" Lauren asked.

"Not really," Pavel admitted. "Most of this is guesswork. It's not like I learned how to operate a U-boat in thirty minutes. Either it works, or it doesn't."

"That doesn't fill me with confidence."

"It wasn't meant to." Pavel turned to Claudia and pointed out a second set of valve wheels. "I want you to operate these. Again, wait for my mark."

"Got it," Claudia said.

Pavel led Mackenzie and Bertram to a pair of seats in front of what looked like large steering wheels. "These stations control the forward and aft dive planes. After we clear the seabed, those wheels should be turned to the left to lower the planes to push the sub's nose up. This will help us keep a semblance of control as we move toward the surface. It's all going to happen pretty fast and you'll need to keep a tight grip on them, so be ready."

"How will we know how far to turn them?" Bertram asked.

"You won't. I'm assuming that they will only turn so far and after that we'll just have to hold them in position."

"What if you're wrong?"

"I guess we'll find out." Pavel turned to Decker. "You have the most important job of all. Operating the blowing distributor. That's what will purge the tanks with compressed air, expelling the ballast water, and allow us to rise." He led Decker to a large hand wheel mounted among the pipes and dials near the planesman's stations where Mackenzie and Bertram were seated. He pointed to a box mounted next to it. "This is the compartment ready indicator box. Whatever you do don't turn the distributor until the valves are open and the lights on that box turn green."

"What happens if he operates it too early?" Mackenzie asked.

"Not sure," Pavel admitted. "My guess is that either we wreck the compressed air tanks, or we rupture the ballast tanks stranding us on the seabed forever. How about we get this right and not find out, eh?"

"Sounds like a fine plan to me," Decker said. "What are you going to do?"

"I'm going to supervise the whole thing and pray to God that I understood enough of that manual to get us to the surface in one piece."

No one commented on this.

Pavel finally broke the silence. "Shall we begin?"

"Is it going to be a bumpy ride up?" Mackenzie asked.

"It'll probably be like the worst roller coaster you've ever been on, and then some," Pavel replied.

"Just great. I hate roller coasters." Mackenzie didn't look pleased.

"Better than suffocating to death." Decker gripped the blowing distributor and tried to ignore the mounting feeling of panic that tightened his chest.

"All right then," Pavel said. "Let's do this thing. Focus on your own assignments. Don't worry about anything else."

"Ready when you are," Claudia said, glancing around the group.

Pavel hesitated a moment, then he stepped over to Mackenzie. "I know there are rules against relationships on the habitat, but after what's happened, I don't care if we get reprimanded." He leaned in and kissed her. They looked at each other for a moment before he spoke again. "If we get out of this alive, I want to have a chat about our future together."

"If you're trying to dump me, you picked a hell of a time to bring it up." Mackenzie forced a smile.

"Nothing of the sort. I was actually thinking we could make things a little more permanent," Pavel replied. He straightened up and resumed his previous position. He glanced toward Claudia and Lauren. "All right, then. Let's open those valves."

Decker watched them turn the wheels and a moment later the compartment ready indicator lights turned green. When Pavel nodded toward him, Decker tensed and inched his own wheel to the right and sent compressed air shooting down the pipes into the ballast tanks to force the seawater out.

The sub shook and groaned.

It echoed with knocks and clangs from deep within the pressure hull, as if they had released a thousand angry demons.

The submarine shifted. It bucked and lifted off the seafloor before settling down again with a mighty jolt.

"It's not working." There was panic in Mackenzie's voice. "The umbilical is holding us in place."

"Give it time," Pavel replied, but he didn't sound convinced.

The front of the sub edged upward. The deck tilted. There was a sharp ping and a thin stream of water shot from somewhere in the conning tower and splashed into the control room, slicking the floor.

Mackenzie screamed. "It's no good. We'll tear ourselves apart. We should stop now while we still can and go back to the habitat."

"Too late for that." Claudia glanced sideways. "For all we know, the umbilical has ruptured and flooded already."

"I don't want to die in here." Mackenzie was close to tears. Her breath came in short, ragged gasps.

"Calm down," Pavel said. "No one's going to die."

As if to prove him wrong, the sub gave one more violent heaving lurch, followed by the sound of tearing metal. Then all hell broke loose.

Chapter 61

WITH A TORTURED SHRIEK the U-909 heaved from the ocean floor, rising bow first and lurching sideways as it struggled to shake free of the umbilical's unyielding grip. From the aft section came a low rumble as the rear of the sub plowed into the soft seabed.

The forward hatch door leading to the front of the U-boat, which had been standing ajar, smashed back against the bulkhead with an echoing crash. The reserve toilet door in the galley flew open, sending the contents of the makeshift pantry spilling out. Cans of food erupted like bullets and smacked into the hull before dropping to the deck plates and rolling away.

"This is insane," Bertram shouted over the melee. "We're going to rip the conning tower off at this rate."

"Too late to worry about that now," Decker said, struggling to maintain his balance. He lost his grip on the blowing distributor and staggered backwards, eventually catching himself on one of the attack periscope's handles and hanging on for dear life.

Pavel was not so lucky. As the sub twisted itself in knots to escape its watery prison, he careened into the forward watertight bulkhead. He let out a pained grunt and scrabbled to hold on. A moment later the wildly pitching U- boat tossed him forward again, sending the marine archaeologist careening into the map table. This time he found purchase, and pulled himself upright, gripping the edge of the table for dear life.

Mackenzie had braced herself against the attack periscope opposite Decker, while Claudia wrapped an arm around a large valve release wheel and was struggling to keep a grip.

"They should put seatbelts in these things," Lauren said, clutching her planesman controls. "I'm writing a stern letter of complaint to the Kriegsmarine if we get out of this with our heads still on our shoulders."

The sub bucked and twisted like a mechanical bull trying to unseat its rider. The pressure hull let out a low, frighteningly long groan. From somewhere in the jungle of valve handles, a second leak sprung, spraying icy water into the control room. A shudder ran the length of the submarine. From the aft section, more items were coming loose and falling. One particularly forceful boom sent a tremor through the deck plates, and Decker wondered if a torpedo had broken its restraints. He was thankful that Thomas had disarmed the deadly weapons. At least the man had done one useful thing.

Another metallic moan reverberated through the sub, followed by a sharp cracking sound. Decker held his breath, expecting the hull to split open at any moment and send freezing seawater cascading down upon them. But instead, the sub righted itself and stopped shaking.

"I think we did it," Pavel said, still gripping the map table. "We must have broken free of the umbilical."

"Does that mean we're rising?" Mackenzie asked.

She didn't need an answer. No sooner had the shaking stopped, than Decker felt his stomach lurch as the U-boat lifted, twisting sideways at the same time.

"Turn the plane wheels to the left," Pavel shouted toward

Mackenzie and Bertram. "Quickly, we need to angle the nose up to control our ascent."

Bertram twisted his wheel. Mackenzie grunted and tried to turn hers. At first, she couldn't move it, but then little by little it shifted, adjusting the hydroplanes on the U-boat's exterior that controlled its angle of tilt.

The submarine's deck slanted. Cans of food, previously ejected from the pantry, rolled toward the forward watertight bulkhead and came to rest there. The sub pitched at a steeper angle.

"That's enough," Pavel called out. "Hold it there. If we go too steep, we'll end up vertical in the water."

The U-boat was rising faster now, barreling through the water at a breakneck pace. A rumble filled the control room, as if the boat had come to life and was roaring as it zipped toward the surface.

Decker felt his legs sliding out from under him and gripped the periscope tighter. He took a deep breath, tried to quell the sudden nausea that threatened to overcome him. "How long will it take us to reach the surface?" He shouted over the cacophony.

"No idea," Pavel said, raising his voice. "At the rate we're moving, not very long."

"Do you want us to do anything else?" Mackenzie asked through gritted teeth. She was holding the controls so tight that her knuckles had turned white.

"I don't think there *is* anything you can do." Pavel pulled himself closer to the map table and wedged his legs around the chair to avoid tumbling backwards. "At this point we're just along for the ride."

The sub shook and vibrated. A valve handle flew off and clattered to the deck, but thankfully whatever was inside the pipe beyond the busted valve stayed where it was.

Moments later, just when Decker thought the crazy ride

would never end, there was a deafening boom, and the entire U-boat shook.

Mackenzie let out a terrified screech.

Then the roar filling the cabin died away. For a half-second they remained stationary, hanging in midair at forty-five degrees, but soon the sub's nose started dropping fast.

"We broke the surface," Pavel said, still gripping the map table. "We're coming down hard. Brace yourselves."

He'd barely finished speaking when the submarine hit the water with a sharp smack that reminded Decker of belly flopping into a swimming hole as a kid back in Louisiana.

The U-boat shuddered one last time, as if protesting its chaotic ride up from the depths, and then came to rest. Somehow, more by good luck than good judgment, they had made it.

Chapter 62

THE SILENCE that engulfed the sub after its perilous charge from the depths was unsettling. Decker let go of the periscope handle and flexed his stiff fingers.

"Did we really make it?" Lauren asked, still gripping the planesman controls as if she was afraid to let go. "Are we on the surface?"

"Looks that way," Pavel said.

The U-boat rocked gently back and forth. Decker thought he could hear waves lapping at the submarine's hull. "Why don't we open the hatch and find out."

"We need to radio the support ship first," Lauren said, finally letting go of her controls. "I don't want to stay stranded out here any longer than necessary."

"I agree," Claudia replied.

"We don't need to use the radio." Decker reached into his pocket and pulled out the CUSP issued phone. He held it out to Claudia. "This should work now we're on the surface."

"How?" Claudia looked confused. "I'm pretty sure there are no cell towers out here."

"Don't need them," Decker said. "This phone works

anywhere in the world. It connects to a network of military satellites, but if anyone asks, I'll deny telling you that."

"Thanks." Claudia took the phone. "I'll make the call now. In the meantime, let's get that conning tower hatch open. I don't know about the rest of you, but I would love to see the sky."

"On it." Decker left Claudia dialing the support ship and went to the tower ladder. He climbed up and turned the hatch release wheel, then pushed the hatch door up and out of the way. A shaft of bright light speared down through the opening and illuminated a patch of deck plate below.

Mackenzie was already climbing up even as Decker heaved himself onto the bridge and basked in the faint warmth of the sun.

"That feels good," Mackenzie said as she exited the conning tower.

One by one the others joined them, with Claudia appearing last.

She handed the phone back to Decker. "Called us a taxi. It will be here in about four and a half hours."

"Can they get here any sooner?" Mackenzie asked. "I'm looking forward to stepping on dry land."

"Not likely," Claudia replied. "They were mighty surprised to get a call from me. They're scrabbling to leave port as we speak, but it will be at least five hours."

"Will the sub float for that long?" Mackenzie looked nervous. "We're not going to sink, right?"

"We won't sink," Pavel replied. "But just to be on the safe side, I'm not going back inside the U-boat unless it's absolutely necessary."

"Me either," Mackenzie said.

"Um, guys?" Bertram interrupted their conversation. He pointed off their starboard side to an object bobbing in the water a couple of hundred feet away. "Isn't that our submersible?"

Pavel spun around. He raised a hand to shield his eyes from the sun's glare. "Sure looks like it."

"Why is it still here?" Lauren asked. "Thomas had a huge head start."

"Maybe the submersible is empty." Claudia leaned over the U-boats bridge rail to get a better look. "He must have had people on standby. I bet he called them from the radio room before he trashed the radio."

"I'm betting it's not empty," Decker said. He was looking in the other direction, at a large oceangoing yacht bearing down upon them. "Looks like we surfaced just in time to see his ride show up."

Everyone turned to look at the new arrival. The motor yacht was sleek, the kind of vessel a multi-millionaire would own. It was at least a hundred and fifty feet long, with three aerodynamic stacked decks topped with communications and marine radar equipment that gave it the appearance of a miniature cruise ship. The sun glinted off its clean white hull and chrome deck rails.

"Thomas's friends aren't slumming it, that's for sure," Decker said.

"Why is it only showing up now?" Mackenzie asked. "Thomas had a good four-hour head start on us, maybe more."

"They were probably at dock in Kourou, just like our own ship currently is. They wouldn't know when Thomas was going to contact them. It would have taken a while to file paperwork with the harbormaster, prepare the ship, and cast off. After that, they still have to get out here. Still, if we'd left it another half hour, they would have picked him up and left already."

"Not that it does us any good." Pavel looked glum. "It's not like we can stop them picking him up."

"We can start the U-boat's diesel engines and maneuver it in between him and them," Lauren said.

"Not going to happen. By the time we figure out how to start those engines, they will have come and gone. There's also the minor problem that none of us know how to steer a U-boat."

"And even if we steered it in their path, they could just change course and go around us." Decker watched the yacht moving closer. He could see figures standing near the back, clearly surprised by the sight of a World War II U-boat sitting in the water ahead of them.

"What about the guns?" Mackenzie asked. She pointed toward the deck below them, and the gun mounted there on a rotating platform. "That deck gun should have enough fire-power to stop them."

"We also have the flack gun," Pavel added. "It was used to defend against enemy aircraft, but I'm sure it will put a few holes in that yacht."

"We don't even know if they're loaded." Decker shook his head. "Or where the ammunition is."

"I know exactly where the ammo is," Claudia said. "Six-hundred feet below us in the habitat. I had Thomas remove all the armaments from the sub the first week we were down there, just to be safe, including the flack gun ammunition and the shells for the deck gun."

"We're defenseless then," Lauren said. "Let's hope the men on that yacht aren't armed."

As if to answer her, a barrage of bullets peppered the conning tower's skin a few inches below the bridge.

Decker saw a figure standing at the yacht's prow. Two other men had positioned themselves along the railing. All three had guns raised.

"Semi-automatics," Decker yelled as a second hail of bullets whizzed past the tower but missed their mark. "We need to take cover." He dropped to the deck, grabbing Mackenzie's arm, and pulling her along with him.

The others followed suit, dropping down as more bullets

flew, and huddling behind the narrow ribbon of extended hull circling the bridge beneath the railing.

"They're at the edge of their range right now," Decker said. "But once they get closer, the conning tower won't protect us anymore."

"What does that mean?" Mackenzie asked, even as another volley of gunfire erupted from the direction of the fast-approaching yacht.

"It means they don't intend to leave any witnesses," Decker said. "And with no way to defend ourselves, we don't stand a chance."

Chapter 63

No sooner had everyone hit the deck, than the gunfire ceased. Decker felt a wave of relief wash over him. They had some breathing room. But he knew they were far from safe.

"Why have they stopped shooting?" Mackenzie asked.

"Saving ammo," Decker said. "They have us pinned down and defenseless. There's a radio in the submersible. I'm sure Thomas told them we don't have any weapons."

"He'd know, because he removed them," Claudia said.

"Exactly." Decker could hear the yacht's engines. They were still far away, but getting closer. "When they get within a few hundred feet, they'll open fire again, for sure. And this time the conning tower won't protect us."

"Then we can't stay here," Lauren said. "We're sitting ducks. We should get back inside the submarine. At least there we stand a chance."

"Maybe then they'll see we aren't a threat and leave us alone," Mackenzie said hopefully. "They are only here for Thomas. They can just pick him up and go."

"That isn't going to happen." Decker shook his head. "We know about the device installed on the U-boat. We know that

Thomas took it. They aren't going to let us live. If we go back inside the sub, all we'll end up doing is trapping ourselves."

"Then they won't need to shoot us," Claudia said. "They can just take out the ballast tanks and sink us. Who knows what other weaponry they've got on that yacht. They could have rocket launchers for all we know. It's too risky."

"Then we fight," Pavel said.

"How?" Claudia looked confused. "We don't have any weapons. Everything is back on the habitat. Thomas even disarmed the torpedoes, not that we'd be able to get into firing position and actually launch one, anyway."

"We don't need torpedoes. I've been studying that translated U-boat manual I found on the web. There's a box bolted next to the deck gun. It has two rounds of ammo in it so the gunners could start firing on enemy ships immediately without waiting for ammunition from below decks," Pavel said. "The deck gun was submerged until now, so Thomas didn't remove those rounds."

"That might be our only chance." Decker said. "I wonder how far away that yacht is now."

"Let's find out," Pavel said.

Before Decker could stop him, he raised his head over the protective bulkhead. A second later, he dropped back down as a fresh volley of bullets flew over his head.

"That was too close," he said, his face white.

"Well?" Claudia glanced toward him.

"They've stopped dead in the water." Pavel looked confused. "They're just sitting there."

"That can't be good," Decker said. He felt a tingle of foreboding. "They must be planning something, otherwise they'd just keep coming and shoot at us."

"The sooner we get to the deck gun, the better," Pavel said. "It takes at least two people to operate it. Three is better." He turned to Decker. "Are you with me?"

"Let's do this," Decker said. "Just the two of us, though.

Three people will be too big a target down on the deck and the gun will only provide minimal protection if they start shooting again."

"Which they're sure to do if they see us playing with that gun."

"Nothing we can do about that." Decker made a mental calculation of how long it would take to climb down from the conning tower and reach the gun. There were rungs for deck access set into each side of the tower near the flak gun. Then they could use the tower itself for cover. They would only be exposed for the last few feet as they ran between the tower and the deck gun. It wasn't ideal, but it would have to do. "Ready?"

"Not really," Pavel admitted. "This might be the stupidest thing I've ever done."

"I wish I could say the same," Decker said. "I'll count down from three. There's no cover on the back half of the bridge, just railings, so we must be quick. And stay low. I'll let you go first, and then I will follow."

"Got it."

Decker counted down. When he reached one, Pavel sprinted forward, bent almost double. He slid under the railing and dropped out of sight. If the men on the yacht had seen him, they didn't fire. Now it was Decker's turn. Without wasting a moment, he lunged forward and grabbed the railing, swinging himself through the gap and down onto the rungs attached to the side of the conning tower. This time a burst of gunfire whizzed through the air inches from his head. He scrambled down the rungs and dropped onto the deck, breathing heavily.

"Now comes the hard bit," Pavel said, eyeing the exposed a gap between the conning tower and the deck gun. "Let's hope their reflexes are not good."

"If they think we're going for that gun, they'll be waiting

for us." Decker wished they had ammo for the flak gun mounted on the conning tower's rear deck.

"It doesn't matter," Pavel said, inching his way to the end of the tower and pausing there. "We can either try to make it to the gun, and give ourselves a fighting chance, or they'll just shoot us anyway."

"Yeah, I know." Decker had already summed up their odds, and they weren't good.

"Want to count down again and go together?" Pavel asked.

"Might as well," Decker said. But before he could do anything, they heard Mackenzie's voice ring out.

Decker looked up to see her standing atop the conning tower, waving her arms at the men on the yacht. "Hey, assholes. Over here."

What she said next, if she said anything at all, was lost in a hail of bullets.

Chapter 64

"Go." Decker gave Pavel a shove onto the pitching deck. "She's drawing their fire."

"Dammit. She'll get herself killed," Pavel said, but even so he sprinted forward, with Decker at his heel. He threw himself down behind the gun, expecting the men on the yacht to turn their firepower from the conning tower onto them. But they didn't. Instead, the chatter of gunfire ceased, giving way to blessed silence.

"We made it," Decker said, sheltering behind the gun's wide girth. "Thanks to Mackenzie."

"They'd better not have shot Mac." Pavel grimaced.

From the conning tower, Mackenzie's voice drifted down. "I'm fine. I ducked back down before they started shooting. They didn't get me."

"Thank goodness for that," Pavel said. He glanced at Decker. "Why do you think they've stopped firing at us?"

"Beats me." Decker shrugged. "They must be done with whatever they're planning. They obviously don't feel the need to waste ammo on us anymore."

"In that case, we'd better get on with it ourselves, and sharp. I'd rather not find out what they have in mind." Pavel nodded toward the long metal box attached to the deck with heavy bolts. "There should be two 14-kilogram rounds in there."

"My guess is we'll only have time to fire once." Decker scooted over to the box and lifted the latches, then threw the lid open. Inside were a pair of lethal-looking shells, each at least two feet long. He raised an eyebrow. "Holy crap. Now that's a bullet."

"Actually, it's a shell." Pavel glanced up at the deck gun. "We need to train the gun on that yacht before we load the round, otherwise they'll pick us off. The gun's shielding will only protect us from frontal assault."

"How do we turn it?" Decker asked.

"There are two traverse wheels on the left side of the turret. We'll have to ignore elevation since we don't have the time or knowledge to use the rangefinder. The gun barrel is horizontal and that will have to do, but we'll need to turn the upper wheel to rotate the gun into position."

"On it." Decker tried to keep as much of the gun as he could between himself and the yacht and reached around to the upper traverse wheel. Little by little, the turret rotated.

Pavel was standing now, shielding himself behind the gun's armor. He squinted through a contraption that Decker assumed was some sort of gun sight. After a while he waved an arm. "That's it. Stop there."

Decker stopped turning the wheel. He risked glancing around the armor toward the yacht. What he saw sent a shiver of fear through him. "We'd better do this quick."

"Why?" Pavel glanced sideways. "What do you see?"

"Remember when Claudia said they might have a rocket launcher? Well, she wasn't wrong." Decker watched a figure approach the bow of the yacht, carrying what looked like a long tube painted a dull army green. "That's why they're not bothering to fire on us. They have a shoulder-fired missile, and it looks like they're preparing to use it."

"Jesus, who are these people? Seriously, who thinks to pack a missile on their yacht?"

"I guess these guys do."

"That's just perfect." Pavel moved to Decker's side and pointed to a latch on the side of the gun. He spoke quickly. "This is the safety latch. Hit that after the shell is loaded and the gun will go off. Word of warning. Don't stand behind the breech when we fire this thing. You don't want to get hit by the shell casing."

"Understood."

"Now we just load the shell."

"Better hurry it up," Decker said, watching the activity on the yacht. "Couple more seconds and they'll be firing on us, and if that missile hits the submarine, we're going straight back to the bottom."

"I know." Pavel kneeled next to the ammunition box and lifted a shell out. He handed it to Decker. "Take this."

"Okay." Decker hoisted the shell, wincing as a stab of pain flared across his bruised chest. "Now what?"

"The deck gun is breech loaded. We need to slide the shell into that groove at the back. Once you push the shell in, the breech will lock automatically."

"Like this?" Decker dropped the shell down into the groove and pushed it forward until the breech lock popped up.

"Yes, just like that," Pavel replied. He said something else, but at that moment, the gunfire began again.

Bullets slammed into the gun's armor in a deadly pitter-patter. One slug embedded itself in the deck inches from Decker's foot.

"I guess they don't like us pointing a gun at them," Pavel said.

"No shit." Decker risked another quick peek around the armor plating. The guy with the shoulder-fired missile was kneeling, the rocket launcher pointed straight toward them. "We're out of time, he's about to fire."

"Hit the safety latch." Pavel dropped to the deck and sheltered behind the gun's armor. "Hit it now."

Decker slammed his hand down on the latch and rolled sideways, away from the breech at the same time.

For a split second, nothing happened. Then there was a deafening boom, and the gun recoiled, spitting an empty shell casing from the gun's rear onto the deck.

Decker turned to look at the yacht, just in time to see a bright flash from the shoulder-fired missile launcher.

Their own shell must have gone wide.

He braced himself for impact, knowing there wasn't time to reload. But then, just as he thought they were doomed, the sub lurched sideways, caught in an ocean swell. Decker gripped the gun mount to keep himself from slipping overboard. Water crashed over the deck, drenching him. The yacht disappeared from view as the U-boat dropped into the swell's wake. He felt a searing blast of scorched air and realized the missile must have passed over their heads without hitting. Thanks to the sudden swell, the men on the yacht had missed. But they wouldn't miss again. They would anticipate the next wave.

"Load again. Quick as you can," Decker shouted, even though the marine archaeologist was already scooping up the second shell and struggling to his feet, pushing it into the breech.

Without waiting for confirmation that the breech was locked, and knowing they had no time to aim, Decker hit the safety latch and fired.

Chapter 65

THE GUN roared and jerked back, ejecting a second shell casing from the breech. Decker, temporarily deafened by the deck gun's report, didn't hear the shell's impact. He only realized they'd scored a direct hit when he saw a ribbon of black smoke curling into the sky from the yacht's direction. His first instinct was to jump up and look, but he hesitated. He did not know how badly they had damaged the yacht and was aware that hostiles may still be targeting the U-boat. He didn't want to get a bullet in the head for his curiosity. But soon it became apparent that the fighting was over. There was no more gunfire. No further missiles launched at the submarine. Deciding it was safe, Decker stood and peeked around the deck gun's armored front. The yacht was dead in the water, its stern on fire and billowing acrid smoke. The ship's stern was dropping lower in the water. The yacht was sinking.

"You did it." Mackenzie's gleeful voice drifted down to them.

Decker looked up toward the conning tower and saw Mackenzie, Bertram, and Claudia standing there watching the distressed yacht.

But they may have celebrated too soon. A new sound

came from the yacht's direction. The rumble of inboard engines. Moments later a large tender, as sleek and trim as the vessel it served, came into view. It rounded the front of the now listing yacht and started on a course that would take it around the U-boat and toward the submersible.

"Oh, hell," Pavel said. "That's not good."

Decker saw men on the tender's deck. They still carried semi-automatic weapons. "They know we're out of ammunition. If it wasn't for that lucky hit to the yacht, we'd be dead already."

"How much do you want to bet they're going to rake us on the way past?" Pavel watched the approaching boat nervously.

"I'd say the odds are around a hundred percent." Decker glanced backwards, toward the submersible. Thomas had thrown the top hatch open and pushed himself up. He now waited for the tender to reach him.

"And after that they're going to collect Thomas and be on their way with the orb," Pavel said.

"How far can they really get in that thing once they do?" Decker asked. "They don't have a yacht anymore."

"They don't need one." Pavel shook his head. "That tender is state-of-the-art. I bet it can travel at fifty knots. Maybe even faster. They can be back in Kourou in under two hours."

The tender drew closer. It was almost upon them now. The men in the back were preparing their weapons and there was nowhere to hide at this range. Even if Decker and the others jumped overboard to escape the initial assault, they would just get picked off in the water.

Then, just when Decker was expecting them to open up, the tender veered sideways, pulled a U-turn, and started back toward the swiftly sinking yacht. It opened up its motors. The bow lifted and the sleek motorboat screamed away, leaving a frothing wake. At the same time, Decker noticed a low thrumming sound from their rear. Decker turned to see a large mili-

tary helicopter hovering fifty feet above the submersible. Two
stubby wings flanked the fuselage toward the helicopter's tail.
Decker guessed these held missiles, although the wings did not
currently carry any armaments. But there was a mean-looking
30mm auto-cannon machine gun mounted to the fuselage.
This was what prompted the tender to do an about tail and
abandon Thomas.

"Holy crap," Pavel said, gawking at the hovering gunship.
"That's an Mi-24. It's like an attack helicopter and troop
transport all in one."

"How on earth do you know that?" Decker asked. He kept
a wary eye on the helicopter, unsure if they were friend or foe.

"I might be a boring marine archaeologist now, but at one
time I was a boy with a fascination for all things military."
Pavel was still watching the helicopter, obviously in awe. "Do
you think they're here to rescue us or kill us?"

"We're not dead yet," Decker replied. "That's a good
sign."

"What should we do?" Pavel said.

"Wait to see what happens next, I guess."

They didn't have to wait long. The helicopter moved
closer and dropped lower, the wash from its rotors roiling the
ocean's surface and sending out circular waves. Water splashed
over the U-boat's deck. Decker risked a glance toward the
yacht. It was going down fast now. The stern was almost at
water level; the bow rising high. There was no sign of the
tender. Faced with the prospect of fighting a helicopter
gunship, the yacht's crew had made themselves scarce, abandoning Thomas and the alien device.

When Decker turned back to face the helicopter, he saw a
door slide open on its right side. A man in a military style
uniform stood on the other side. Decker suspected he
belonged to the Ghost Team, CUSP's version of an elite task
force. They were charged with mopping-up operations and
transferring dangerous subjects to the high-security facility

called The Zoo. The last time he'd encountered them, although he hadn't seen them in person, was in Ireland after they defeated Grendel. His suspicions were soon answered.

"John Decker?" The man leaned out of the helicopter.

Decker raised an arm. "That's me."

"Excellent." The man shouted over the din of the rotors. "Adam Hunt sent us. He said you guys might need a ride home."

Decker wondered how Hunt had known of their predicament. Then he remembered that Claudia had placed a call to the support ship from his phone after they surfaced. Either the support ship had contacted Hunt, or his phone was being monitored and Hunt had intercepted the call. This team must have been waiting in French Guiana for this very eventuality. He made a mental note to ask Hunt if his phone was being monitored, but right now he was simply happy for the help. It had saved their lives.

"What about him?" Pavel shouted, pointing toward Thomas in the submersible.

"He'll be coming too," the soldier on the helicopter replied. "Adam Hunt told us to make recovering the orb our first priority. He's going to be extremely happy."

"That's all very well," Mackenzie called out from the submarine's bridge. "But you think we could get off this U-boat? I would really like to go home now."

"Me too," Pavel said. He glanced up toward Mackenzie and smiled at her. "First thing I'm going to do is take you on a real date."

"I'd like that." Mackenzie returned the smile.

Decker watched the exchange with a bemused grin, then turned his attention back to the helicopter. It had moved off and was hovering once more over the submersible. A line dropped from the open hatch and a soldier rappelled down, while a second man kept an assault rifle trained on Thomas. He wondered if Hunt would confine the treacherous munitions specialist to The Zoo, or if a different fate awaited him. Then he decided it didn't matter. Thomas's plan had been foiled, and they were safe. Even so, one question nagged at him. Who did Thomas, and his companions on the yacht, work for? And more important, would he run across them again?

Chapter 66

The U-boat sat in a sheltered inlet hidden from the ocean. It was moored to a wooden dock with a new set of steps attached to the conning tower and leading up to the bridge. It had taken several days for CUSP to tow the sub up from French Guiana; the trip made longer by their desire to avoid the shipping lanes and stay out of sight. But Decker hadn't been there for that. He'd flown home to Nancy and spent the better part of two weeks recovering from his ordeal. His chest still hurt, but only slightly. A full checkup had confirmed one cracked rib, but otherwise he'd escaped unscathed. Nancy was happy to have him home and disappointed when Hunt summoned him to the private island that housed both The Zoo and an operations center for CUSP. Now he stood looking at the sub—which had survived its brush with Thomas's men surprisingly well—and waited for Hunt to give him permission to do what he'd came here for. In the meantime, he still had questions.

"I'm sure this is above my pay grade," Decker said. "But what happened to Thomas? Did you put him in The Zoo?"

"It is beyond your pay grade," Hunt admitted. "But I'm at liberty to share pertinent information with my operatives, and I choose to believe that this falls into that category. No, we did not put Thomas in The Zoo. He might be a monster, but he's a human one. The Zoo is more suited for monsters of the supernatural kind."

"Where is he then?"

"I can't give you his exact location, but suffice to say that he won't be seeing the light of day for an awfully long time. Actually, he won't be seeing it ever again."

"You didn't—"

"Relax. We didn't kill him. He's in a high-security facility."

"Has he spoken?"

"Not a word. We don't know who he works for or who those men on the yacht were. All we know is that they were well-funded and well-armed. We know one thing, though. Thomas Barringer is not the man's real name. It's a cleverly constructed false identity. His school attendance, work history, and personal life were all faked. It would pass all but the deepest level covert background checks. He's been working under that identity for at least a couple of years, maybe more. We put our extensive resources into finding out who he really is, but came up blank. The organization he works for is clearly well-connected and sophisticated."

"Are you aware of any such organizations?" Decker asked.

"Not until now." An expression of concern passed briefly across Hunt's face. "Our organization may have a less ethical and much more dangerous rival, possibly sponsored by a hostile foreign power, so secrecy is even more important than ever."

Decker didn't reply to this. He watched operatives coming and going from the sub. They had already fitted the orb back in its cradle in the control room. They had also recharged the U-boat's batteries.

Adam watched for a while too, then he turned to Decker. "Are you sure you want to do this?"

"Not really, but I think we have a duty." Decker took a deep breath. "Those submariners have been trapped in a living hell for decades. I think it's time we set them free."

"Just thought I'd ask."

"What will happen to them after their rescue?" Decker asked. "You're not going to put them in the same place as Thomas, are you?"

"Heavens, no." Hunt looked hurt by the suggestion. "We can't just let them go, obviously. The culture shock alone would be immense, not to mention the stir it would cause if a bunch of men from the second world war suddenly showed up on their descendant's doorsteps. We reintegrate them into society, give them new identities, and swear them to secrecy. Of course, we must monitor them to make sure they don't contact their families back in Germany."

"That's harsh." Decker wondered what it would be like to find yourself almost eighty years in the future with no idea what had happened and all your loved ones long dead.

"It's not meant to be harsh. It's a necessity. We can't risk revealing the technology on the submarine, or how those men survived all these years without aging." Hunt's eyes trailed up to the submarine. "That's assuming we can actually bring them back."

"We're about to find out," Decker said, watching the last of the CUSP operatives climb down from the conning tower.

One of them approached and addressed Hunt. "Everything's ready. Good to go when you are."

Hunt glanced at Decker. "I think that's your cue."

"It just might be," Decker said. He took a deep breath and stepped toward the submarine. "Might as well get this over with."

Chapter 67

DECKER CLIMBED down into the control room. A low hum permeated the air, emanating from the direction of the box containing the orb. The box itself stood open, front panel resting on the floor. Hunt's men had already set the six knobs on the control panel to the exact coordinates of the island, and the position which the sub already occupied. This was important. In order to bring back the submariners stranded between dimensions, they would have to power the orb up and activate it, just as the submariners themselves had done back in the Second World War.

Only this time there would be no accidents. The orb would fully engage. But they didn't want the U-boat to take a trip to anywhere else on the globe. Instead, it would stay right where it was, and if Decker's theory about the alien device was correct, it would finish the job it had started decades earlier and bring the men home for good. Or if something went wrong, Decker might find himself trapped along with them, trapped for eternity on another plain of existence. It was a chance he must take, not only because someone had to operate the device from inside the U-boat, but because he couldn't live with himself if he walked away without trying to help. Even so, he hesitated, finger poised over a red button sitting to the left of the dials. A button that would activate the alien orb. He thought of Nancy, and what would happen if he didn't come home. Then he pushed those thoughts from his mind and pressed the button.

Chapter 68

AT FIRST NOTHING HAPPENED, and Decker wondered if Hunt's people had reinstalled the device correctly. Then, little by little, the hum coming from the alien device rose in pitch. The air came alive, as if filled with electricity. The hairs on Decker's arms stood up. He felt a tingle coursing through his skin. The U-boat started to vibrate.

Metallic groans echoed inside the tight space and Decker held his breath, wondering if the submarine would pull itself apart under the immense stress the orb was clearly exerting upon it.

This continued for a few moments more, with the hum rising to a deafening crescendo. A blinding white light erupted in the control room, so intense that Decker lifted an arm to shield his eyes. When he dropped it again, he was no longer on the sub, but instead found himself standing amid a bleak and barren landscape that appeared solid and non-corporeal both the same time. The land was flat and featureless beneath a sky filled with a whirling vortex that rose into the heavens and coiled between myriad motionless planets of all shapes and sizes that hung above the landscape like baubles on a Christmas tree. He looked around in terrified awe. Then he realized he was not alone. Standing in a group several feet to his left were the U-boat's crew, or at least what remained of them. They watched him, wide eyed, clearly surprised to see another living soul.

One man stepped forward. He carried a Luger. Decker recognized him as the same man that had shot him weeks before in the engine room. This time, apparently, he meant to finish the job.

Then another man stepped forward and placed himself between them. He turned to his comrade and shook his head, motioning for the man to lower the gun.

He turned back to Decker and spoke.

"Why are you here?" The man said in English. His voice sounded strange, modulating up and down in pitch and echoing even though they were in the open.

"I came to save you." Decker raised his hands, palms out. "I'm unarmed. The war is over."

The man nodded.

Decker scanned the group and counted ten men. "Where are the rest of you?"

"This is all we number. The others didn't survive. We don't know what happened to them." The man held out his hand in greeting. "My name is Otto Sauer. I'm the First Watch Officer, but now I'm in charge. We lost our commander along with most of the crew when we activated the device."

Decker lowered his hands and stepped forward to accept Otto's greeting, but before he could grip the First Watch Officer's hand, the strange world around them shifted and faded.

Decker stopped, surprised. He looked up, taking in the magnificent sky filled with alien worlds, and then in a flash the unearthly realm melted from view and he was back aboard the U-boat with the ten startled submariners by his side. The hum that had filled the submarine moments before now gently dissipated and the orb fell silent. It had done its job and pulled the men back to the real world, before closing the portal. From outside the submarine, Decker heard excited voices. An operative clambered down through the conning tower, followed by another. There would be more of them arriving, Decker was sure, to contain the situation and escort the newly freed submariners from the U-boat. Decker sighed and leaned back against the attack periscope, the stress of the last few minutes evaporating as he realized it was over. He wouldn't end up trapped in some far-flung and timeless dimension after all. This was a good day, not only because he had survived another perilous mission but also because he'd fulfilled the promise made to Nancy before leaving for the island, that he would stay safe and come back to her in one piece.

Yes, today was indeed good.

Epilogue

Three months later - An undisclosed location in the Sierra Nevada Mountains

THE CORRIDOR WAS LONG, ending in a reinforced steel door. A uniformed man of stocky build approached and placed his palm against a panel mounted next to the doorframe, then waited while the door locks disengaged. He opened it and stepped through into a windowless chamber with an identical door on the other side. The room was furnished only with a metal desk upon which sat a computer monitor. Behind the desk was another man wearing the same uniform. A patch on his right side, above a military style name tag, contained a single word stitched in block capitals. CUSP.

The newcomer approached the desk, his hand resting lightly upon a holster containing a service pistol. "I need to see the occupant of cell fifteen."

The soldier on guard duty looked up, a bored expression on his face. He reached toward his keyboard. "Authorization?"

"It comes from the top. I need to speak with him right now."

"I still need to know who authorized the interview." The guard jabbed the keyboard. The monitor woke up. He typed in a password to unlock the terminal. "What's your authorization code."

"Just open up and let me in," the man nodded toward the inner door. "We're wasting time."

"Not without the proper authorization code." The guard looked up, defiant. "You know the rules."

"How about we skip the code," the man said, sliding his service weapon out of its holder in a swift, fluid movement and pulling the trigger.

The guard hadn't even registered what was going on before the bullet crashed through his forehead and opened the back of his skull, spraying the wall behind him red.

The man holstered his weapon and turned to the computer monitor. His hands flew over the keyboard, accessing systems he should not have been able to, and disabling what was designed to be an impenetrable security system. A moment later, the inner door's bolts drew back with a clunk. He went to the door and opened it, then stepped through into a long and featureless corridor with rows of cell doors on each side. These he ignored, until he arrived at one in particular, identified by the number fifteen stenciled above the door frame.

He held his hand up to another featureless black panel next to the door. When he placed his palm against it the panel lit up green. This had been the hardest part—getting his biometric profile into the system—but it hadn't proved impossible, especially with the vast resources at his disposal.

He turned from the panel back toward the cell door. There was no handle. There didn't need to be. Exactly five seconds after the biometric print had identified him, or at least the false identity crafted for him to break into this facility, the door slid open.

The man known until recently as Thomas Barringer stood on the other side. "You took your sweet time."

"I don't think we took much time at all, given the complexity of getting in here."

"Whatever. You're here now and that's all that matters." Thomas stepped out into the corridor and drew in a long breath. "How about we make ourselves scarce before someone notices this little jailbreak? I'd like to get back to work."

Acknowledgments

I would like to say a big thank you to my VIP team, who spot the occasional typo, give me feedback, and make the books so much better. Thanks especially to Zac Martin for his history advice on this and previous books. Lastly, I would like thank my wife, Sonya, who wishes I wrote anything but monsters, but still edits my books and tells me to go back and do it again when I get lazy.

About the Author

Anthony M. Strong is a British born writer living and working in the United States. He is the author of the popular John Decker series of supernatural adventure thrillers.

Anthony has worked as a graphic designer, newspaper writer, artist, and actor. When he was a young boy, he dreamed of becoming an Egyptologist and spent hours reading about pyramids and tombs. Until he discovered dinosaurs and decided to be a paleontologist instead. Neither career panned out, but he was left with a fascination for monsters and archaeology that serve him well in the John Decker books.

Anthony currently resides most of the year on Florida's Space Coast where he can watch rockets launch from his balcony, and part of the year in beautiful New England, with his wife Sonya, and two furry bosses, Izzie and Hayden.

Connect with Anthony, find out about new releases, and get free books at www.anthonymstrong.com.

Made in the USA
Coppell, TX
04 October 2022

84064029R00157